# THE
# MERIDIEM

## CEDRIC: BOOK 2

C.  A.  LEAR

This is a work of fiction. Names, characters, places, and incidents either are the product of the author's imagination or are used fictitiously.

Copy Editing by Angie Chen

Cover Design by Kit Foster

ISBN-13: 978-0-9992908-3-5

First edition
10 9 8 7 6 5 4 3 2 1

For Dad.

.

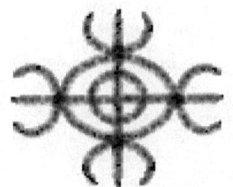

# 1 - AFTERMATH

## MAY 1799, Vos Castle

In the counting chamber beneath Vos Castle, Lord Domitian stood over the remains of his beloved Countess Marie. Beside her body—still in her bloodied gown—rested her severed head and hands. Domitian frowned at her murky eyes sunken into the orbits of her skull, her once luxurious brown hair sullied and snarled. It was the scene of her assassination, and his sadness and anger had only grown since Headmistress Abigail announced Marie's death a week ago, alleging that a lowly boy servant had killed her.

*A boy could not have done this*, thought Domitian.

Memories of Marie clung to him like the sweetness of decay. Marie used to spend days, weeks, even months in this counting chamber, dressed in her finest gown, sitting at her Louis XIV table, zealously counting jewelry, buttons, and pieces of gold and silver. She would tally and contain all of it in lovely pouches, sacks, and lockboxes. When done, Marie basked in vainglory of her accomplishment. This would go on for several more weeks until the unremitting desire to retotal slowly dissolved her contentment and calm. All at once, she would snap with fits of rage, sadness, and laughter. She would rip the sacks open and tear box-lids off their hinges, spewing all the contents and wallowing in it like a rooting pig until her emotions finally settled. After bathing and putting on a clean and resplendent gown, she would begin again, methodically sorting and counting the riches and storing them in new plush pouches, sacks, and lockboxes.

Domitian dabbed melancholy from his eyes with his kerchief. Though Marie never really afforded him the affection he so craved, he pined for her, needed her. He could not have dethroned their former master without her.

He carefully moved about the room with an investigative eye, looking for clues to refute Headmistress Abigail's allegation of who the murderer was. A child of any disposition would not have the strength to kill the powerful and clever countess. Those corpses still chained to the walls ought to explain what truly happened here. On second thought, those pitiable souls would probably reveal nothing of the assassin, focusing instead on Marie's gluttony—devouring them all in a day!

Eleven boys, he counted. Eleven chained and drained of blood. He thought Marie had been feeding on merely a child a week and in the privacy of her bedchamber, but no. Obviously, she misled him. She was addicted. Her cravings to hover were uncontrollable, which explained her aloofness, rapid aging, drooling pustules, and constant bloating in the latter months of her existence. Their former master warned of the dangers of child's blood.

*It is a poisonous drug—the most addictive substance known to our kindred—producing euphoria, which lifts the abuser on a cloud of limitless pleasures and hallucinations that we call the hover. Beware the hover, for want of reproducing its effects will lead to more and evermore consumption of the poison until no amount will satisfy the relentless cravings or stave off the gradual and inevitable rotting of mind and body.*

Domitian had not tasted child's blood in weeks, and had unexpectedly lost his appetite for it. Perhaps the warnings, or Marie's death and his sudden rise to power, or a castle barren of children contributed to his surprising rehabilitation.

"You should have told me, my sweet...the seriousness of your affliction," whispered Domitian to Marie's remains. His eyes roamed the ravaged chamber, taking in each of the eleven bodies. "Despite all this, the cheating, the waste, the distrust, I still love you." Pink tears squeezed from his eyes, spattering on a fractured wooden lockbox on the floor beside his boot. He nudged the box over, uncovering something of interest beneath it. He knelt down and used his kerchief to pick it up. It was a piece of dried flesh the size of a pea.

"Odd," he muttered, turning it over, wondering if it was a mole or a nipple, how and why it was removed, and from whose body. "Definitely a nipple..." His eyes analyzed the chained bodies—all boys. He glanced over at Marie's headless and handless body. Her gown was filthy but intact and unmolested. He folded the evidence inside the kerchief and placed it in his coat pocket whilst pacing and mulling over the possibilities.

The once sizeable storage loft and everything on it lay in ruin—splintered beams and joists telling of a ferocious fight, of thrown bodies careening through structural timbers. Much of the clan's wealth—wall-to-wall coins, buttons, jewelry, and even crucifixes—twinkled like stars in a black sky. He sniffed the air and stratified smells into layers, filtering out odors of mold and rot, detecting remnants of Marie's henchman who had gone missing, of Headmistress Abigail, and of a man—probably her brother Pierce van Fleming.

Domitian scowled at the thought of Pierce—the Englishman who had been prophesied to rule his clan. Obviously a false prophet, thought Domitian, and a coward...running from battle and abandoning his sister. A scant but lingering scent of a girl made Domitian flare his nostrils, and drew his attention to Marie's prized French table.

It sat askew at the center of the room—severed rope tied to each of its legs, a strand of hair glued in blood to the tabletop. These clues told of a girl whose fairness attracted Marie, and of the countess's inability to entrance the girl and the boys all at once. Too many of them, thought Domitian, would be too exhausting even for Marie to entrance. That is why they were fettered and chained.

He lifted the strand of hair and brought it near the candle-flame—copper blond, long and wavy. He saw a set of empty shackles, the only empty set. Uncharacteristic of Marie to fill all but one set. With plenty of orphans still available in the castle at that time, there ought to have been twelve boys in shackles, and one girl bound to the table. Where are they, and was the evidence—the nipple—taken from the girl?

He brought to mind the battle four days ago. On that day, his sword skills were unrivaled. He killed so many that he lost count. From the top of the staircase, he saw Abigail and Pierce leading child-servants through the castle. It was a puzzling sight. Did Abigail and her brother kill the countess and steal the servants? He understood why they might want to kill Marie, but why take the servants? Had they intended to sell them, eat them, or worst of all, free them? Domitian remembered Marie's plan to sell orphans to the dreaded upyrian vampires of the east.

Upyrian, otherwise known as upyr, were Russian sired vampires. Differences between upyrian and western vampires were many, including language, religion, traditions, and rituals. A select few upyrian were capable of shape-shifting and even mind-meddling. Unlike mindbending, which was erasing or modifying memories and thoughts, mind-meddling was a form of telepathy and shared senses over vast distances. Though vampires in the west believed they were more sophisticated and culturally superior to their eastern counterparts, the upyrian queen, Žofie Cervenka, disagreed.

Not only sophisticated and powerful, Queen Žofie united most of the eastern vampire colonies. From the Baltic to the Bulgars, through the Magyar and Ottoman Empire, she conquered the colonies and made them worship the Titan god Kronos. Malefactors were quickly quashed and summarily sentenced to death by ritual execution called *Nabídka*. This was a sacrificial killing, an offering to Kronos who supposedly devoured his own children. The ritual required the condemned—known as a child, though all were adults—to be stripped naked and suspended head down on an upside-down crucifix. An ornate athame was used to flay the arms. When enough blood was collected to feed all witnesses, they filled their cups, gave thanks to Kronos, and drank the blood. After that, the head was severed and the body and crucifix were burned or buried depending on the mood of the queen and location of the event.

Marie ignored those stark differences, focusing instead on the similarities between east and west. By developing stronger ties to the east, especially to Queen Žofie, untold wealth and power ought to be had. To that end, Domitian was content to know that Marie had secretly nurtured a cordial rapport with Žofie.

Suddenly, Domitian heard a guard approaching and stiffened until he appeared at the doorway to the chamber.

"Milord," said the guard.

"What is it?" said Domitian, waving him in.

The guard stepped inside, averting his eyes from the body parts. "Milord, the Prussians and Romans are leaving. The exterior gates are repaired, and the castle is in order."

"What of the dead?"

"The Romans and Prussians recovered their own. Shall we bury all ours, milord?"

"Not all of them. Identify the traitors and toss them in the rubbish pit."

"Yes, milord."

"And what of Count Marcel's remains?"

"We placed them in a lockbox in your bedchamber, as instructed, milord."

Domitian nodded and gazed over at Countess Marie's head. "There lies my greatest advocate." He covered his quivering lips with a tightly clenched fist. "We owe everything to her. We dare not disturb her remains until I know exactly what to do with them." Domitian looked for more clues. "Where is the traitor Sir Michael?"

"In the dungeon, milord..."

"Complaining of rats, I hope. What more have you to report?"

"I have news concerning the boy servant, Cedric Martens, milord."

Domitian sneered. "Go on."

"The boy was captured outside Brussels—"

"Excellent!"

The guard's posture slumped.

"What is it now?" grumbled Domitian.

"Swordsmen came...and the boy escaped with them."

Domitian lifted an iron crucifix from the floor and threw it with such velocity that it embedded in the guard's forehead up to the cross arms.

The guard fell to his knees, wincing and trembling.

Domitian approached the ailing vampire. "We sent three of our best to capture that boy, did we not?"

The guard squeaked something incomprehensible.

"Speak up, idiot!"

"Yes, milord!"

"What *army* rescued him?" spat Domitian.

On his knees, crucifix protruding from his eyes, the injured vampire said: "Two swordsmen attacked..."

Domitian's eyes widened. "I knew it!"

"They beheaded two of us—all as witnessed by Sven."

"And Sven just stood by and did nothing?"

"The attackers and the boy fled north by horse—"

Domitian took hold of the crucifix, placed his boot against the guard's face, and yanked it out. He then bent the cross in half and threw it against the wall. "What is the problem with Sven? Is he fat and slow?"

"Milord?" asked the guard, his eyes realigning.

"Must be if he is unable to outrun horses for a short distance."

"Forgive me, milord, he observed the rescue from afar. However, Sven has a knack for stalking. I told him to go and pursue them to the north. They likely went to Amsterdam or Rotterdam."

"Or Copenhagen or London!" seethed Domitian.

The guard lowered his head. "Sven has a keen sense of smell, milord."

Domitian scoffed. "Good ole Sven." He began to pace, turning after every third step. "They attempted to capture the boy in a field, you say?"

"Yes, milord."

"Witnesses?"

"None, milord."

"And what of our guards' remains?"

"Sven collected them and returned them to the castle, milord."

Domitian paused to stare down at a gold coin. "Who were these swordsmen?" he whispered to himself. "Perhaps I shall capture them, turn them, and make them eat garlic." He retrieved the folded kerchief from his pocket and felt the shape of its contents. "What of Abigail, is she still locked up in Marie's boudoir?"

"Yes, milord."

"Bring her to me."

"Yes, milord."

## 2 - FLEEING NORTHWARD

Rescued by the Fortune Brothers Klaas and Gert, Cedric was holding on for dear life, fleeing by horse, riding tandem behind Gert. Cedric had no other choice than to trust these men, who had come out of nowhere and dispatched his vampire abductors in a few seconds outside Brussels. Gert followed his brother Klaas on their black steeds, hooves hammering northward, a yolk-orange sun touching the horizon.

A week ago, Cedric narrowly escaped the battle at Vos Castle with his life and with the lives of his friends, Lily and Jacob. He had promised Lily—his precious Lily—to go to Amsterdam if they were separated. They agreed to find each other at the church in the middle of the city. That is where he must go.

At a hairpin curve, Cedric grabbed hold of Gert's cape nearly toppling the both of them.

Gert glanced back at Cedric. "Let go of my cape! Hold on to my belt!"

"Sorry, sir!" shouted Cedric, gripping Gert's weapon's belt. He leaned forward, securing him closer to Gert and let his mind wander. *God only knows what would have happened if the brothers had not rescued me from those bloodsucking monsters.* In his mind, Lily's face appeared, her smile somewhat faded, though they had been together earlier in the day. What became of Lily and Jacob? Had they been captured? Are they en route to Amsterdam?

"Will those devils ever stop hunting me?"

Voices in his head answered in unison: *Yes, yes, they will stop hunting you, when they capture you! Stupid boy, run as far as you can else we are all going to die...*

Exposed to the supernatural, Cedric struggled to understand vampires. If God created all things, then He must have created vampires, too, but why? Even blood-sucking mosquitoes, though despised by all, have purpose—food for fishes, birds, and bats. Yet, vampires have no such worth. They prey on man, woman, and child. Why would God create such people? And what of the orphaned, unwanted, and defenseless children seeking refuge only to be enslaved and consumed by those perverted creatures?

*Vampires!*

They made no sense to Cedric. With each passing day, his darkest memories dulled and his feelings of those iniquitous manifestations hardened until analyzing them no longer offered even the illusion of understanding, empathy, or solace.

After traveling swiftly for a long mile, Gert and Klaas slowed their horses to a trot and continued on until arriving at a roadside inn. The moon was nearly full, and the brisk of winter lingered like an unwanted guest in late May.

After booking rooms, Cedric met the brothers in the dining hall and took seats at a long table shared by others. Cedric counted twelve chatty patrons, mostly travelers by the sound of them. An elder woman was drying a goblet behind the counter. An elder man swept the floor. They appeared to be the proprietors, probably husband and wife or related in some way. A young girl who reminded Cedric of Lily stepped from the kitchen to ask the woman a question.

The man set aside his broom and came to serve them. "Well, if it is the Brothers Fortunate," said the barman, revealing a toothy smile beneath his shaggy gray beard.

"Good evening, Mister Williams," said Klaas.

"You look well, Mister Williams," said Gert. "May I introduce our associate, Cedric Martens of Linder?"

Williams' smiling eyes greeted Cedric's. "Welcome, Mister Martens. Drink and food, gentlemen?"

"Ale, to start," said Gert.

"Same here," said Klaas.

"Have you any milk or juice?" asked Cedric.

Williams shrugged his shoulders. "We ran dry of milk and juice an hour ago. I recommend the cider. We uncorked the barrel just today."

"Splendid," said Cedric.

After Williams delivered the drinks, the brothers lifted their mugs.

"To Cedric," said Gert with a broad smile, "and fancy meeting you again!"

"Here, here!" said Klaas, guzzling half his ale down. He enjoyed a belch and set his mug on the table. "We have questions."

"Indeed we do," said Gert, wiping ale from his mustache with his sleeve.

"I suppose you want to know why those monsters attacked me," said Cedric.

Klaas raised an eyebrow. "Monsters?"

"Yes, from Vos Castle," said Cedric, certain they knew what he was talking about.

"Castle?" said Gert, eyes widening.

Klaas lowered his head, looked left and right, and whispered: "What do you know about the castle?"

Cedric leaned forward and whispered in kind. "I was a servant there."

Klaas and Gert sat back, sighed, and nodded in unison as if agreeing to some inaudible opinion.

"Go on, then, brother," said Gert to Klaas, waving his hand.

"I defer to you, brother," said Klaas to Gert.

Gert turned to Cedric and shook his head. "*Nee*, we do not wish to discuss the castle."

Cedric felt confused. The brothers slew his abductors. They saved his life back there. What was more important than that?

"We want to talk about Amsterdam," said Gert. "Have you any business there?"

"Forget business," said Klaas. "Do you want to go there?"

"With us?" added Gert.

The question surprised Cedric. Suddenly, the castle and its horrors dissolved into a sea of luck. He intended to go to Amsterdam—not only to meet Lily and Jacob but also to get as far away from Vos Castle as possible, perhaps board a ship, and sail away.

"As you know," said Gert, "we are performers."

"Masters of blades, extraordinaire!" shouted Klaas followed by a swig of drink.

"We have several engagements in Amsterdam and could use someone strong like you to help us set up the stage—"

"And take down the stage," added Klaas.

"Tend to errands as well," said Gert.

Cedric's only thought was, "Yes!" The need to find Lily tunneled his awareness into a space that only she could fill. "Yes, of course. It is the least I can do after all you have done for me. I would be honored to go with you to Amsterdam and assist you in any way," said Cedric, also knowing that safety came in numbers.

"Then, it is settled!" said Klaas, raising his goblet.

After they toasted to companionship and drank their cups empty, Klaas immediately looked for Williams. "Mister Williams! Wherefore art thou, Mister William?" shouted Klaas to the barman. "More drink, Mister Williams!"

Cedric was relieved to be traveling with honorable, fearless, skilled swordsmen who slew monsters with no want of mentioning it. Was it bad form to speak of such things in a crowded room? No matter, he felt obligated to express gratitude. "I, erm...I wanted...I mean..."

"Let me guess," said Klaas. "You are grateful beyond words."

Cedric blurted laughter. "Yes! I am grateful...very grateful! I owe my life to you both."

"You owe it to my younger brother," said Klaas. "It was he who saw your predicament. He suggested that we intercede. I disagreed, especially in the light of day. What if someone had seen us? What then?"

"Seen us?" said Gert, as if the question was absurd. "No ogler would risk neck-in-noose to explain what was ogled, brother!"

All three went silent as Williams came by with full cups and set them on the table.

Cedric leaned forward, feeling the effects of the cider, and spoke softly. "I am also thankful to you," said Cedric to Gert, "for pointing me in the direction of the forest. Do you remember?"

"Ah, yes," said Gert, "and I apologize for pointing you in the direction of the forest."

"Why?" asked Cedric, surprised at the comment. "You warned me of the dangers and how to avoid them. I failed to listen. I spent the night in a small cave and met a strange woman, too."

"Spending the night in a cave with a strange woman is dangerous business if you ask me!" said Klaas.

Gert laughed. "Very strange—!"

Cedric chuckled politely. "The woman was blind and spoke in riddles," he added. "She told me to leave the forest at once."

Klaas rested both hands on the table and leaned forward. "We should discuss this later," said Klaas, staring at Gert as if communicating by telepathy.

Gert nodded. "Besides, there will be plenty of time to speak of your adventures—"

"In the company of gray crows," said Klaas.

"And pink sheep," added Gert.

"And green insects," offered Cedric.

Gert and Klaas stroked their knotted beards and stared at Cedric as if he was the odd one.

## 3 - UNCLE & AUNTIE DUNKEL

The next morning, Klaas and Gert mounted their horses, Cedric behind Gert as before, and they resumed their journey. It was a beautiful day with many travelers sharing the road. Some would smile back at Cedric and nod, while others appeared locked in thought, perhaps listening to or trying to quiet the voices in their heads as he often did himself. The land was flat and vast, as far as he could see, green fields and grazing livestock, winding streams and windmills, the scent of wildflowers and hay crops. Not since the time Cedric rode horses with his father had he felt so free. He missed his family, especially his father. Until his sixteenth year, he had spent more time with his father than with anyone else. Cedric confided in him and learned from him how to farm and mend and build useful things such as fences, gates, containers, furniture—anything of wood. His father taught him to hunt game in the small forest near their home. There was so much more Cedric wanted to learn from him. He never expected his family to suffer and forever vanish as they had—the whole of their existence reduced to fading memories.

"Are you thinking?" asked Gert.

Cedric opened his eyes and took a look around. "Yes."

"Me, as well. At this rate, we will stop and spend the night at the home of my auntie and uncle. Good news for you, Auntie is a wonderful cook and you will leave on the morrow in a saddle of your own."

"A horse? I will receive a horse to ride?"

"Something like that," said Gert.

By sundown, they arrived at an old barn beside a stand of trees. If not for the bright moon and clear skies, it would have been too dark to see the barn. Gert placed two fingers on his lip and whistled.

After Cedric hopped down from Gert's horse, he heard latches on the side of the barn and watched the top half of a door open. An old man with a long gray beard, pipe in mouth, smoke snaking up, peered out from the doorway. Upon recognizing the brothers, he unlatched the bottom half of the door and stepped out with lantern in hand.

"Uncle Dunkel!" said Klaas to the old man.

"Evening, Klaas, my boy!" said Dunkel.

"We apologize for arriving so late," said Klaas, leading his horse to his uncle. Klaas pointed at Cedric. "He is to blame."

"Always blaming others," said Dunkel, winking at Cedric.

"We need an animal for him to ride," said Klaas. "May we take Molly on the morrow?"

"Yes you may, but must you speak of leaving," Dunkel said, frowning, "whence you have only just arrived?"

"Setting expectations, Uncle...Remember the last time we dropped in and failed to let you know that we were leaving the next day until we were leaving."

"That was rude of us," said Gert.

Klaas nodded. "Nothing would make us happier than to spend more time with you and Auntie, but we have commitments."

"Jammer!" shouted Dunkel. "Where must you go this time?" He took the horse by the reins.

"Canal town," said Gert.

"Shall I prepare the usual provisions?" asked Dunkel.

"No need, but thank you, Uncle," said Klaas.

"Very well," said Dunkel. "Your Auntie is inside."

Cedric followed the brothers to a house behind the barn and up a flight of stairs onto a sizeable balcony. As soon as they entered through a door, a plump elderly woman put down a dish and beamed.

"There you are!" said Auntie, coming to greet them. "How long has it been?" she asked Gert as she hugged him and then stepped back to size him up. "Handsome as always...!" She turned to Cedric and smiled. "And who is this?" asked Auntie.

Gert swept his hand out to introduce him. "Cedric Martens of Linder..."

"How do you do?" said Cedric.

She squinted at him. "How is your appetite?"

"We ate," said Klaas.

"Breakfast on the morrow, then?" she asked.

"You are too kind, Auntie," said Gert, "and yes, please!"

She winked at Cedric. "Gert will show you to your room."

Gert led Cedric through a short hallway and stopped at a green door. He pushed the door open and stood aside.

Cedric entered the room. It was modestly furnished with a small window—*perfect*, he thought. Cedric turned to Gert but saw that he had gone. Cedric closed the door and put down his bag of possessions. After he washed his face and hands in a basin of water, he fell back on the bed exhausted and closed his eyes.

The next morning, the brothers and Cedric entered the dining room where Dunkel was already seated and Auntie was busy bringing plates of food from the kitchen.

"Good morning, Auntie!" said Klaas, kissing her on the cheek as she put down a bowl of potatoes.

"Good morning, Klaas, Gert, Master Cedric," said Uncle.

"Good morning, sir and Auntie," said Cedric, finding a seat next to Klaas.

"So," started Auntie as she rubbed her otherwise clean hands on her apron, "what brings the fabulous Fortune

Brothers and their fine young friend to our modest abode, eh? And where are you off to in such a rush this time?"

"Amsterdam," interjected Uncle Dunkel.

"Amsterdam again?" she said in a tone somewhere between disappointed and despondent. "Will you stop in Ghent on the way?"

"Yes," said Klaas. "Only for a night..."

"To collect Adina," said Gert.

"Of course," said Auntie. "Such a pretty thing... I imagine she looks like yesteryear."

"As always," said Klaas.

Cedric noticed the uncle lowering his chin and bringing his hands together.

"We thank the gods for the bounty we are about to receive," prayed Dunkel, "and we humbly ask the gods to watch over Klaas, Gert, Adina, and Cedric, to protect and deliver them from wickedness." He opened his eyes and smiled. "Let us eat!" Dunkel reached for a plate of cheese and sausage.

"You should both come with us," said Gert to his aunt and uncle. "Mother misses you."

"We seldom travel anymore," said Auntie. "Our world is here in this quiet little valley. No troubles, no bother... Not many neighbors round here but the few we have are kind and giving."

"Thank you for this delicious meal," said Cedric to Auntie.

"Have some eggs and muffins, dear boy," said Auntie, handing him a plate. "I cannot allow you to leave on an empty belly."

"Heed her words, Cedric," suggested Klaas, mouth bulging with food.

Cedric took a muffin and compared Auntie's facial features to the brothers'. He saw a family resemblance, the same blue eyes, prominent nose, strong chin, straight brown hair, though Auntie's hair was gray and tied in two little buns like bear's ears.

After a hardy breakfast and tearful goodbyes, the brothers mounted their horses, Cedric on a mule, and merged back onto the road to Amsterdam. It was a spectacular day. The road was uncongested, the weather bright and still. Cedric enjoyed riding alongside the brothers, even upon a mule. She was a gentle creature, long ears, stable gait, and as tall as the horses.

"What is her name?" asked Cedric.

"Molly," said Gert. "She is as old as I am."

"Will you return her to your uncle and aunt?"

"Henceforth, she will live in Ghent."

"Did you say you juggle?" asked Klaas of Cedric. "We can use a juggler in our show."

Recalling they had asked him this question before, Cedric shook his head.

"Does that mean you cannot juggle or that you are not interested in juggling in our show?" asked Klaas.

"I have never juggled," said Cedric. "I can learn to."

"Perhaps..." said Klaas.

"Who are your friends in Amsterdam?" asked Gert.

"Friends?" asked Cedric.

"You mentioned them two nights ago, something about meeting them in Amsterdam," said Gert. "Who are they?"

"We were..." Cedric lowered his voice, "servants at Vos Castle."

Klaas stroked his beard and stared at Cedric. "Yes, about that..."

"You are fully aware that your attackers were vampires, then?" asked Gert.

"Yes," said Cedric.

"How much do you know about the vampires at Vos Castle?" asked Gert.

Cedric had always wondered if magical beings existed and at one time wished they had. The fables of creatures such as trolls, gnomes, elves, vampires, wizards, and dragons told by the fathers in his village were as fantastic as they were frightening. As he grew into his own thoughts, he decided that those magical beings were not real and merely used to spice otherwise insipid stories of morality. Now, he was giving into different thoughts of uncertainty—that such things might be real.

"Go on," said Klaas. "Tell us what you know."

"I know who the royals are," said Cedric. "I know their names."

"Royals?" asked Gert.

"The proprietors of the castle," said Cedric, "members of the Royal Flemish clan. I have met them. I accompanied Countess Marie de Vos to England."

Gert choked and coughed. He lifted his canteen, took a drink, and wiped his mouth. "Go on."

"I know Headmistress Abigail and her brother Pierce van Fleming," said Cedric, feeling somewhat relieved to tell them of his experiences. "Do...do you know them?"

Klaas tapped his chin and stared at Gert.

"Except for Pierce van Fleming, I am familiar with all those names," said Gert.

"I, as well," said Klaas.

"That is understandable," said Cedric. "Mister Fleming is from England."

"I presume you met this Mister van Fleming when you accompanied the countess to England," said Klaas.

"Yes, sir," said Cedric.

Klaas wrinkled his nose, and focused his wide-set eyes on the boy. "Please call me by my given name, which is Klaas."

"Klaas," said Cedric, feeling odd to address an elder by his forename.

Klaas lifted his finger in the air. "However, in the presence of our audience, I am Mister Fortune, Master of Blades!" Klaas flashed Gert an apathetic smirk. "You may call my brother—"

"Gert!" blurted Gert. He turned to Cedric. "Please address me by my first name as well."

Klaas butted in: "I think your stage name is—"

"No, brother, Gert is my given name. And regardless of circumstances, please do not address me as Smaller Fortune, Mister Misfortune, nor Fortuneless the Fearful." He glared at Klaas. "Those are stupid names, brother." He waggled a finger in the air. "Henceforth, I shall be known as Gert."

"Humdrum," muttered Klaas, "Your stage names have always been—"

"No," said Gert, shaking his head.

"—more interesting," finished Klaas.

Gert glared at his brother. "Elder brother, you may plan our tours. You may plan our shows. You may even plan to plan our plans, but you shall not plan to overrule our parents who named us. Therefore and henceforth, either onstage or offstage, I shall be called—"

"Gert the deluded," grumbled Klaas. "We use stage names to protect our anonymity." He sighed and acknowledged Cedric once more. "Have you any siblings, Cedric?"

"Not anymore," replied Cedric, picturing an image of his little sister, a smaller version of his mother.

"Please forgive me, Cedric," said Klaas, still leering at his brother. "Shall we go, then, dear brother *G-g-g-ert?*"

Preferring to move past the bickering, Cedric changed the topic. "Well then, brothers Klaas and Gert, shall we be on our way? I am for one excited to see Amsterdam. I hear it is a floating city with hundreds of bridges and boats. Is that true? How many days journey is it? I presume the church defines the city's center. Is it a large church?"

Gert's arms unfolded. "Amsterdam is three days by horse."

"Depending on how quickly or slowly the horses move," added Klaas.

Cedric never felt more grateful to be traveling with these men. They seemed to bring him luck and certainly a broader level of safety. He was planning to go to Amsterdam because he and his dear Lily and friend Jacob planned to meet there in the event they were separated. Separated... He imagined what they probably had to do when the vampires came—*run*. A flood of worry washed over him. Did Lily and Jacob make it safely to Amsterdam, or were they abducted and taken to Vos Castle? He reminded himself that Jacob and Lily carried weapons and were prepared to use them. Nevertheless, he prayed for them, for their safety. He believed they were waiting for him in Amsterdam, probably worrying for him the same.

Cedric heard a whisper, a voice he had not heard for quite some time. Even though he was fairly successful at suppressing the voices in his head, they were always there in the background, an undercurrent of disparagement.

*The boy is older but none the years wiser*, whispered a crotchety voice that reminded Cedric of a blacksmith near Linder whose temper was as hot as a forge.

*He fears for his friends because he's guilty of failing them*, added an elder woman's voice.

*He endangered them*, added a girl's voice with a whining drawl.

*Your friends are no longer your friends, boy!* shouted the crotchety voice.

*They will never forgive you*, whispered all in unison.

Cedric shook his head and hummed a song, trying to drown the voices out. When that failed, he closed his eyes, held his breath, and swallowed, hoping the voices—like hiccups—would stop. It worked, and in the comfort of silence he thought of Lily again. *Beautiful Lily.* He longed to be with her, to grow old with her. If only he was free to do so.

## 4 – ABIGAIL'S ARANGEMENT

A castle guard jostled Abigail forward through the entranceway of the counting chamber wherein Domitian had been investigating the murder of his beloved Countess Marie de Vos.

"Milord," said the guard, "Headmistress Abigail is here."

Domitian waved her in.

The guard shoved her so hard she tripped and fell onto the cluttered floor.

Domitian turned to see Abigail flat on her stomach, plumes of dust rising. Domitian sneered at the guard. "Leave us, and close the door!"

Abigail slowly lifted herself to her bare feet and instinctually dusted off her ragged servant's dress she was made to wear. The tattered and dirty garment was too small and short to cover her knees yet not too filthy or unflattering to annul her beauty. A bath and a new gown was all she needed to seduce nearly anyone.

Had it been a different time and place, Domitian would have been delighted to see her, but the mere presence of Abigail van Ness amidst the body parts of Countess Marie de Vos angered him. Like an arrow, Domitian sprung at her, taking her neck in hand and shoving her back into a stone wall. He peered into her violet eyes, puffy and seeping pink tears, and took in her delicate features—petite nose, long eyelashes, chapped full lips gaping like a suffocating fish. He might have squeezed her head right off, but the pathetic condition of this love-goddess beauty somehow assuaged his fury. He loosened his grip and pressed his body to hers.

Abigail cringed as his lips touched hers and his tongue began to probe.

Domitian drew back and spat on the floor. "You taste like rat!" He wiped his mouth on his sleeve. "How can you stand it—the taste of vermin?"

Abigail ran her finger across her violated lips.

"Your diet disgusts me. How can one so beautiful be so..." He shook his head and paced back and forth in front of her. "I need answers..." He stopped and squinted at her judgingly. "First question: why did you betray the countess?" He turned and pointed at the countess's remains. "She saved your life!" He wagged his finger at her. "She saved your life, yet you betrayed her. Why, Abby? Revenge?" He scowled at her. "I know your little story—how you were made to watch villagers stone your mother to death in the street. They would have stoned you and your father, too, had Marie not come to your rescue. She killed them all to save you, to make you one of us."

Abigail said nothing.

"She gave you freedom. She gave you power and purpose. You were her favorite daughter. I should know. She spent more time with you than me or anyone else for that matter! So, again, why, Abby?" After a pause, his lips began to quiver and he placed his trembling hands on Abigail's shoulders. "Help me to understand why." Domitian turned away for a brief moment in thought, then turned back to Abigail and gripped her jaw, forcing her to look at Marie's remains. "Look at her! Look at what you did to my love!" Domitian let go of Abigail's face and pointed at her with contempt. "You did this to her. You conspired with your brother to kill her. Do you deny it? The boy servant could not have done this alone!" Domitian's tone dropped and became steadier, more purposeful now. "Marie was too powerful for a mere boy to defeat her. No, I think something completely different happened here." He peered into her eyes. "You and your brother came to kill the countess. You overpowered the guards and attacked her here in this room. So, Abby, which one of you butchered her? Was it you or was it your brother?"

Abigail said nothing.

Domitian threw her against the wall so hard the plaster cracked on impact. She crumbled to the floor. "Tell me! Who killed the countess?"

Domitian straightened his waistcoat and moved toward the table at the center of the room. He righted two overturned chairs and sat in one. He flipped his locks behind his back and stared at the chair in front of him. "Come...crawl to me." He waited as she cautiously moved on knees and hands to him. When she tried to stand and sit in the available chair, he kicked her to the floor. "Did I say to sit in the chair?" He glanced over at the corpses on the walls and then at Marie's head. "Who killed Countess Marie, and why?" Domitian's eyes shifted back to Abigail. "Was it jealousy? Were you jealous of her or of me? Was it your brother who wanted her dead? I might understand that."

"He did not kill her," whispered Abigail.

"Speak up!"

"I said neither my brother nor I killed her."

"Then who did?"

"I told you—"

"Yes, I know you would have me believe a boy singlehandedly killed her, but that is absurd!"

Abigail's eyes found a dent in the wall where her brother had slammed Marie's head into it. "The countess murdered my father."

Domitian clicked his tongue in disappointment. "I do not understand you, Abby. Why avenge your father? Vampires are supposed to consume their mortal relatives, not honor them. Yet, you go around collecting grudges. Most unhealthy, you know—grudges. Grudges to us are like constipation to humans." He quivered with disgust. "Why retain all that dirt inside you?"

Abigail turned away.

"Marie held grudges, too, you know, but not ad infinitum. She let them go, in spiteful ways, of course. Well, she was infinitely spiteful as you know." He sighed.

"Child's blood ruined her," said Abigail.

"I would normally disagree with you simply because I dislike you, but this time I must concur. I mean, just look at all these corpses! Holes in their eyes and bite marks on their arms prove a voracious addiction. Oh and, Abby, observe the only set of empty shackles on the wall there, and those cut bindings on the Louis table. My guess is Marie had lashed a girl to that table and filled every shackle with boys." He lifted his chin and sniffed the air. "Can you smell her, the girl? I can. What do you know about her and the missing boy and their whereabouts?"

"They were servants. I know nothing of their whereabouts."

"Who set them free?"

"I led a few children out of the castle, but the children you speak of escaped through the airshaft in the catacombs."

"Who released the boy and girl from this room?"

Abigail averted her eyes and said nothing.

"Your silence is an admission of guilt." Domitian felt the urge to poke Abigail's eyes out but settled down and began again. "I saw you and your brother escorting orphans out of the castle. It was during the battle, which—by the way—I won. You were inside the castle during the time the countess was killed. So, tell me, tell me now, who killed the countess? Was it you? Did you kill her, Abby? Or is the killer your brother?"

"No," said Abigail.

"Did you witness her murder?"

Abigail went silent again.

"Really, Abby, your silence tells volumes, and I suppose you will hold fast to your story about the boy killer. All right then...explain how the boy was able to do it."

"With a sword," said Abigail.

"Aha! You were there, and I have *this* to prove it." Domitian reached into his pocket and lifted out the kerchief-wrapped evidence of flesh. "Missing something, Abby?" He stared at her bosoms and smiled. "Show me."

Abigail turned away.

Domitian leapt on her and tore her dress open, exposing her breasts. One was perfect, the other missing a nipple. "I believe this belongs to you." Domitian carefully placed the dried nipple where it ought to be.

She remembered when Countess Marie had pinched it off and put it in her mouth. Abigail thought the countess had swallowed it. Perhaps it was knocked out of her mouth in the fight.

When Domitian saw that Abigail was going to cover her breasts, he pointed at them. "Wait! I just need to be absolutely certain..." Almost instantly, the dried nipple began to hydrate and heal in place. Domitian crossed his legs and waved two fingers at her to cover herself. "Did you really think you would outsmart me, Abby? You were here when the countess was murdered. It was you. You came to murder her, but something went wrong, and your brother helped to finish her." He sighed and closed his eyes in thought. "Your betrayal is punishable by death, you know this. What to do, what to do with you?" He sat back down in his chair and crossed his arms. "In your case, I think the best punishment is to hunt down your brother, Pierce van Fleming, and have him pay for your treachery. Oh where, oh where has he gone?" Domitian stomped his foot. "Where is he?"

"I suppose he is en route to the other side of the world," she said, holding her torn dress together over her chest.

Domitian jumped up from his chair, this time knocking it over. "Why must you play games, Abby? Gerda will extract what I need from your vermin brain!"

"She will fail, for my thick vermin skull is impenetrable—"

Domitian laughed at her gall and placed his hand on her shoulder. She was trembling, and that pleased him. He drew her locks out of her face and over her ear. "How do you prefer your brother to be tortured, hmm? You know that I will find him. It is only a matter of time. This century or the next, this continent or the other, anywhere he goes, I will find him; and when I do, I will have him tortured every day for a year. He will beg for death, but I will not kill him. Instead, I will separate his fingers from his hands, his hands from his arms, his arms and legs from his body, and bury him alive with all his parts in separate boxes deep in the ground. Do you understand?"

Abigail nodded.

"So, what are you willing to do in exchange for your brother's freedom?" He stood up and looked down his nose at her.

Abigail sighed. "What would you have me do?"

Domitian laughed. "Your mother was a necromancer, yes? She resurrected your brother, obviously with half a brain. You know, Abby...I asked Marie to kill your brother, but did she listen?" He shook his head. "Now, your brother is thrice born and as dumb as a squirrel! What does that all mean?" Domitian paused and bounced his fist on his chin. "It means that you will resurrect Countess Marie. That is what you will do in exchange for your life."

"I am no necromancer."

"I heard differently. I heard you resurrected a dog."

Indeed, Abigail had reanimated a canine, but it came back different. It was uncharacteristically irritable. It ran off into the forest, probably to avenge its own murder by killing a small pack of wolves. It was never seen again. "Have you a dead dog?" asked Abigail. "I will do my best to resurrect it, but not in exchange for my life."

"What in Hades' name do you mean? I will torture you to death if you refuse to do as I say."

"Do it, then. Torture me to death. I care not."

Domitian was growing tired of Abigail's obstinacy. "Why so stubborn, Abby?" He shook his head with growing frustration. "What is it that you want if not your life?"

"I want to save my brother's life."

Domitian laughed. "No, no, no not that, anything but that. He must be punished for his crimes against our clan."

"Lord, I will resurrect the countess if you grant unconditional freedom to my brother Pierce van Fleming."

"I hate that name," hissed Domitian, face twisting. "Oh how I loathe him!"

"Is your hatred for my brother greater than your love for Marie?" said Abigail, glancing over at Marie's head. "Would you forgo her resurrection for Pierce?"

Domitian wilted in his chair. He needed Marie and was certain Abigail could bring her back. How could he trust Abigail? Was she really unafraid to die? He reached into his coat pocket and retrieved a small device that he had found in Sir Michael's dungeon. It was an iron vice. He held it out for Abigail to see. "Do you know what this is?"

Abigail nodded.

"We vampires are endowed with certain gifts: speed, strength, heightened senses, and longevity. Many of us claim to be immortal. Yet, someday all of us will die." He curled his finger for Abigail to come closer. "Do you know what this little clamp is called?"

Abigail shook her head.

"Pilliwinks..." He giggled. "Delightful name is it not—pilliwinks? Now, please place both thumbs in it here like this." He demonstrated by inserting his thumb between the clamps. Then he tossed the tool onto the floor in front of her. "Pick it up and insert your thumbs, please."

Abigail stared down at the device.

"Pick it up!"

Abigail lifted the tool with her left hand.

"Place your right thumb between the clamps."

She did as she was told.

"Now, the other thumb."

"Why must you do this?" asked Abigail. "This will hurt me, but it will not change my mind."

After she inserted her left thumb, Domitian leaned forward, took hold of the pilliwinks, and started to turn the screw. As the clamps began to squeeze Abigail's thumbs, he carefully studied her expression. "Feel the pain, Abby. I will not stop until either you agree to resurrect the countess unconditionally or your thumbs are crushed." He continued to turn the screw. "Tell me that you will resurrect her, and I will stop."

"I will not," refused Abigail.

Domitian kept turning the screw.

Abigail cringed and yelped in pain.

"Oh, now you feel it! This, is merely a small taste of what has yet to come. Do you remember the rack, Abby? Do you remember how it felt to have your limbs pulled out of the sockets? Tell me again that you do not want to be tortured to death. Tell me that and the next level of torture will be the rack."

Abigail shook her head. "Tortured me to death! I will only resurrect the countess if you grant me one request of my own."

"After I torture you to death, I will hunt down your brother and do the same to him! Agree to resurrect her!"

Domitian stopped turning the screw and stared at her flattened thumbs, blood dripping onto the floor between them. "Stubborn, stubborn, woman!" He let go of the pilliwinks and sat back in his chair. "Remove the clamp."

"How," she squeaked, her face contorted with pain. Abigail placed the wing nut between her teeth and struggled to unscrew it. Finally, the pilliwinks slipped off her smashed digits, clanging to the blood spattered floor. Abigail remained on the floor in front of Domitian, staring down at her ruined thumbs.

"They will heal," said Domitian.

"Who will resurrect your precious countess when I am dead?"

Domitian saw now that Abigail indeed cared more for her brother than she did for her own life. In order to return Marie he had to let Pierce go. "You are a shrewd one, Abby. Very well...you will resurrect the countess in trade for your brother's freedom."

"And if I fail to resurrect the countess, what then? Will you hunt my brother?"

"What do you think?"

Abigail closed her eyes, taking a moment. When she opened them, she nodded. "Agreed..."

Domitian's grin lifted his ears. He crouched to her level and gently took her damaged hands into his. "Your thumbs are already healing, see?"

Abigail ignored her injuries, locking her eyes onto his.

"When can we start?" asked Domitian, standing and turning to face Marie's remains. "I will provide everything you need."

"I need a deadwood tree..."

"A what...?"

"A deadwood tree. Magic feeds the tree until the essence of the before-life flows through its roots and into its branches and leaves. The necromancer need only draw the essence out."

"That all sounds completely absurd. Where is this tree?"

"In the forest..."

"Abby," said Domitian in a deeper tone. "Whether you care to die or not, trick me and I will kill you and your brother. Do you understand?"

"Yes, milord."

## 5 - THE HOUSE OF MERIDIEM

Cedric felt it in his bones the scraping fear of becoming cynical and contemptible. He had worked hard to keep a positive spirit and ignore the critics in his head. He was fortunate to be traveling with the brothers and hoped their friendship would grow. Still, Cedric felt alone and aimless, numbed by the sadness of losing his family to the Black Death and his friends to implausible evil.

In a year's time, Cedric had seen so much wickedness that he hoped and prayed to eradicate all of it by simply waking at home in Linder. Problem was, this was no dream, bad or otherwise. Bloodthirsty creatures were pursuing him. He detested the fact that he had killed Countess Marie de Vos. Though it was an unfortunate kill-or-be-killed circumstance, his burden of guilt remained. Had he not returned to the castle to free Lily, he would have killed no one, but that argument led back to the question of what would have happened to Lily had he not returned to the castle.

Who was the countess? Why was she so evil? What is a vampire, exactly? At first, he thought they were godless people going mad in a dingy castle. As time went on, no explanation adequately filled the ever-widening and deepening mysteries concerning those hellish manifestations. Perhaps they were demons or people who had been possessed by demons. Cedric had heard of such things. Yet, time spent with the evil Countess Marie and troubled Pierce van Fleming—the man she tried to seduce and kill—revealed other possibilities.

Perhaps vampires were afflicted by a disease. Perhaps they were not of this earth. Perhaps they were fallen angels. Cedric saw that ordinary people were as much caretaker as prey to them, and a select few were neither. They were singled out, as Pierce was. Marie had traveled by land and sea for many days to find him, and when she did, she changed him. At first, the change made him very sick. He was irritable, delusional, feverish, and aloof. Over time, he got better. He became extraordinary, like the rest of them. He rapidly healed from wounds from which ordinary men died. He leapt with ease from London Bridge onto a moving ship. He conjured lightning from his hands. Cedric saw all of it with his own peeping eyes but struggled to believe them.

The vampires usually slept by day and stalked by night, but not because of some aversion to sunlight. He had seen them outside in the brightest of days. They appeared no more sensitive to sunlight than he was. He posited that stalking prey under the veil of darkness and mist was a tactical strategy.

"Are you thinking again or napping, Cedric?" asked Gert, turning back to smile at the boy whose eyes had been closed and head had been bobbing for quite some time.

Cedric shook his head and let out a soft chuckle. "Thinking..."

"What of?"

"Life, death, family, friends, *them*..."

"Them?" asked Gert, yawning and stretching his arms. "Easy to lose oneself in reverie on days like this... I was thinking of home. I look forward to introducing you to my wife and our entire family."

"Our staff as well," added Klaas.

"And especially Adina," said Gert.

"I will be honored to meet them all," said Cedric, noticing a gray raven soaring above them. Cedric knew it was an unusually large bird by how slowly it flapped its wings. Gray, too. He had never seen a gray raven before. "Look at that bird," said Cedric, pointing up at it.

Gert and Klaas saw it, then looked at each other and shrugged.

"A sign of good luck," said Gert, cheerfully. "We have seen all sorts of wondrous animals, Cedric. Silver birds, golden wolves, green foxes..."

"Green foxes?" asked Cedric.

"A word of advice," said Klaas to Cedric. "Do not believe everything my brother says."

Cedric scanned the sky for the raven but saw only a few clouds. He looked to see where it had gone. "How far is Amsterdam from your home?"

"A day's trot is all," said Gert.

"A half day's gallop," added Klaas.

"The bird landed behind yonder rock," said Gert, chuckling, "if you are still looking for it."

It was near dusk when they arrived in Ghent. Cedric followed the brothers along a fern-lined trail to a big pile of rocks. Behind the rocks was a gate made of vines. The gate swung open and they sauntered for ten minutes through a lush garden. The garden contained marble statues of Greek gods and a voluminous fountain with water-spouting mermaids reclining on a rock in a pool of water-lilies. He looked toward the edges of the property and saw a dense wall of trees. They appeared to be tall pine trees growing so tightly together that no child could fit between their trunks and the branches interlaced to form a solid barrier. A palatial house came into view. Cedric had seen large houses in London and Brussels before but nothing quite as big as the building directly ahead of them.

The stately building was many floors tall and as wide as Buckingham House in London, but slightly curved as if wanting to wrap itself around anyone approaching it. A wide glass dome rose at its center, adding another three levels to its overall height. There were too many windows of various shapes, sizes, and colors to count. The entrance door resembled a fortress gate of iron and timber, with all sorts of interesting carvings of mythical creatures such as griffins, gargoyles, dragons, and beasts with multiple heads. Compensating for a lack of glitzy elegance with rustic zeal and oddity, the walls were of chiseled stone and brick and exposed timbers shaped by carpenters to retain much of their tree shape and features.

Inside the house, a sudden waft of baked foods reminded Cedric of home. Brick, stone, and wood continued throughout the interior of the house. Cedric wondered if the fellers who fell the trees carved the ornamental effigies similar to the ones outside of unworldly creatures perched and peering from random ledges in the massive foyer. In the center of the space stood the most interesting feature of all—a massive tree, rising up to the glass and iron dome ceiling. Its sparse foliage of red and yellow star-shaped leaves and clusters of pink flowers contrasted beautifully with its otherwise thick and gnarled branches. Dozens of bizarre little birds like feathery bumblebees, fat and round, smaller and more iridescent than a hummingbird, buzzed and darted from flower to flower in a dizzying display of aerial acrobatics.

*What sort of tree is that?* Cedric thought. *Just look at those birds. Everything is so wondrous.* Utterly distracted, he had not noticed four women approaching until Gert tapped him on his shoulder.

After Klaas and Gert respectfully greeted the eldest woman, calling her "*Grootmoeder*", which Cedric knew to mean grandmother, and the next eldest as "Moeder," they turned their attention to the two younger women.

The grandmother approached Cedric and studied his face. She took his hand in hers and smiled as if satisfied to have confirmed something she had always known. "Welcome, Mister Cedric Martens. I am Lidia, Mother to Isa, grandmother to Klaas and Gert."

Cedric bowed. "I am honored, madam. Thank you for welcoming me into your beautiful home." Suddenly, Cedric realized that Lidia had called him by name. Had someone mentioned his name to her? When?

Klaas hugged his wife Sanne, and turned to introduce her to Cedric. "Mister Cedric Martens of—of—"

"Linder," Gert reminded his brother.

"Right," said Klaas, "Linder is a farming village somewhere, uh—"

"Southeast of the Sonian Forest," said Gert, in stride as if his job was to remind Klaas of such things.

"How do you do?" said Cedric to Sanne.

"This is Roos," said Gert, pulling his wife closer.

"Pleased to make your acquaintance," said Cedric. Cedric was beside himself, dizzied to be in a home with family again— any family—and utterly confused that Lidia knew his name.

Suddenly, a young woman bounded into the foyer. Lidia turned to her. "There you are, Adina. Meet our guest, Mister Cedric Martens of—"

"Linder," blurted Klaas followed by a click of his tongue.

Gert broke away to meet Adina. He kissed her cheek, hugged her, and led her to Cedric. "Cedric, this is my sister, Adina."

Cedric bowed and took her hand, but when he tried to kiss it, she withdrew and crossed her arms.

"Mister Martens," said Adina.

Obviously, the Bezuidenhouts were no ordinary family. As wealthy as they were attractive, even the grandmother dazzled with youth in her eyes. Klaas and Gert's wives were beautiful, and Adina was stunning. Not since Cedric had laid eyes on Headmistress Abigail a year ago had he found it difficult to look away from a woman until now. Perhaps it was the lively glow of her skin and thickness of her blonde hair draping over her shoulders. Yet, Cedric thought her eyes were her most striking feature. Her right eye was the color of bluebells in spring while the other was as green as moss on a log. Her comfortable but modest maiden's gown revealed enough of her graceful proportions to rouse him. He smiled at her, moved his eyes to Grandmother Lidia, and wondered how old Adina might be.

Klaas raised his hand and said, "There will be time on the morrow to visit. Now, if you will excuse us, Sanne and I will bid you a good evening." He patted Gert on the shoulder as he and Sanne moved to Lidia. They kissed Klaas's mother on the cheek and continued on to the stairs, up two flights to a vestibule, and out of sight into a corridor.

Lidia turned to Adina. "Adina dear, please show Mister Martens to his bedchamber." She smiled at Cedric. "Rest well, my dear."

"Thank you, madam."

Cedric followed Adina through wide and winding corridors deep into the house. After what seemed to be an impossibly long trek, Adina opened a large door and let Cedric inside. In the bedchamber was an elaborately carved canopy bed with blue velvet curtains. Along the walls he counted six windows, each one unique in shape and size. A peculiar mirror hung on the wall among the windows. Not only irregular in shape with distorted reflections, the mirror was also softly glowing. Cedric was certain of it.

"Do you like the room?" asked Adina, standing at the doorway.

Cedric turned to her. "Very much, yes."

"Help yourself to the wardrobe. New clothes have been selected for you." She pointed to a door at the far side of the room. "You may freshen up in there. No need to go outside."

"Thank you, um..."

"Adina. Good evening, Cedric."

"Good evening, Adina."

Cedric heard the latch drop after Adina closed the door and quickly went to check if it was locked. During his time at Vos Castle, he developed a fear of being locked in a room. After Adina's footsteps faded to silence, he placed his thumb on the latch and pressed it. He pulled the door open and peered into the corridor but saw no one. He closed the door and went to the bed on which a nightgown of linen was neatly placed. He found a washbasin and vase of rosewater on a table, and a wardrobe of handsome new clothing in the armoire. Holding the garments against himself, he wondered how it was possible they knew his size. What were these people?

He opened the door to a room wherein he saw a wooden box about knee-high against the wall below a tall window. Two washbasins and vases of fresh water, including cups and a stack of wash rags and towels, were arranged on a cabinet. He slowly lifted the box-lid and looked inside. The first thing he noticed was a porcelain bowl with a fist-sized drain hole around which the wooden box was built. It was a commode, similar to those he had seen in England.

After relieving himself and washing off with a sponge, he put the nightgown on, got into bed, and immediately fell asleep.

# 6 - THE HARVEST

At dawn, after Cedric arrived at Klaas and Gert's home, Domitian and his sentry followed Abigail into the Sonian Forest to collect a seed from the deadwood tree. After an hour of moving swiftly through the woods, they arrived at a clearing. A burned-out stump stood near the center of the opening, and a pile of rocks and a bouquet of dried flowers marked a gravesite nearby. Abigail went directly to the stump. She placed her hand on a few pieces of tree bark and gently pulled them off, but found nothing beneath them. She looked into the hollowed base. Nearly a shin's length down, she saw her reflection peering back at her. She leaned over the stump, reached inside, and submerged her hand into water. Reaching as far as she could, the bottom was too deep to touch. The jagged top edge of the stump prevented her from reaching any farther without actually inserting her head and shoulders into the hollowed space.

"Lift me up and hold me over," said Abigail to the guard who was standing in front of her, arms crossed, blasé face. She quickly tied her long hair back into a knot, placed her hands on the top edge of the stump, and waited for the guard.

He took hold of her ankles and lifted her legs until she was suspended upside down. He held her over the hollow of the stump and lowered her in. To fit into the confining interior, she extended her right arm and the other up behind her back.

"Lower," she insisted.

The guard lowered her until her shoulders were inside the stump.

Domitian giggled at the sight of what appeared to be a woman being stuffed into a tree stump. He wrestled his attention away and focused on the gravesite. Was this the burial ground of a dog or of Abigail's brother?

Suddenly, the serenity of the forest was shattered by screaming. Abigail's torso slid to her waist into the stump.

"Up! Pull me up!" Abigail's screaming was muffled. "Lift!" Eyes-deep in the water now.

The guard struggled to lift her. "Milord!" yelped the guard to Domitian.

Domitian joined the guard and took hold of her thighs to help lift her out, but they were getting nowhere. He squatted and gripped her legs tightly. "Lift together on the count of three!"

The guard quickly took a similar position opposite Domitian and nodded.

Domitian counted. "And one, and two, and lift!"

With enough strength to pull her up without tearing her legs off, Abigail's shoulders finally emerged from the stump. She took hold of the top edge of the stump with her left hand, and shouted, "Lift again!"

While the guard held onto her legs, Domitian reached into the stump and took hold of Abigail's right arm. Then he began to pull. With every two inches of arm gained, she was tugged back down an inch. Slowly, but painfully, they were winning the battle. When her wrist broke the surface of the water and was now a few inches from the top edge of the stump, everyone finally got to see what had latched onto her.

From the depths of the deadwood tree stump appeared a red, slimy hand with long, bony fingers that gripped tightly around Abigail's fist. What made the stump dweller even stranger was the green eyeball on the back of the hand, which now looked more like a serpent with a mouth in the shape of a hand. Bulging veins pulsated and wriggled like earthworms beneath the creature's red and nearly translucent skin. Black thorns grew in rows down its body. The guard grabbed hold of the creature's body, and the thorns extended through his hands. The guard was now moaning in pain alongside Abigail.

With her free hand, Abigail quickly plunged her fingers into the creature's green eye. It hissed and clamped tighter on her fist. Abigail cringed with pain and anger as she took a firm hold of its eye and yanked it out of its socket. Finally, the serpent writhed in silence and released Abigail. It retracted its thorns, and slinked back into the unknown depths of the hollowed tree trunk.

Domitian kneeled beside Abigail and saw the lacerations on her crushed hand. "What was that?"

She shook her head, her eyes still wider than ever. "My mother never told me of such things."

"It appeared very upset, as if it was guarding something valuable," said the guard.

"It was," said Abigail as she gingerly opened her damaged hand. There in her bloody palm was a seed the size of a robin's egg, multicolored with short spines. In her other hand was the green eyeball. She tossed the eye into the stump and stood up. "I will need to plant this seed near the countess's remains."

As the guard and Abigail behind him started back into the forest, Domitian noticed an ethereal cloud of light floating above Abigail. The light moved down to the base of a tree surrounded by ferns and began to glimmer there. At first, Domitian wanted to say something to the others, but pursed his lips and waited. When Abigail and the guard turned to look for Domitian, he waved them on. "I wish to spend time alone," said Domitian. "Gaétan, take her so she can plant the seed."

"Yes, milord," said Gaétan, ushering Abigail to move on.

Domitian turned to the light and saw an image of a woman sitting in a golden chair.

She wore a jeweled tiara and a royal blue gown with slits up the sides. The chair was really a throne resting atop a mound of dazzling riches.

She turned to view Domitian squarely and smiled, revealing an impressive pair of fangs. She extended her bare leg seductively across the arm of the golden throne and winked at Domitian. "You must be Domitian Augustus de' Medici," said the woman as she ran her tongue over her retracting mandibles. "You look exactly as she described—Marie's little *chelovek.*"

Domitian was struck by wonder. How could she know his name or Marie's for that matter? Was this the legendary queen of the Upyrian Empire? "Yes, it is I, Lord Domitian." Domitian quickly surveyed his surroundings to see that he was alone. "What trickery is this?"

"What stupidity is this?" replied the woman, pointing at him.

Domitian raised an eyebrow at her comment. "I ask again, what sort of witchy trickery is this? Who are you, and how is it that I can see you like—like this?" He reached out to touch the image but his hand went through it.

"You know who I am." The woman squinted as if trying to recognize Domitian's surroundings. "Where are you?"

Domitian looked up through the canopy at the sky. He was taken aback by the woman's daring. Yet, what if she really was the queen? "Forest," whispered Domitian. "I am in a forest."

"Which forest?"

"Sonian Forest, to be precise."

"Why are you there?"

"Oh, taking a stroll."

"Stroll? What is stroll?"

"A walk, I went for a walk, a trek, a jaunt. Do you not do that in Russia?"

She moved her leg off the throne's arm and stood up. She placed her hands on her hips and sneered. "What is my name? Say my name."

Domitian wanted to repeat *"my name"* or to say *"tiny witch,"* but restrained himself. Then, as if someone had taken over his body and certainly his voice, he spoke loudly and clearly. "Žofie, Queen of Upyrian." A jolt of fear entered his body. He had spoken someone else's words.

The woman giggled as if completely mad. Then, silence and an air of seriousness came over her. "You may address me as Eminence or Majesty if you prefer."

Domitian chuckled politely at the insult. "I feel as if I am in a dream, with little control over my thoughts and voice. Are you really Queen Žofie?"

"Your Eminence or Your Majesty!"

A sharp pain in the center of his head caused Domitian to cringe. When the pain subsided he felt even better than before. "How is it possible to communicate like this, er, Your Eminence?"

Žofie sat back down and drank from a golden goblet. When she put it down, a spot of blood remained on her lips. "So delicious, child's blood. You drink it?"

Domitian brought his hands together and recalled the last time he had tasted child's blood. Not since before the battle at Vos Castle, and at least two months before that. "I have tried it, Your Eminence."

"It is best when fresh! I convinced your Countess Marie de Vos to drink it. She drank even more than me."

Domitian wondered if the queen had something to do with Marie's excessiveness.

"I miss her very much. Is she really dead?" Žofie asked.

"I am afraid so—"

"She was magnificent woman—more upyrian than some upyrian."

"Indeed, Your Eminence. I miss her dearly as well. She is the reason for my existence—"

"Quiet! Continue to say stupid things and I will silence you forever."

The sharp pain returned.

"In this world you exist only because I allow it." She huffed as if annoyed. "Now that I see you, I question Countess

Marie's taste in men. I thought she had better judgment. Perhaps she made mistake and you are accident, da?"

Again, the pain subsided and Domitian felt better than before and astonishingly not as offended by her insults as he normally would be.

"Maybe Countess Marie realized too late that you come from powerful family, important to your clan. For that reason Countess Marie cannot kill you. So she made you into a little vampire man." The queen smirked at Domitian's good nature. "You have thick skin, Domitian. That is good. Perhaps henceforth I will call you Thick Skin Domitian." She appeared to be listening to something or someone as she went quiet for a moment. Then, she looked directly at him and smiled. "So, you still want to know how I communicate like this?"

Domitian nodded.

"It is magical, a sort of meddling of minds. Not so deep like bending of minds."

"I feel it, a sort of tickling sensation in my head."

"I can know what you are thinking if you allow me. I cannot control you entirely, like a marionette, but enough to make you see and hear me—like now. It is easiest to meddle with simpletons like you. It is difficult to meddle with smart minds like Countess Marie. I can only do smart minds when they sleep or when they are unaware or too weak to stop me."

"I see, I think..."

"Do not see. Do not think. Free your mind to me."

Domitian looked inward and tried to detect Žofie's presence. A slight dizziness came over him and he felt something like a splinter inside his head.

"Your mind is so full of holes to hide in, you will never find me."

Domitian felt as if his energy was being drained. The ache in his mind had dissolved into a comfortable dizziness.

"Are you aware of my agreement with Countess Marie de Vos?"

Domitian massaged his temples. "Are you referring to the orphans, Your Eminence?"

"Yes."

"Yes, Countess Marie shared details of this agreement. I know the trade routes, mode of transportation, expected quantities—"

"There is one condition," said Žofie.

"Yes, Your Eminence?"

"You must tell me where my sister is."

Domitian was instantly baffled. He expected conditions concerning payment, quotas, border restrictions, but her sister? "Your Eminence...?"

"My twin sister. It's like looking in mirror, but I am prettier version of us. She has one blue eye, one green eye, like a snow dog."

"Ah, I see! She should be very easy to identify. Where is she now?"

"If I knew that, why would I need you?"

"Forgive me, Your Eminence. Can you provide a general location and her name? I will send my soldier to find her and capture her—"

Žofie laughed. "You cannot capture her! She is too powerful for little vampires. You need only to find her and tell me where she is. Her name is Adina Cervenka, but she goes by a new surname: Bezuidenhout. She resides in the House of Meridiem. No one knows exactly where that is. Also, Adina is immortal not vampire."

Domitian was suddenly fascinated. "Immortal, but not vampire—human? Human immortal...is that possible?"

"She is twice born, resurrected by a Meridiem necromancer. She is powerful but not so pretty. The color of her eyes are different, one blue other green, like a dog"

"I—I see." However, Domitian had only heard of Meridiem sorcerers. They were supposedly bound by a pact to guard the western border from invading upyrians. Was there any truth to that? If so, would he endanger the west by helping Žofie capture her sister Adina, a Meridiem immortal?

"You need only tell me where she is. I'll take care of the rest. Then, we'll discuss delicious orphan trade and border, da?"

"Yes, yes, of course, Your Eminence. When shall we meet again, or rather, how may I contact you?"

"You need only open your mind and call to me, and I will find you."

Domitian watched the image slowly fade into the ferns, and he dropped to his knees when it had fully vanished.

# 7 - BREAKFAST AT THE BEZUIDENHOUTS

## JUNE 1799

Disharmonious cockerels woke Cedric from a deep slumber. He slid the bed-curtain open and squinted up at the unusually shaped windows and the strange mirror among them. The mirror was no longer glowing or distorted. Curiosity coaxed him out of bed to examine the mirror. He touched the surface of it—smooth and ordinary. Satisfied it was just a mirror, he looked through a lighter colored window pane at a large fountain in the gardens below.

A knock at the door startled him.

After opening the door, Cedric was happy to see Gert there.

"Slept well, Cedric?" asked Gert with his signature cheery smile.

Cedric rubbed the back of his neck and smiled back. "Yes, thank you."

"Moeder insisted that we bathe before breakfast—no exceptions."

"I washed last night," said Cedric, not feeling the need to bathe again.

"Not sponge bathing, tub bathing, and worry not. Our breakfast will still be waiting for us, fresh and hot afterwards. Take a robe from the armoire. I will wait outside. Be quick, for the sooner we bathe the sooner we eat!"

The bathing room was located at the far end of the house, which was difficult for Cedric to know, as the labyrinth of hallways to get there twisted not only right and left and up and down, but also slanted one way or the other. Along the way, dozens of doors of all shapes, sizes, and colors caused Cedric to wonder what was behind each one.

The bathing room was more like a big cave in the side of a mountain because it had one enormous abstractly-shape window with views of a lush valley. The cavern appeared to be carved from solid stone. Four bronze tubs large enough to fit two persons in each were separated by a stone partition that was not straight but meandered in an *S*-pattern. Flowering plants and vines grew on the partition, which was tall enough to lend privacy but low enough for bathers to communicate.

"This one is yours," said Gert, pointing to the tub nearly filled with steaming water. "Enjoy."

Cedric saw a pipe jutting out of the rock partition beside the tub—water was flowing out. "Where is the water coming from?" asked Cedric.

Gert turned and pointed at a wall of rock. "Behind that wall is hot spring water."

"Spring water?"

"Yes, it bubbles out of the ground."

"I've never heard of such a thing."

"Do you know what a volcano is?"

"Yes."

"This house is built atop a volcano. We believe that one day everything here will sink into a lake of fire."

"Really?"

"No." Gert chuckled at Cedric before moving behind a flowery wall to bathe.

Cedric went to his tub. Flowers were floating on the surface of the water. He disrobed and slowly got in. After an acclimating moment, he slid all the way under the water and stayed there for as long as his breath lasted.

After bathing and returning to his bedchamber, Cedric put on his new clothes. Except for the white shirt, everything else was black like the Fortune Brothers' clothes. He ventured out into the corridor and followed his nose at the beckoning of his stomach. Through the maze of hallways, passing countless doors, his hand wandered to a pewter doorknob in the shape of a raven's head. He wanted to know what was behind that green door. Just as he turned the knob and found that it was locked, a voice from behind scared him into a defensive spin.

"Good day, Cedric," said Adina.

Cedric felt guilty for snooping. "Good day, Adina." He searched for the look of distrust on her face but saw only her penetrating blue and green eyes looking through him at the interesting door knob. "I...I was marveling at the enormity of your home. There are just so many rooms and...and doors."

She waved at Cedric to step aside, which he did, and she went to the door, placed her hand on the doorknob, easily turned it, and pushed the door open. "Go on, have a look inside."

Cedric peered into a very large and sparsely furnished room. He looked up and saw a row of ceiling beams carved in the shape of arms from elbows to fingertips. Each of the enormous hands held a chain from which dangled candle chandeliers made of elk's horns.

"This is the ballroom," said Adina, following Cedric into the cavernous space. She pointed to the far end. "Over there is where performers set up." She pointed to doors around the room. "Those doors all lead to a corridor. Many rooms are quite big and have more than one door. Therefore, many of the doors you see lead to the same room." She stepped out into the hallway. "Breakfast is ready."

Cedric quickly stepped out of the ballroom, closing the door behind him, and followed her to a dining hall large enough to seat fifty people. Laid out on one of two long tables was an assortment of food, enough to feed twenty mouths. Cedric had never seen a finer bounty served all at once. The most food he had ever seen in one sitting was a large pot of vegetable stew in the dining hall at Vos Castle.

Lidia was already seated at the head of the table. At the center sat Klaas and Gert, their wives Sanne and Roos beside them, and beside Sanne sat four children, twin girls and twin boys. Each set of twins appeared to be a year apart in age.

"Uma and Elissa are seven," said Sanne to Cedric. "Bjorn and Karl are eight."

"What is your name?" asked Uma to Cedric.

"Cedric Martens."

"Why are you here?" asked Elissa.

"Where do you come from?" asked Uma.

"What is your business?" said Bjorn, with a serious face to match his tone.

"That is quite enough," said Sanne to the kids. "Master Cedric is a guest. He is not required to answer such questions." Sanne smiled at Cedric. "I apologize for the inquisition. They are a curious lot and obviously interested in you." Sanne shook her head at her children. "Mind your manners and allow our guest to enjoy his breakfast."

"Sit where you like," said Klaas to Cedric.

Cedric searched for Adina, but his vision got lost in the crowd of people that were flowing in and around the dining hall. Cedric found Gert and Roos and sat next to them at the center of the table.

"Believe it or not, Cedric," said Gert, "all these people are family."

"And most live here," said Roos.

Cedric finally saw Adina, sitting at the end of the table.

Roos followed Cedric's eyes to her. "You know, Cedric," said Roos. "Adina is a blade master."

"Really?" said Cedric, forcing his eyes away.

Gert nodded affirmatively. "The best of us all—but do not tell Klaas I said that."

Lidia stood up, and the room went silent.

Cedric's attention now shifted to Lidia. He wondered if she would lead a prayer. His father always had before meals.

Lidia's smile was bright but teary when her eyes fell upon Cedric. "We welcome our newest friend, Mister Cedric Martens of Linder."

Cedric was not expecting to be recognized by the matriarch.

Lidia continued. "We humbly ask the gods to look favorably upon Cedric Martens and our family, to watch over Adina, Klaas, and Gert on their next assignment and to escort them safely home to us." Lidia's eyes roamed over the food. "Bless the harvest and our noble beasts whose lives were sacrificed to nourish us." Lidia offered her hands to guests sitting to her left and right, and everyone then took their neighbor's hand in theirs. Lidia closed her eyes and whispered something that Cedric could not understand. When she was done, she sat down and said, "Eat well, live well."

Activities resumed at an even greater pace and volume.

"So, Cedric of Linder," said Roos, stabbing a slice of salted ham and placing it on Cedric's plate. "You appear too young to be playing with Gert and Klaas."

"I will be eighteen soon," said Cedric.

"Already a man, then," said Roos.

"He is older than his years," said Gert. "He has seen a great deal—a large gray raven, for example."

Cedric turned to see Adina conversing with Lidia, both smiling and laughing and filling their plates.

"How old is Adina?" asked Cedric to anyone who might know.

"I would say, nineteen, or so," volunteered Roos.

*Is she attracted to me?* he thought. No sooner had his heart began to race toward the possibility of something romantic between them before it paused at the thought of Lily. A man came to pour juice into his goblet. Another man came around with water, and Cedric redirected his attention to those sitting near him.

After breakfast, Cedric and the brothers joined Adina at the stable outside. This time, there were four horses.

"This is your horse," said Adina to Cedric.

Cedric took the reins. His horse was a tall, gray mare with shaggy ankles and a long mane. The tail had been cropped and tied, and the finest brown leather saddle Cedric had ever seen had been cinched on.

Adina and her brothers mounted their Belgium black horses, and allowed Cedric to catch up as they rode slowly toward the palatial entry where Lidia, Roos, Sonne, and her children were assembled.

After brief goodbyes, for the second time, Klaas turned his horse toward the garden and led the others away from the house. Klaas's children ran beside them through the gardens, waving and cheering until they got tired and faded back. The four continued on through what really appeared to be a fairytale garden surrounded by a solid wall of trees and boulders the size of carriages, until they reached the hidden gate of vines at the farthest edge of the property.

## 8 - FREDERIC DE ROTHSCHILD

It was afternoon when Amsterdam came into view, faint, many miles yet in the distance. Farmlands and waterways between them told of a bountiful city. They came upon a farmhouse beside a river southeast of Amsterdam. With Adina there, Klaas was less persnickety, though still rambunctious. Gert rode up to Cedric and lifted off his Dutch hat. "How are you getting along, Cedric?"

"Very well, thank you," said Cedric.

"This farm belongs to Frederic de Rothschild. We have agreements with him as well as with other generous friends of the family. They provide lodging in exchange for private performances. Tonight, we will perform and hopefully shed no blood this time." Gert dismounted and walked his horse toward a barn.

Cedric followed, wondering what Gert meant—no blood this time. Were they perhaps not as skilled with blades as they purported to be?

The home of Frederic de Rothschild was perched on a knoll overlooking a meadow. It was a simple but large house of wood and brick. Cedric guessed three main floors with a fourth level that popped up near the center of the roof like some sort of observation tower in the shape of a gazebo. As Cedric followed the siblings to the main entrance, the front door swung open and out stepped a well dressed lady and a clean-shaven gentleman.

"What took you so long!" said the man, smiling and rushing to meet Klaas.

Klaas shook the man's hand and patted him on his shoulder. "Is a year so long, Frederic?"

Gert bowed and kissed the woman's hand. "It is a pleasure to gaze upon your beauty again, dear Linda."

Klaas turned to Cedric. "May I introduce Mister Cedric Martens of..."

"Linder," said Gert. "Mister and Missus Rothschild are dear old friends."

"How do you do, Mister and Missus Rothschild?" said Cedric, and he bowed.

"Welcome, Mister Martens," said Linda, taking Adina by the hand, the two women smiling but saying nothing to each other. "Please, come inside, everyone."

Dinner time that evening, Cedric and the siblings were seated at a long dining table with the Rothschilds' sizeable family to feast. Mister Rothschild sat at the north end of the table. Klaas sat to his right. Missus Rothschild sat across from her husband and Adina sat to her right. Gert sat next to Klaas and Cedric sat next to Adina. The remaining seats were occupied by three sons, two daughters—all young adults—a potential son-in-law, two aging aunts, and the eldest member of their family, Missus Rothschild's mother. Cedric observed the butler, though tall his hair was so short and white that his head may as well have been bald. Waiting the table with him was the first footman, even taller and younger that the bartender. A daughter could not remove her eyes from him as he poured wine and generally helped the house maids serve the table. The Rothschilds appeared extremely wealthy to Cedric who wondered how they earned their wealth.

Cedric noticed Mister Rothschild's stare. He glanced over at Mister Rothschild and smiled.

"Mister Martens," said Rothschild, finally. "Curious to know how you came to know the Bezuidenhouts?"

"We met during our travels, a year ago," said Cedric. "I was en route to Brussels—"

"We were en route to Luxembourg, as I recall," added Gert.

"Yes, that would be right," said Klaas.

Mister Rothschild lifted his glass of wine and waited for everyone to join him in a toast. "Honorable friends, new and old, may our amity grow lavishly and unremittingly in both quality and harmonious polytonality! It has indeed, been too long. Proost!"

"Proost!" everyone cheered.

Though Cedric happily conversed and joked with everyone at the table, Gert and Klaas had asked earlier that he not mention the castle or discuss vampires. Secrets felt like guilt, to Cedric. He wanted to confess them not hide them. Yet, he endeavored to honor their requests, learning the appropriateness of various subject matters. Challenged by etiquette, he was also burdened by his feelings for Adina. She was sitting beside him to his left. Every now and again, when they would bump elbows, he would feel a tingle of energy from his limbs to his heart. He felt both excited and vexed, as his friends, especially Lily, were becoming less prominent in his daily thoughts. Who was Adina? He began to wonder. She acted older than her years. She reminded him of Countess Marie in that way. Clearly, she was no monster, no vampire.

Drowning in a sea of multiple and unrelated conversations from all sides, he suddenly felt Adina's hand on his leg and her lips to his ear.

"Will you help us set up the stage tonight?" whispered Adina into Cedric's ear.

Cedric nodded, trying not to let her words and breath weaken his composure.

"We may call upon you to join us on stage if only for a minute."

Adina removed her hand from Cedric's leg, straightened and instantly engaged the hostess in lockstep timing, as if she had never left their conversation.

After dinner, everybody retired to the music chamber, which was a sizeable room with a raised stage at one end. Rows of armchairs and side tables offered comfortable seating. Cedric offered to help the siblings set up the stage.

They erected a circular plank, a coffin-shaped box, and pots of oil along the front edge of the stage—all items that had been stored there at the house. After everything was set, Cedric stepped off the stage and wandered to the back of the room, behind the Rothschild family, to watch. One of the Rothschild girls waved Cedric over to sit in an empty chair with them. Cedric thanked her and took the seat.

Gert stood at center stage. He held out his arms and smiled brightly. "Friends, families, on this evening of evenings, together we shall celebrate life, amuse death, and tempt fate, all from the comfort of your chairs. I give you the Fabulous Fortune Brothers, featuring the one and the only, Mister Fortune, Master of Blades!"

Klaas stepped forward and bowed to enthusiastic applause.

"The beautiful and incomparable Adina!" announced Gert.

Adina stepped forward with three unlit torches in hand.

Klaas introduced Gert as Mister Misfortune, Master of None, drawing laughs and a brief sneer from Gert that probably only Cedric noticed.

Gert and Klaas started juggling three swords while Adina explained the nuances and obvious dangers of the stunt. She then ignited the torches in a firepot and started to juggle them. The effect was something of a firestorm on stage. She turned to her brothers and share-juggled the swords and torches among them. It was mesmerizing and terrifying to see, especially Adina, whose beauty lit the stage in Cedric's eyes.

What if they dropped the fire or cut themselves? He worried for them. No wonder Gert hoped they would not draw any blood.

They juggled oddly shaped objects, too: small knives, daggers, balls, and torches. Literally stacking danger, they stood on one another's shoulders—Gert on Klaas's shoulders, and Adina on Gert's shoulders—juggling torches and blades up and down the human tower.

The smell of burning oil and the swooshing sounds of whirling fire captivated Cedric. He suddenly found himself on his feet along with the Rothschilds who were every bit as enthralled by the performance.

Cedric admired Adina's bravery and trust in her brother when she was strapped to a round panel and spun like a pinwheel, slowly at first, then faster as Klaas—blindfolded and smiling—threw daggers at her from twenty paces, each one lodging within an inch of her body. When she was set free, all that remained on the panel were the blades in the outline of her body. Then, Adina took those blades, two at a time, and threw them back at Klaas as he juggled three muskmelons, until all three melons was bristling with daggers. Just when Cedric thought the demonstration had ended, Klaas tossed each melon high into the air toward Gert. Adina unsheathed her sword and sliced the melons in midflight. Slices of fruit fell onto a table and Gert collected the daggers.

"Cedric," said Adina. "Would you be so kind as to bring the fruit to the audience to enjoy?"

Cedric quickly entered the stage, received a platter from Gert, and arranged the sliced melon onto the platter.

"Dear friends," said Gert, "our trusty associate Mister Cedric Martens will arranges slices of delicious fruit on a platter for your enjoyment!"

Cedric did as asked, taking the platter of fruit to the Rothschilds. As the family ate the melon, the siblings continued their show with swordplay so quick and precise and dangerous that Cedric feared for the sibling's safety.

Blindfolded, Adina defended herself with a sword in each hand against her brothers' circling attacks. Just as Cedric decided that the whole thing was masterfully choreographed and practiced, the brothers stood down and Gert asked Cedric to join them on stage again.

Gert handed his sword to Cedric when he returned to the stage. "Dear friends," said Gert, "please watch as Mister Cedric Martens—who has never raised a sword in our presence before—puts Adina's mastery to the test." He lifted a finger for emphasis. "Bearing in mind, ladies and gentlemen, Adina is thoroughly hoodwinked! She can see nothing."

"How does she do it?" hollered Mr. Rothschild.

Klaas stepped forward. "How? This is how! Watch!"

Gert nudged Cedric toward Adina, whose stance appeared aggressive with her swords crossed in front of her chest, black cloth masking her eyes.

Uncertain what he was supposed to do, sweat formed on Cedric's brow.

Gert nudged him again. "Go on," whispered Gert to Cedric, "Fear not, my friend. She is in no danger."

Cedric nodded. He ineptly pointed his sword at her and took a step forward.

Adina brought both swords downward, filling the room with the slicing sound of metal-on-metal. She turned sideways to Cedric and pointed her swords at him.

Cedric timidly lunged so that his sword would fall short if she failed to parry.

Adina quickly stepped aside, catching Cedric's sword in the crux of her re-crossed swords. A circular movement twisted his weapon away from him. Cedric felt awkward and helpless, watching his sword launched into the air.

Klaas caught his weapon by the handle and bowed as if that was the best part.

Before Cedric could move an inch, Adina was in front of him, her blades touching his neck. A lump formed in his throat as he froze, staring at the blades and then at her lips, searching for a smile or smirk. As soon as it started, it ended with Adina withdrawing her swords and removing her blindfold. Cedric's fright turned to relief as he finally noticed the Rothschild family on their feet, clapping and cheering.

"The Incomparable Adina and Mister Cedric Martens, ladies and gentlemen!" shouted Gert.

Later that night, while lying in bed, Cedric relished the performance, and Adina occupied his every thought. He had never met anyone like her before. Her blade skills really seemed to be superior to her brothers'. He wondered what traveling and performing as they do might be like. Would he ever consider a life like theirs if it were possible? It was Cedric's good fortune to have met the Fabulous Fortune Brothers. It was safer to travel with them than by himself to Amsterdam. He wanted so much to see Lily and Jacob there. Yet, a sudden yearning to juggle drew his thoughts back to Adina. Everyone in her family had been so hospitable, all but her.

Would she warm to him? He imagined Lily and Adina side by side. Lily was such a pretty girl, not yet an adult perhaps; but neither was Cedric, or so he felt, lacking depth of experience in matters of the heart. Until he became a hunted man, he and Lily had planned a future together. He ached to be with her. She was the reason he returned to Vos Castle. She was now the reason he was going to Amsterdam. Adina, on the other hand, acted exceedingly mature for nineteen. She was a full grown adult. Cedric was growing certain of it.

Tired yet still unable to sleep, when Cedric started counting imaginary sheep, memories of Countess Marie's compulsive need to tally everything disrupted any chance of sleep. As he tossed and turned under the covers, he heard the soft rumble of voices from behind his door. Curious, he got out of bed, went to the door, and pressed his ear to it. The voices grew fainter until he heard nothing. He quietly opened the door and crept out into the hallway. The voices were barely audible and fading to his left. Following the voices to the music chamber, he crouched in front of the closed door. He peeked through the lock but saw little more than the backs of five armchairs that had been rearranged closer to the inglenook. Cedric saw no servants. It was very late, and everyone was supposed to be asleep. With nothing to see, he pressed his ear to the keyhole and managed to make out some words.

"How many are they, dear?" Mr. Rothschild spoke softly to his wife.

"Four," whispered Mrs. Rothschild.

"Yes, four," affirmed Mr. Rothschild.

"Where are they sleeping?" whispered Klaas.

"Where, indeed," said Mr. Rothschild. "They have been moving, you see. They were spotted in the Luis Te Vraag Cemetery night before last."

"And last night?" asked Klaas.

Mr. Rothschild sipped his tea. "There again, but if you find nothing, then stand down and await further instructions."

"Have you any names?" asked Adina.

"Descriptions only," said Mr. Rothschild. "Light brown hair, blue eyes, farmer's clothing."

"On wing, too," added Mrs. Rothschild.

"Yes," confirmed Mr. Rothschild. "I am afraid so."

"Payment...?" asked Klaas.

"Mother received payment before we left," said Adina. "When should we go?"

"At dawn," said Mrs. Rothschild.

When it seemed that the sibling's discussion with the Rothschilds was concluding, Cedric quickly returned to his bedchamber, wondering what they were being paid to do.

# 9 -SIR MICHAEL'S PROMISE

In his chambers in the highest tower at Vos Castle, Domitian placed his hand on a lockbox in which the remains of the former master known as Count Marcel Marc de Vos were contained. Marcel had ruled the clan for over four hundred years. Pity he had to be killed, and by his trusted advisor Sir Michael, thought Domitian. Domitian took hold of the padlock and removed it. He was about to open the lid when he heard something from inside the box. He leaned closer to the lid.

"Yes? Are you in there? Can you hear me?" Domitian gently knocked on the box and intently listened. "If by chance you can hear me, I wanted to remind you that had you abdicated peacefully, I would not be talking to a box." Domitian returned the padlock to the latch. "Wait here," he said to the box with a giggle.

He quickly moved through the catacombs to a small chamber conveniently called the dungeon because many devices of torture—mostly broken and stacked in a pile—were stored inside it. A guard stood beside a heavy timber and iron door. "Open the door," said Domitian.

The sentry did as he was told, and Domitian stepped inside. He signaled his guard to close the door behind him. A torch on the wall illuminated the room's clutter and something moving on the floor.

Sir Michael Livesey appeared to be dead, or sleeping, in a semi-standing position against the wall—arms shackled at the wrists above his head, bare feet chained to the floor. Two fat rats were gnawing his toes, over and over again in the same spot that miraculously healed over and over again.

Domitian stepped on both rats, but they would not die. He lifted a squealing rat by the tail into the torchlight and observed its teeth. Not that it was possible for a vampire to sire vampire rats, just to be safe Domitian twisted off their heads and tossed the body parts at the other rats moving among the clutter of torturing devices. He shuddered with disgust for having touched the vermin. He hated rats—could not imagine eating one even if he had to.

"Greetings, Sir Michael," said Domitian, lifting the torch to Michael's face, causing the man to turn away. Michael was suffering from starvation with bits of disgust, disgrace, distrust, and anger all mashed together. "You look simply awful!" Domitian followed his comment with a chuckle. "The effects of starvation are interesting, are they not? When the frenzy comes, the moisture in your body will evaporate, leaving you dry like leather, with a burning sensation in your guts. You may drift out of consciousness for relief, but that is only a temporary departure from the hellish reality of the frenzy. You are looking a bit leathery now, Sir Michael. Why are you made to suffer, you may ask? The answer is simple. You will suffer until you agree to help me. Since the average lifespan of a vampire is potentially...centuries, that is a long time to suffer. You might ask, *what does Domitian want?* Well, you see, without the countess, I am at a disadvantage. She had always been the brains of our efforts. I think you know that already." Domitian waited for Sir Michael to react, but the man remained stubbornly motionless. "What I want is what you know."

Sir Michael remained silent, eyes closed.

"Being that you were Count Marcel's advisor, you must know things—knowledge that under normal circumstances would have transferred from Marcel to me had he abdicated peacefully. Countess Marie had told me that you are privy to such valuable information." He slapped Sir Michael's face. "Wake up, my dark knight!"

Sir Michael opened his eyes and turned to Domitian's grinning face.

"Guard!" said Domitian.

"Yes, milord," said the guard.

"Bring us a lamb."

"Milord?"

"A living lamb, and be quick."

"Yes, milord."

Domitian patted Michael's cheek. "There, now we are all alone to talk."

"I have nothing to say to you," grumbled Michael.

"I suggest that you talk if only to make conversation. You must be lonely down here in the company of rats."

Michael scoffed. "You must be lonely in the company of your dead countess."

Domitian marveled at this shackled and suffering man's gall. Sir Michael was gutsy. "Why do you think I am lonely? I am the master of this clan. Clearly, you are the loneliest one here."

Michael grinned to bare his canines already long and hard, eager to penetrate. "I am suffering, yes, but I am not as desperate to survive as you will be when Orfeo comes for you."

"Master Orfeo? Come here, all the way from Rome, to do what—to hurt me? Why would he do that? We are allies."

"Your alliance was based on your promise to provide soldiers. How can you do that when your clan has been whittled down to no more than half dozen? Without the countess to mastermind your next move, your days are numbered."

Domitian cringed and bit his knuckle. "Doomed, you say?" Domitian was getting deeper into his head, it was agonizing. "We are eleven—no, wait, nine, I think. Two of our guards were recently slain by swordsmen."

Sir Michael coughed up a hoarse chuckle. "Who killed your guards?"

"Men dressed in black, rescuing the orphan who Abigail claims to have killed the countess."

Sir Michael let out a few humored puffs of air through his nose.

"Do you know who those swordsmen might be, or who that wretched orphan is?" asked Domitian.

"You know who the boy is. He escorted Countess Marie to England—"

"Yes, of course! How could I have missed that? His name was on the declaration Marie had presented to the council."

Michael scoffed.

Domitian immediately punched Michael, hearing a loud crack of a breaking rib. "Do not forget who I am!"

Michael closed his eyes, as if feeling the pain in his damaged chest. "Orfeo will destroy you and take this castle," he mumbled. "Then he will bring war to the east. That is his plan."

"How do you know?"

"How can you not know?"

"I am getting very tired of your *snideness*."

Michael laughed with greater vibrato. "Snideness is not a word."

"You know what I meant! Must you be so rude?" Domitian bit his lip, clenched his fists, and forced himself to settle down. He sighed. "Please, Sir Michael. All I ask is that you provide information and advice. Surely, that is not too high a price for cleaner accommodations."

"Fine, I advise that you kill yourself before Orfeo kills you."

"That is not funny."

"Then I advise that you ask Abigail to resurrect the countess so she can provide the information and advice that you so desire." Michael looked into Domitian's eyes and sneered. "You...you have already asked her."

Domitian continued to stare back at Michael, marveling at his shrewdness. "Yes, I have, by way of the countess's wishes. She told me years ago that Abigail was a necromancer."

"And if Abigail fails to resurrect her, what then?"

"She will not fail."

"Not planning for failure is your failure."

Domitian bit his knuckle again, worried that Sir Michael would not cooperate. "Please, please, my dark knight. Will you not advise me? I have no one, as you say. I am a master of a small clan, but I will grow it to something greater than it ever was."

"Not an easy thing to do without humans noticing."

"Yes, I know. It takes time."

"Time, you do not have."

The guard came to the door with a lamb in his arms. "Milord?"

"Come," said Domitian.

The guard brought the lamb to Domitian.

"Put the lamb down and take your position outside," ordered Domitian.

When the guard closed the door, Domitian knelt down beside the lamb and stroked it. It had been entranced not to panic. He lifted the animal to Michael's face. "Feed."

Michael turned away.

"This is only to delay the frenzy."

Michael finally accepted the offering, sinking his fangs into its carotid artery.

Before the animal was drained to death, Domitian took it away and walked to the door. "Guard, return this animal to its pen. We need these beasts to feed the new supply of orphans we expect to receive in the coming weeks." He wagged his finger at the guard after he took back the lamb. "Do not think of tasting this animal's blood."

"Yes, milord," said the guard, trying not to look at the fresh blood oozing from the wound.

## 10 – JOSEHPUS BERTONELLI

Cedric followed the Bezuidenhouts along the River Amstel, stopping near the Magere Brug, which was a narrow bridge crossing the river. After stabling their horses there, they continued on foot over the bridge and toward the City of Amsterdam.

Amsterdam was unlike any place Cedric had ever seen—a dizzying array of waterways, bridges, and roadways over which people traveled betwixt narrow and grandiose buildings of multicolored facades and geometrical parapets. The people appeared just as interesting as the architecture. The men wore coat, breeches, and waistcoat but their collars were to-their-ears tall, and their hats were of all shapes and sizes—from old fashioned tricornes and to tall beaver hats with straight and shaped brims and knitted whaler's caps both fresh and worn. Older men wore wigs while many of the younger ones over-styled their hair like those Incroyable French elite. Some women, especially the younger ones, dressed simply but attractively in low cut bodices with elbow length sleeves, cotton skirts, or colorful open skirts revealing quilted petticoats, while others wore wentke gowns that looked more like robes of silk with exotic floral patterns. Nearly all the women wore some form of hat or bonnet of straw or cotton and lace, in every geometrical shape and adornment, while others emphasized their tall merveilleuse hair with tiny hats and ribbons. Amsterdam was a fashion purgatory that Cedric had not expected to see. Amsterdam must be a very special and lenient city for no one to take any offense or inclination toward uniformity. Everybody moved by foot, horse, boat, or buggy at a relaxed pace, going about their day.

The sights reminded him of his friend Pierce van Fleming. Cedric recalled that Pierce desired to experience the world. He would have liked this city, thought Cedric.

Cedric and the siblings walked along Herengracht to a tall house and up a short flight of steps to the front door. Klaas looked right and left as if to gain his bearings, knocked on the door four times quickly, and four times slowly.

An older gentleman wearing a white servant's uniform answered the door. "Good evening, masseurs and mademoiselle," the servant said to everyone in a French accent. "Mister Bertonelli has been expecting you." He let everyone inside and closed the door.

It was a fairly large home with mosaic tile flooring in the entry, interesting but drab portraits on the walls, and practical but solidly built furnishings. A stately longcase clock, with a large pendulum swaying behind its glass doors, captured Cedric's attention. By the looks of the wooden cabinet, it probably chimed loudly and beautifully. The time was 5:38, so Cedric would have to wait to hear its voice.

Soon, a well dressed and groomed gentleman with graying hair rushed in to greet them. He vigorously shook Klaas's hand. "Welcome back, my old friend, Klaas!"

Cedric noticed the man's Italian accent.

The gentleman turned to Gert. "Master Gert, as stylish and handsome as ever. Welcome back." He took Adina's hand in his and kissed it gently. "As lovely and ageless as ever, my dear, Adina." His eyes finally wandered to Cedric.

Klaas placed his hand on Cedric's shoulder. "May I introduce Cedric Martens of...of..."

"Linder," said Gert.

The gentleman smirked jokingly at Klaas and chuckled. "Not the smoothest introduction, Klaas. Thank you for rescuing your brother, Gert." He took a step closer to Cedric and extended his hand. "Josephus Bertonelli of Firenze, at your service."

Cedric shook his hand. "How do you do, Mister Bertonelli?"

"I do quite well, thank you," quipped Josephus with a giggle. "Welcome to my humble home. All of you must be very tired, no?" He snapped his finger and shouted, "Francois!" When the servant reappeared in the vestibule, Josephus said, "Please show our guests to their chambers. Also, everyone, dinner will be served at"—he glanced over at the longcase clock—"eight o'clock—plenty of time to recover from your journey. We have much to discuss!"

The servant led them upstairs to their rooms, and once again, a feeling of gratefulness rushed over Cedric as he was let into a luxurious bedchamber. He set his satchel down on a table beside three crystal decanters, each one containing a different colored liquid. He lifted a decanter, removed its stopper, and sniffed the contents. It contained whisky. Pierce van Fleming had taught him a few things about drink. From the satchel he retrieved a purse. He opened the purse and shook out a dozen gold broads. On each coin was an image of the King of England, but Cedric's eyes imagined Countess Marie's bust on the head's side. She had awarded him his first gold broad after solving her mathematical riddle. He cherished that coin.

He avoided the whisky, pouring himself a glass of water instead, and wondered what to do with the money. He originally wanted to buy a farm for Lily, but the dream of being with her was fading into a life of constant fear and running. Yet, he promised to meet her and his friend Jacob at the church in the center of Amsterdam.

He heard a click followed by soft chiming from the mantle clock above the inglenook—six o'clock in the evening. He lit a fire in the inglenook, sat on the bed, and leaned back against the headboard.

So far, he had managed to survive by running, hiding, and being extremely lucky. He attributed his good fortune to good friends and God's will. His faith was the only constant in his life. He prayed each day not only to God, Son, and Holy Spirit, but also to his parents. He wished the disparaging voices in his head belonged to them. Though he was on the run most of the time, there were times when he had no choice but to stand and fight; and in those situations, when luck smiled upon him and the tang of victory quenched his ego until those voices in his head spouting fear and failure went silent, he walked away triumphant. Indeed, he had been lucky—lucky to be alive and in the presence of the Fortune Brothers.

A sudden knock at the door jolted him awake. He knocked over his glass of water getting up to answer it. When he opened the door, he saw Adina down the hall, walking away.

"Eight o'clock," she said, without turning or stopping. "Dinner is served."

That evening, after a delicious meal and lively discussion with Mister Bertonelli, all moved to the parlor for games and desserts. Cedric went to a window and saw a few boats drifting by. Coaches were traveling along the road between canal and buildings; apart from the grinding of steel-clad wheels and horses clopping on cobblestone, all was as pleasant as the weather in early July.

"I suppose we should not discuss business at this time," whispered Josephus to Klaas.

Klaas and Gert nodded.

Cedric was on the other side of the room, too engrossed in thought to know what was being said.

"Is the youngest in the know?" whispered Josephus so quietly that the brothers had to lean in to hear.

"No," said Adina to Josephus. She glared at Klaas and then at Gert and whispered: "He should not be here." When the brothers provided nothing but blank expressions, she broke away and went to Cedric. Standing beside him, she followed his gaze to boats on the canal outside. "What do you think of this city?"

"Wet," replied Cedric.

Adina chuckled.

Cedric turned to her and said softly, "How do you know Mister Bertonelli? How do you know so many people in so many places?"

She smiled. "Our family travels and has many friends who are willing to provide food and lodging in exchange for private performances."

Cedric was skeptical that it was really that simple. "That is what Gert said."

Adina glanced over at her brothers. "Our wealth is old money, Cedric, very old money. Despite that, we are paid handsomely for our performances. You might be surprised."

"Everything surprises me," said Cedric.

"Cake?" asked Francois, standing behind them with a silver tray of sweets.

Adina lifted a bite-sized yellow cube and gave it to Cedric. "Do you like lemon cake?"

"I like lemons," said Cedric.

Adina lifted a pink cube from the tray and popped it into her mouth.

After three hours of cards, drinks, desserts, and discussion over Josephus's desire to establish a care-home for the elderly, they finally retired for the night.

The first night in Josephus's house was a restless one for Cedric. As excited as he was to go and find Lily, aside from the satisfaction of seeing her, of knowing she was well, and talking with her even for a brief but cautious moment away from public view to provide her with like satisfaction, his hope of marriage to her or anyone was fading. Why on earth would he settle down and start a family while murdering creatures were hunting him?

After a sleepless night, and before morning's first light, he snuck out of the house. He stopped to ask a man sweeping the sidewalk the whereabouts of the church. There were so many churches. Cedric guessed that it would be the oldest or largest of them all, for which the man provided directions and a name: Oude Kerk.

When Cedric arrived at Oude Kerk, the city was coming alive with buggies, boats, and people calmly moving in every direction. He observed the church's interesting design, its multiple gables and tower.

*Is this the church?*

Hopelessness fell over him. What if he never saw his friends again? He shook off the pessimism and decided to visit that church and all the churches along the way back to the house each day for a week. If his friends were in the city, they would surely find one another.

He returned to Josephus's house and spent the day with the Fortune Brothers while Adina went off on her own. Whenever Cedric asked about Adina, one of the brothers responded with: *She is complicated* or *Perhaps she should be the one to ask*—which made Cedric wonder if there was some sort of rift between the brothers and their sister, and if he was the cause of it. Though no one had asked him to leave, perhaps he had overstayed his welcome.

The second night was almost as restless as the first, and when the clock chimed four o'clock, he heard door latches, creaking hinges, and footsteps in the hall. The Bezuidenhouts were up. Cedric slipped out of bed and listened from behind his door. The siblings were out there, trying to be quiet, but the old house gave them away. When all was quiet again, he quickly put on his clothes and left his room to investigate.

He moved through the hall and heard the entrance door opening. Peering down from the top of the stairs, Cedric watched Francois let the siblings out and close the door. When the servant exited the foyer, Cedric descended the stairs and peered through a window beside the entry door. He saw the brothers and Adina boarding a carriage parked out front. When the coach started to pull away, Cedric quietly opened the door and exited the house.

The streets and walkways were devoid of people and traffic at that hour so he was able to run unimpeded, staying within view of the coach.

Two miles later, winded and close to quitting the chase, the coach finally stopped beside a cemetery. Cedric watched from a safe distance as the siblings entered the graveyard through an iron gate, carrying bags. Because the coachman was lighting a pipe and staying behind, Cedric kept his distance, scaling the perimeter wall and stalking the siblings to a crypt near the center of the cemetery. Beside the crypt, the siblings placed the bags on the ground, opened them, and removed additional weapons.

They were going into battle and Cedric's heart started to race with fear and excitement.

After the siblings entered the building, Cedric rushed to peer inside. It was dark, too dark to see anything. He cautiously entered the building, feeling the floor drop a step and then another until he was spiraling down. He wished he had a torch to light his way. About two flights down, he saw a faint glow of blue light. Suddenly, the silence was shattered by clashing blades followed by beastly growling and screeching. The sounds were terrifying—as if ungodly creatures were being tortured to death. Were the siblings in danger? Were they being killed? How could he possibly help them? It was too dark. He had no weapons. Suddenly, a waft of rotting flesh rose up. Terror took hold of Cedric. He clambered upward on hands and feet and stumbled out of the building. He ran through the cemetery toward the coachman waiting outside. Just as he got to the gate, the man met him with the points of a sword and wooden spear.

Cedric skidded to a stop and held up his hands. "I am Cedric Martens of Linder, friend of the Bezuidenhout brothers and their sister Adina. I fear they are in danger."

"Do not move!"

"Please, sir—"

"Quiet! Stay where you are. The siblings will return shortly. They always do; and when they do, they will confirm your so-called friendship, ya?"

"Did you not hear what I said? I believe they are in danger!"

The coachman sniggered. "They are always in danger."

Cedric turned to look for the siblings but saw only darkness. "They need help. I heard horrible screaming..."

"Did you now?" The coachman sounded indifferent as he puffed on his pipe.

"You have weapons. Please, give me a sword and I will go help them."

"Help them? You will burden them." The coachman looked over Cedric's shoulder. "Look now. Here they come, all three of 'em," he said casually, as if no other outcome was possible.

"Master Cedric?" said Adina, shocked to see him.

"Cedric, what are you doing here?" asked Gert.

"Did you see anything other than Cedric?" Klaas asked the coachman.

"No, Mister Fortune," said the coachman.

"Come on, Cedric, get inside," said Klaas, ushering the boy into the coach.

# 11 - THE DEBATE

In the carriage, Cedric sat beside Gert. He glanced across at Klaas, whose normally worry-free face appeared tense. Adina continued to stare out the window and Gert's eyes were closed. The more Cedric thought about what he had done, the sorrier he felt. The brothers had saved Cedric's life, and their family had shown only kindness and generosity to him. He was beginning to realize that secretly following them was a bad idea. He had jeopardized their trust in him. The voices in his head thought so—they scolded him for meddling in others' affairs. Yet, curiosity was a driving force and so were good intentions. Cedric meant no harm. He merely wanted to show how interested he was in what they were doing. The Bezuidenhouts were a good family, and Cedric desperately missed his own family—the love and camaraderie of his parents and sister. He wanted to work for the brothers, to help them, to be closer to them and their family.

After arriving at Josephus's house, they approached the entrance, and Klaas knocked on the door—as usual—four times quickly, four times slowly.

When Francois let them in and saw that Cedric was with them, Cedric expected a raised eyebrow or comment, but Francois's face was as expressive as a resting stone.

"Good morning, Francois," said Klaas as he bounded into the foyer. "Guess who we found? Evidently, Mister Martens wanders the streets in his sleep..."

Cedric entered the foyer, fearing he was going to be asked to gather his things and leave.

Klaas placed his hand on Francois's shoulder. "We will be in the library."

Francois nodded once. "Understood, monsieur."

The siblings moved quickly through a corridor toward the back of the house.

"Please," blurted Cedric, hand reaching out as if he might hold them back. "May I speak with you?"

Adina stopped and pointed at him. "You may not, not at this moment. This is a family matter—"

"I apologize," said Cedric. "Please allow me to explain."

Gert stepped between Adina and Cedric. "Sister, can Cedric wait for us in the library?"

Adina shrugged her shoulders and muttered, "Fine."

Gert smiled at Cedric and waved for Cedric to follow them.

Cedric fell in behind the siblings as they continued on toward a pair of red doors. Klaas opened them and let everyone into the library. Gert went straight to the inglenook, smoke trickling upward from a pile of leftover embers. He tossed two logs into the firebox and poked around, successfully coaxing a small flame to feast on the wood.

Meanwhile, Klaas moved to a tall bookshelf and steadily pushed against it until it slid back into a space behind the wall.

"Mister Martens," said Adina. "Please wait here." She nodded at her brothers to enter through the opening, and they did. Before Cedric could utter another word, Adina slipped inside and the bookshelf slid back into position.

Dumbfounded by what had just happened, Cedric went to the wall of shelves and books to investigate how it worked. He removed books, pulled and pushed the shelves, but the wall would not budge. He listened closely for voices but heard nothing except those in his head:

*Look at what you have done, boy!*

*Ruined everything again, you have!*

*Curiosity killed your friends, and now...!*

Cedric shook his head and moved to the fire. He stared into it, ignoring the disparaging words. He placed his hand over the fire until the heat became unbearable. He quickly pulled back and rubbed the pain out of his hand, and with it the voices out of his head.

Inside the secret room, Adina lit gas lamps while Klaas poured three glasses of cognac from a crystal decanter.

"Whose pea-brained idea was it to bring the boy to Amsterdam?" said Adina scathingly. "He should not be here with us. He should not know what we do."

Klaas handed her a glass. "Two should-nots in a row, sister?"

"Here is a third should-not," said Gert. "We *should not* discount Cedric so hastily."

"May I remind you, little brother," said Adina, her eyes beginning to glow, "we are in this quandary because you asked him to travel with us!"

Gert crossed his arms. "Grootmoeder approved."

"On your ill-advised recommendation probably..." hissed Adina so angrily that a mirror on the wall started to glow blue and green to match her eyes. After an uncomfortable moment, Adina shook her head.

Gert turned to his brother and tilted his head with a nod to say something.

Klaas sighed. "Yes, well, Grootmoeder approved because she saw Cedric...he is important. She said that he will change the future for us all," confessed Klaas.

Adina's eyes darted between her two brothers. "What do you mean?"

"Grootmoeder saw the future, or was at least shown the future," said Gert.

"Lidia mentioned nothing of this to me, why? When were you going to mention this?" Adina looked as if her family had conspired to withhold important information from her.

"It was Grootmoeder's idea to wait," said Gert.

"Wait, why?" asked Adina indignantly.

"You know why," said Klaas. "Grootmoeder feared you would not appreciate her premonitions."

"Lidia is not a seer! That is not her strength." Adina took in a deep breath and closed her eyes. When she exhaled and opened them, the mirror stopped glowing. "Was Lidia alone or did someone help her? Who else was involved?"

"Elida, in the Sonian Forest," said Klaas. "Grootmoeder met with her. Cedric's stories of the castle, the forest, England, slaying the countess, everything, is all true and foretold!"

"So, they conjoined..." said Adina.

"Yes," said Gert. "Cedric is prophesied to help us fight your sister and the Upyrian Empire."

Adina shook her head with disappointment. "Grootmoeder was wrong not to tell me. I would have challenged that prophecy, and we would not be in this predicament."

"This predicament is what we were working towards," said Gert.

Adina shook her finger at Gert. "Cedric is not the one. He is no fighter. He is weak, not to mention overly-inquisitive and meddlesome to a fault—"

"Traits of a good spy," said Klaas.

"Terribly clumsy to be caught so easily," rebutted Adina.

Cedric has potential to be a strong fighter," said Gert. "We can train him."

Adina ignored the comment. "Honorable he may be, we need a born-fighter—someone who can keep secrets, bend the truth, and kill if need be. Otherwise, he is a liability."

"Or asset," countered Gert.

Adina exhaled sharply. "He is lucky to be alive! Luck has no place here. Our work is dangerous, too dangerous for someone like him. For his safety and ours, we must ask him to leave."

"For his safety, he is better off to stay with us," said Klaas.

"He is being hunted," added Gert.

"Hunted? By whom?" asked Adina, placing her hands on her head and burying her fingers in her thick blonde hair.

"Guess," said Klaas.

"He was being abducted by castle guards in a field outside Brussels when we saw him," said Gert. "We finished off the guards and freed Cedric."

Adina's brows tilted. "Were those guards from Vos Castle?"

Klaas and Gert nodded in accord.

"Are you both out of your minds?" She struggled to control her temper, eyes glowing again. "We are forbidden from meeting members of the League, let alone kill them. Doing so violates the pact! Have you forgotten?"

"We have not forgotten," said Gert.

"It was right to free Cedric," said Klaas.

"They were going to take him," Gert reminded her. "You know what that means. Cedric would have been tortured and killed."

"You should not speculate, little brother," said Adina. "We cannot know what goes on inside that castle," retorted Adina.

"I think it is fair to speculate that his story was not to end well," said Gert.

"Is that our problem?" asked Adina.

"I think it is," said Klaas.

"We have made it our problem," said Gert, "and I do not regret it."

"Obviously," said Adina. "What could they possibly want with the boy?"

"Why not ask *him*?" suggested Klaas.

"What, and draw the ire of Vos Castle upon us?"

"Let us be rational," said Gert. "The *fangers* know little of us because the *corvus* have shielded us for centuries. We should continue to use magic as we have and protect Cedric."

Adina scoffed at his comment. "Magic may have concealed our identities all these centuries, but we are not invisible or invulnerable. You know that magic is not always reliable or infallible, especially when applied to vampires. Not all vampires are susceptible to it."

"Most upyrians are," said Gert

"I fear they know our faces now," said Adina with a sigh.

"We would not make any decisions without you," said Klaas.

"No?" she said before drinking some cognac. "Then why was I not involved with your decision to invite the boy to Amsterdam?"

"We told you," said Gert.

"Besides, you have been away these past two months," snipped Klaas.

"I was visiting *your* father," said Adina.

Klaas drank half his cognac and exhaled. "You should leave him be."

"Why is your heart so cold to him?" asked Adina. "He is your father."

"I cannot forgive him," said Klaas. "Father would have willingly betrayed our entire family had we not stopped him. Even if Cedric gambled, I doubt the boy would sell his family's secrets to pay off his debt, knowing the transaction would destroy his family."

"Well..." said Adina, approaching the hidden door, placing her hand on it. "Convince me the person behind this door will not get us all killed."

"He is loyal," said Klaas.

"He is a fast study," said Gert.

"He will learn quickly," said Klaas, lifting his glass of cognac to his lips.

"We have never taught an outsider," said Adina.

"Grootmoeder might not be so opposed," murmured Gert.

Klaas stepped between them and held his hands up. "Now, now, our voices are equal. We are here to discuss and resolve, and we are not leaving this room until we do."

After much debate and cognac, the brothers achieved little more than a headache. Adina disagreed with all their opinions concerning Cedric, how he would be of no use to them, and why he needed their protection.

"Are we ready to see him?" asked Gert, defeat in his voice.

"I think we are," said Klaas with a sigh.

"Let him in," said Adina, "and remember this, I am unconvinced, and I will not sweeten my opinion just because you like him."

## 12 - THE ROMAN IS COMING

In the counting chamber, Domitian watched his guards remove the last corpse from the wall. He stood where Countess Marie's body parts had lain before they were carefully collected and placed in Abigail's charge. The eldest of Domitian's guards, Gaétan, was ordered to stay with Abigail, which meant he was to kill her if she tried to escape. Domitian heard footsteps approaching. He turned to the entranceway and saw Gerda.

Gerda was of Polish birth. Orphaned at sixteen years of age, she found her way to Brussels as a servant where she was poorly treated. Hearing of an orphanage near the forest, she and another servant ran away to Vos Castle. Both girls would serve at the castle until their eighteenth years. In 1661, after being charmed by Count Marcel to attend one of his blood orgies, he made Gerda a vampire. Gerda's friend, however, disappeared.

After becoming a vampire, Gerda quickly discovered a great power from within. During a violent argument between two guards over Gerda's attention, she tried to separate them. She was pushed aside and the guards began to fight. Gerda could do little more than to wish they would stop. Then it happened.

The vampires stopped fighting. Her wish penetrated their minds like a spear of emotions, enabling her to see as they saw, feel as they felt—anger, lust, and fear—and more importantly, shape or bend their main beliefs into what she wanted them to believe.

Domitian had always liked Gerda. She never argued with him or refused any of his demands. "Gerda, I was just thinking of you; but then again, you probably already knew that!" He giggled at his *mind-bending* joke.

"Milord," said Gerda, smiling sweetly. "It is difficult enough to know with my own thoughts. Why on earth would I want to know yours?"

"So good of you not to be in my head, Gerda."

"I have come to inform you of Romans entering the realm. Master Orfeo is among them."

"Orfeo? How many of them?"

"Twelve in all."

"Dear me... There are more of them than there are of us." Domitian giggled nervously.

"When will they arrive?"

"Soon... milord, what shall we do?" asked Gerda.

Domitian's first thought was to abandon the castle and good luck to all, but avoiding Orfeo was impossible, and Sir Michael predicted this. "Gerda, send word. We are to assemble in the courtyard to receive our guests. After the formalities, I will show Orfeo to the library so we may talk in private."

"Yes, milord."

"Oh, and Gerda? How many servants have we in the castle?"

"None, milord."

"What? Why?"

"All were killed in the battle, or escaped. Even the human count and his son are dead. We have not received any newcomers."

Domitian sighed. "Hopefully Orfeo arrives on a full stomach. Go, my dear, tell the others to assemble in the courtyard."

When Domitian stepped out into the courtyard with three guards, Abigail and Gerda were already there with two others. It was a pleasant August evening—not how Domitian envisioned the day of reckoning. Domitian remembered the scene in that courtyard just three weeks ago. Two armies ready to battle—Count Marcel and his Prussian allies on one side, and Domitian with a few tired soldiers on the other. Clearly, Domitian would have been destroyed had Sir Michael not run Count Marcel through his back with a javelin.

Defeating Marcel brought an immediate end to the conflict. The Royal Flemish Clan and all its property went to Domitian, but at what cost?

Domitian heard Orfeo's Romans entering the barbican. If Domitian's clan was stronger, he would have positioned bowmen with pots of fire-oil upon the ramparts. He imagined Orfeo's Romans, trapped between the high walls of the barbican, fire and death raining down on them. If only his clan was stronger, he thought. As the first of the Romans entered the courtyard, layers of anxiety overwhelmed any fantasies of ambush.

Domitian stepped forward. "Welcome, Master Orfeo! Welcome all to Vos Castle."

Orfeo dismounted his horse, cinched his black leather gloves up on each finger, and walked past Domitian toward the castle's entrance. He waved a finger up and backward. "Take care of my men and their horses," he said to the castle guards. "Come, Domitian."

Domitian scurried to catch up to Orfeo as the Roman master barked orders: "Show my soldiers to their chambers and stable the horses! Bring humans for my men to feast on. We are hungry and tired and disappointed."

Domitian led Orfeo to the library, closed the doors behind them, and joined Orfeo at the center of the spacious room.

Orfeo paced the room, gazing up at the books, and then paused to glare at Domitian.

Domitian trembled and managed an awkward smile. "It is so nice to—"

"Shut up," said Orfeo, finally removing his gloves. "I delivered on my promise to you, Domitian. I provided an army to help you defeat Count Marcel. Now, I expect you to deliver on your promise to me."

"Yes, of course—"

"I need fifty soldiers."

"Fifty?"

"Yes. Fifty, or have you forgotten the details of our agreement?"

"I remember, fifty, yes." Domitian fidgeted with his cuffs and began to tap his foot.

"What is the matter?"

"Oh, nothing. I will call upon my Prussian allies and—"

"No. They are already providing fifty soldiers."

"I see, the Parisians then—"

"They are already sending soldiers as well. How many soldiers have you?"

"I apologize, Master Orfeo, but it has only been three weeks since the battle..."

"How many soldiers can you spare?"

"Well..." Domitian had half a dozen men available, but the castle would be defenseless without them. "Not...not quite enough."

Orfeo took up a quill from a side table and came at Domitian with blurring speed.

Domitian braced for impact. The quill entered his eye and continued into his brain until the tip touched the back of his skull.

Domitian fell against a shelf of books, knocking some to the floor. "Master Orfeo," whimpered Domitian, "was...was that really ne-ne-necessary?"

"Was it *ne-ne-necessary?*" mocked Orfeo. "Was it necessary that I send soldiers to fight your battle for you? No, it was not! Yet, I sent them because you promised to provide fifty soldiers when I needed them. That was our agreement! Do you not remember?"

Domitian nodded. "I...I re-re-remember."

Orfeo shook his head at the sight of the quill protruding from Domitian's eyeball and waved his finger at it. "Go on, remove it."

Domitian slowly extracted the quill from his eye, globs of fleshy matter stuck to the barbs. "Oh, oooh," groaned Domitian. He steadied his balance and managed a lopsided smile. "Master Orfeo, I would provide a hundred soldiers if I had them. My clan is de-de-decimated. I have but a few men and women here, but I have something better to offer—something more valuable than fifty soldiers."

Orfeo sat down in an armchair and Domitian took a chair beside him. Domitian's punctured eye was still tearing, but the wound was closing and his vision was being restored. Orfeo offered a handkerchief. Domitian took it and swabbed his eye.

"Proceed," said Orfeo, crossing his arms.

"Thank you, Master Orfeo. You are fair and just. I share in your hatred of the east. Unfortunately, the cost to defeat Count Marcel was much higher than expected. Not only have I lost most of my clan, I lost Countess Marie de Vos."

A sadness softened Orfeo's expression. "I heard, and that is the other reason I came."

"Thank you, Orfeo."

"Not to consol you—fool—but to collect the collateral owed to me. All your property, including this ugly castle, is mine now. You see, since you cannot honor our agreement, you cannot honor me. Since you cannot honor me, my consolation is everything you have. Now, what were you going to say about something more valuable...?"

Domitian thought back to his discussions with Sir Michael. He predicted this would happen. "Yes, well, thank you for coming all this way to inform me. I do honor you, Master Orfeo, and I am your loyal servant."

"You are as much a liar as you are a disloyal servant. Now, if you have nothing better to offer, show me to the counting chamber. My soldiers will secure my riches."

"Yes, Master Orfeo."

"Curious to know...how has your clan remained anonymous here for so long? What is your front?"

"Our front was the rightful owners of this estate—the human count and his son. We used mind-bending techniques to remove their suspicions and fears of us. They provided a human face to the world concerning this estate. Unfortunately, they were killed."

"I see. Well, then, my soldiers will remain here to ensure my interests are secured from the likes of you and your kindred. I will return to Roma to prepare for battle in a fortnight."

"Battle, Master Orfeo? May I ask who your opponent will be?"

"Romania, of course."

"Of course... Will you be leading the attack, master?"

"Why are you probing, Domitian? Are you scheming?"

"No, master! A battle against the east is, well, serious. Are you not concerned that such a battle might restart the *Lunabellum*?"

"The Moon War? Perhaps that is precisely what I intend to do. Start it and end it, destroying the east. Imagine, our kind thriving throughout all of Europe and eastward into Asia with no upyrian to stop us." Orfeo planted his eyes on Domitian as if to read his face. "Curious, Domitian, how do you prefer to die? I cannot have you running around thinking of ways to kill me, as you killed Count Marcel, now can I?"

"Master Orfeo, I assure you—my loyalty to you is true. You are the master, clearly you are—"

"Beheading, staking, fire perhaps?" asked Orfeo, eyes narrowing. "Of course, before you die, you will be tortured, and your little brain will be emptied of useful knowledge, if any."

Domitian giggled timidly, rubbing his knees with his hands. "Well, I suppose beheading would be the least painful way to go—and torture would only sully the luxury of a painless execution, would it not?"

Orfeo looked down in thought and raised a finger. "I almost forgot, what were you trying to tell me earlier...? Oh yes, something more valuable than fifty soldiers."

Domitian cleared his throat with a cough. "I am sure you are aware of the upyrians' insatiable appetite for child's blood. I suppose they have drained and licked the east clean of its orphans. However, the west is still crawling with them. Vos Castle has been a sanctuary to orphans for generations. At our peak, we sheltered over a hundred on any given night."

Orfeo closed his eyes and grumbled impatiently. "Get to the point."

"I have an agreement with Queen Žofie. She will buy orphans from me—I mean, us."

The queen's name captured Orfeo's attention. "Go on."

"Obviously, you will receive a percentage. We may discuss—"

"Ninety percent."

Domitian forced a smile. "Eh, seventy-five, master?"

"One hundred percent and you keep your life, Domitian."

Domitian sat back in his chair, realizing that he had no leverage to negotiate and his mistake was mentioning the upyrian deal. "My life and no torture, please. I loathe suffering, even my enemies. Though I have tortured a few in my day, I enjoyed it not."

"Very well," said Orfeo, "one hundred percent busy no torture."

"Thank you, master."

"Tell me, Domitian, how does it work, this sale?"

"Very good question, Master Orfeo. We have selected two points of delivery, one in the south and the other in the north. Only you and I will know the trade routes. Half the payment will be released in advance of delivery; the remainder will be released after delivery. I have a bank in Brussels, but we may establish one in Roma instead, if you prefer to. I will pro-pro-provide the goods. You can provide guards to deliver. I will be happy to control the money—"

Orfeo laughed. "You will control nothing." Orfeo stood up. Domitian stood up with him.

"Domitian. If you speak the truth, then your agreement with the queen is a better-something after all." Orfeo grinned. "Queen Žofie is the only upyrian worth meeting. Arrange a meeting between us. Do this, and I will know you are speaking the truth."

"Yes, Master Orfeo."

## 13 - MONSTERS AND HOW BADLY THEY DIE

Cedric was sitting in the library when the wall of books suddenly shifted back into the void. He expected the siblings to pile out, but no. Cedric stood up and cautiously inched toward the opening.

"Come, Cedric, join us," said Gert from within.

Cedric slipped through the narrow opening into the secret room. As his eyes adjusted to the dim candle lighting, the hidden door noisily slid back into the closed position.

"Welcome," said Klaas, standing beside a chair on which Adina sat, clutching her drink, staring forward at nothing in particular.

Cedric's eyes explored the room. It was not a large space—about ten paces square with a high ceiling and no windows. Weapons and old books of all sorts covered nearly every inch of wall space to as high as one might reach.

Klaas poured cognac into a fourth glass and handed it to Cedric. The Fortune brother lifted his glass, and after Adina finally lifted hers, Klaas grinned and said: "To Cedric Martens of...of..." He raised his hand to Gert. "...of Linder."

After everyone drank, Cedric wondered if this was going to be a polite reprimanding and send-off. He latched his now fully adjusted eyes onto the impressive collection of swords, daggers, crossbows, wooden stakes, maps, and an oversized book resting on a wooden podium. His eyes turned upward to the ceiling on which stars against a black background twinkled like actual stars.

"Mirrors," said Klaas, "the stars, just reflections."

"You followed us, why?" asked Adina.

Cedric turned to her. "I apologize—"

"Why?" said Adina, more forcibly.

"I...I was sleepless and curious to know what you were doing, where you were going."

"Had it not occurred to you that you were not invited?" said Adina. "Or is that what you do—show up unannounced and unwelcomed? My brothers and I have a difference of opinion concerning you. Whereas they believe your excuses, I believe you were spying—motivated by something other than curiosity."

"I was not spying in the sense of betrayal," said Cedric, worry turning to fear, eyes turning to Gert for advocacy. "I only wanted to know what you were doing and to assist if allowed. Please, accept my apology. I...I meant to cause no trouble."

"Curiosity and trouble are quarrelsome comrades," said Adina. "Tell me, was your curiosity satisfied?"

"I...I have more questions than answers."

"What did you expect?" asked Adina.

"I had no expectations."

"What did you see?"

"I saw you, your brothers, and a coachman. All of you were carrying weapons."

"Did you follow us into the crypt?" asked Adina.

"Yes, but not all the way in."

"Describe what you saw," said Adina.

"I saw a blue light, glowing from below." Cedric noticed the brothers nodding at his comment.

"What else?" asked Adina.

"I heard dreadful noises, growling and screaming."

"Animal noises, perhaps?" asked Adina.

"No, more like...demons," said Cedric. "I had experienced those sounds before."

"Where and when?" asked Gert, beating his sister to the question.

"At Vos Castle..." A voice in Cedric's head told him not to confess to Marie's murder. *Murder?* Cedric had not thought of it as murder but as self-defense. What would she have done to his friends and to him had he not killed her? Erasing that knee-buckling event from his mind was impossible—he tried. Salvation was confession, and he was ready to confess. Cedric sighed and then looked steadily into Adina's eyes—one blue, the other green. "I was at the castle during a fierce battle between Count Marcel and Lord Domitian. I rescued my friends...

*Foolhardy endeavor, that was!* said the crotchety voice in his head.

*Indeed, especially when you are the one in need of rescuing,* added the woman's voice.

Cedric clenched his eyes and massaged his temples, trying to dispel the voices.

"Is something the matter?" asked Adina.

*There most certainly is!* grumbled the crotchety voice.

Cedric took in a deep breath and allowed his eyes to search for the words. "In defense of my friends, and I considered no other option than to defend them. Had I hesitated, even for the briefest moment, she would have killed them and me. I had to what I did. There was no other choice. I had to."

"What did you do?" asked Adina.

Cedric looked into Adina's eyes and swallowed. He felt sick to his stomach. "I... I killed Countess Marie de Vos." Cedric felt as if the walls were closing in on him. It became so quiet in his head that he heard his heart pounding in his ears and even the fire popping in the library.

Klaas lifted his glass. "To monsters and how badly they die!"

Gert drank with his brother while Adina gazed steadily at Cedric.

"I am aware of some aspects of your life, Cedric," said Adina. "My brothers tell me that the plague took your family, and the vampires at Vos Castle took your friends. Luck has smiled upon you, helping you to escape serious injury and even death. Luck, however, is an unreliable friend. Have you any money, a clutch of gold coins perhaps?"

"I do," said Cedric.

"Then why not go where it is safe and make a new life there?" said Adina.

"Where is it safe to go?" asked Cedric, truly wanting to know. "I fear there is no safe place for me, for they will never leave me be."

"If I may, Adina," interrupted Klaas. "You are right, sister, luck is a fickle friend, an unreliable rascal, a shady charlatan, a—"

"Please stop," said Adina, cringing, "and get to your point."

"Cedric Martens is as good as dead," said Klaas, obliging his sister. "They will find him, and because of that, I say we have common enemies."

"His enemies are not necessarily our enemies," said Adina.

"Not now," said Gert, "but change is coming, and it involves the Flemish clan."

"Cedric can be useful to us," said Klaas. "He knows Elida."

"What?" Adina was clearly surprised at this new information.

"Go on, tell her, Cedric," said Gert, a glint of fun in his eyes.

"Yes, do tell," said Klaas.

Cedric was uncertain where this discussion was leading him, but it felt good to let everything out. "It was the day after I had met your brothers. I was on my way to Brussels and wandering through the forest—"

"Sonian Forest," clarified Gert.

"It was mid-summer, last year. I came upon a small house in the forest and saw no one there. I decided to carry on, but when I turned to leave, a woman was standing behind me.

Startled, I backed into vines growing over a pile of rocks. They immediately coiled around me, binding me. She told me to remain calm else I strangle. Then she gave me some food and told me to leave the forest before it was too late."

Adina's eyes narrowed. "Elida went missing a few weeks ago. Do you know what happened to her?"

"No," said Cedric. "Is she not well?"

"How well do you know Abigail van Ness?" asked Adina.

"Headmistress Abigail was always kind to me. Her brother, Pierce van Fleming, is my friend. Together, we helped Count Marcel and his men into the castle."

"My, my, all the count's horses and all the count's men," said Klaas.

Gert stepped into the brief pause with his glass raised. "I think I have heard enough. I offer a motion—that Cedric Martens of Linder joins us, becomes one of us. What say you, brother, sister?"

"I say no," said Adina, her eyes darting between the brothers. "I know what you see... I see it, too... There is much to admire. Cedric is kind, curious, and brave. Yet, those qualities alone will not protect him from the dangers we face." Adina slowly circled Cedric, sizing him, scrutinizing him. "Who is this person, standing here? Is he a fighter? He carries no weapon. Is he a boy? He is nearly eighteen years of age. Is he a man? He is nearly eighteen years of age. Is he a spy? He says no." Adina stopped in front of Cedric and stared at his face. "I think this person is standing between dark and light, fearlessness and folly. This person is lost and conflicted, with voices of doubt cluttering his thoughts. How can I protect him when I am struggling to protect you both?" she asked her brothers. "This person is a risk." She turned to Gert. "No brother, I cannot support your motion." She moved away from Cedric. "I do not mean to offend you, Cedric. That is simply the truth, my truth."

Cedric nodded, disappointed by her comments but in control of his emotions.

Adina lifted her glass of cognac and drank some. She put the glass down and turned to Klaas. "I motion that Cedric Martens of Linder leaves us."

"Sister?" said Gert.

"It is either him or me, Gert." Adina paused to let her words sink in. "I will not compromise us for him." She turned to Cedric and lowered her eyes. "It is decided. Please gather your belongings and leave in the hour."

With a long face, Gert opened the secret door and let Cedric out. Behind Cedric came Klaas and Gert, and after a longer moment came Adina with two weapons in her hands.

"Cedric," said Adina. She held out a dagger. "This is for you." She glanced down at the sword in her other hand. "This as well..."

Cedric shook his head. "Thank you, but I've taken too much from you already. I will leave at once." He turned and left the siblings in the library.

# 14 - HUNTED

Cedric stood in the foyer, his satchel of personal belongings resting on the floor. Francois opened the door and said something to someone standing outside. Noticing a carriage, Cedric moved to Francois. "Please, ask the carriage to leave."

Francois's eyes shifted to Klaas.

"Cedric," said Klaas, "the carriage will take you to the stable where you will receive your horse."

"I have no horse," said Cedric.

"The one you rode in on, that is your horse," Klaas reminded him.

"That is *your* horse," said Cedric. "Thank you for allowing me to ride her."

"Cedric," said Gert, "take the horse, please."

Cedric smiled at Gert and shook his head. "It is a nice day, and I prefer to walk." He turned to Adina and noticed a bit of sadness lurking beneath her smile. Cedric also noticed a sword handle protruding from his satchel but decided not to mention it. He just wanted to leave. He slung the satchel over his shoulders and turned to the siblings. A farewell smile and nod preceded his exit into the warmth of an early August afternoon. In minutes, Cedric was heading north, feeling more alone and vulnerable than ever before.

Francois closed the door and turned to the siblings, who appeared anything but relieved or cheery.

"We should follow him," said Gert. "Watch his back until he leaves the city."

"That boy was a good friend," said Klaas. "Do you not agree?" Klaas asked Adina, who was staring at the door as if waiting for Cedric to return at any moment.

"The sword," said Klaas. "Which did you give to him?"

"Blood iron," murmured Adina, "short blade."

"I know the one," said Gert. "Really short...oversized knife, really."

"And the dagger?" asked Klaas.

"Same as the sword," said Adina.

"She means blood dagger," said Klaas.

Gert's eyes widened. "I thought there were no others."

The blood daggers were believed to have been forged by Hephaestus, who was the blacksmith of the Olympian gods. He used wine to temper the blades, for he often drank copious volumes of the red alcohol, and fashioned a collection of daggers, swords, and shields that in a certain light reflected a red sheen. Sometime later, threads of wood were tightly woven and inlaid into the fuller slot on each side of the blades. The type of wood used, which facilitated the slaying of vampires, is unverified. Applying a bit of magic, these blood weapons would come alive. Adina could make them dance in air or in the hands of their master. Thus, not only practice and natural ability facilitated the Fortune siblings' superior fighting prowess.

"You thought correctly," said Adina.

"Did you give him one of yours?" asked Klaas, a glint of satisfaction in his eye.

Adina ignored the question.

"I knew it!" said Klaas. "You do have a heart for the man-boy after all."

"What will Grootmoeder say, when she finds out that we turned him away?" Gert asked Adina. "She said that he would change the future, our future."

"I will speak to her if need be," said Adina, softly, as if reconsidering her decision.

"I am going to follow him," said Gert, moving to the door.

"Ah, the price we pay for guilty consciences," said Klaas, falling in behind Gert.

Francois opened the front door and let the brothers out. He then turned to Adina, who appeared to be frozen in thought. "Do you wish to go with your brothers, mademoiselle?" asked Francois.

She shook her head at first, but when Francois started to close the door, she sprung past him and onto the porch. Sensing the whereabouts of the blood-iron blades, she quickly pursued her brothers.

On that fair day in Amsterdam, unaware that he was being followed not only by the siblings but also by Sven, who had been tracking Cedric since Brussels, the young man of Linder felt that it was safe enough to see the sights in daylight. Traversing the canals and bridges, he eventually came upon a street fair. There were scores of people enjoying the festivities among dozens of vendors and artists.

Not far behind was Sven, sniffing his way closer to Cedric, walking quickly but not too quickly as to draw unwanted attention. He stopped at the edge of the fair and scanned the crowd. If only he could see Cedric, then it would be a matter of following him to a secluded ending.

Cedric purchased freshly baked bread, cheese, sausage, and carrots, and walked to a nearby park to enjoy the food. He sat down beside a tree, completely unaware of the looming predator. As he ate, he opened his sack and fished out the dagger. It reminded Cedric of the brothers' daggers. It looked exactly the same. The handle was simple, wooden grips riveted to the tang. The uniquely defining aspect was a circle with a twin-line cross of equal length arms carved into the handle, and a thread of wood fibers woven through the blade. The stitching was centered on each side of the blade, terminating a knuckle's width from the pointed tip. The fiber was very fine and flush with the surface. Cedric turned it over and over, trying to figure out how it was made, why it was made like that, but he could only speculate.

He gazed through the park's mature trees to the street and saw men, women, children, dogs on leashes, entire families, walking to and fro, enjoying the splendid day. Just as his eyes refocused on the blade, his mind processed an unexpected sighting. He looked to the street again and saw them.

*Lily and Jacob?*

It was them! They were leaving the street fair together, arm in arm, turning a corner and walking away now. Before Cedric could stand, a leather strap came across his chest.

From behind the tree Sven caught the other end of his whip as it came around the trunk, and he pulled back tightly.

Cedric tried to free himself by pushing the whip upward and slinking downward, but that only made things worse when the whip tightened across his neck.

Sven tied both ends together and went to the other side of the tree to collect his prisoner, but found a severed whip, a satchel, and Cedric sprinting toward the street fair. Sven fell into pursuit, dodging the dagger Cedric threw at him.

By the time Cedric reached the edge of the fair, Sven was close enough to pounce on him, but Cedric turned quickly between two vendors' booths and ran behind them. On the opposite side of the booths, Sven moved in parallel with Cedric.

Cedric stopped and doubled back.

Sven shadowed him. When Sven was held up by a large group of people, Cedric sprinted to the busiest section of the fair. Sven relentlessly pushed his way through the crowds to close the gap between them.

Cedric had no other choice than to pull objects onto Sven's path to slow him down. Buckets of flowers, shelves with books, paintings on easels, stacks of brooms—anything that might slow his pursuer was tipped over. The commotion was drawing the attention, confusion, and panic of everyone there.

Under the guise of darkness, Sven might have leaped over the obstacles and pounced on Cedric like an owl, but in the light of day, and with so many people around, he was relegated to act ordinary. As long as Sven kept Cedric in view, catching him was inevitable. Fortunately for Sven, inevitability came early when Cedric tripped and fell. Just as the boy was scrambling to get to his feet, Sven took hold of his arm. Unfortunately for Sven, Cedric was also in the grasp of an affluent businessman.

"What have we here?" said the businessman. "What do you think you are doing, young man?" He demanded an answer from Cedric. The man was elderly but fit. His clothes were of the finest threads, and he stood with the air of stewardship.

Cedric turned to Sven. The intensity in the vampire's eyes revived ghastly memories of Vos Castle.

"Do you know him?" said the businessman to Sven.

"Yes, he is wanted for crimes against the state of France," Sven lied.

"Crimes?" said the businessman, lifting an eyebrow. "What are his crimes, and who are you?"

"My name is Charles-Édouard Boucher, constable to the First Consul, Napoleon Bonaparte," he lied again. Sven stared deeply into the man's eyes. "This person is wanted for treason." Gasps came from the gathering crowd.

"No!" yelped Cedric. "He is lying—"

"What is the meaning of this, Jon?" said a woman to the businessman, damaged flowers in her hand. She glared at Cedric. "Just look at what you did to my flowers!"

Sven pulled Cedric closer to him. "You will release my prisoner," he said to Jon. "Release him now."

"What about my flowers?" asked the woman.

"What about my paintings?" asked an artist.

Sven lifted a moneybag from his waistcoat and shook it in front of them. They smiled at the sound of jingling coins.

Cedric was panicking. He saw what was happening. He struggled to free himself, but Sven's grip was so firm, his arm was going numb. "Please, sir," he appealed to Jon the businessman. "I am guilty for damaging their goods. Please take me to the constable. I must be held accountable for my disturbance here. I must be questioned, if not punished!"

"He will be punished in France. Now, release him, sir," Sven commanded Jon.

Jon nodded. "Yes, of course, Mister Boucher." He released Cedric and stepped back.

Sven gazed at the crowd. "This man is wanted for participating in the peasant uprising against the state of France. Clear the way!" Sven tossed his moneybag to the flower woman as he dragged Cedric away. "That should be more than enough to pay for all damages associated with this man," shouted Sven to the vendors.

Several blocks later, Sven pulled Cedric into a lonely side street. At the moment Sven became distracted by a hissing cat on top of a wooden box, Cedric swung his elbow into his abductor's nose. It was enough to loosen Sven's grip. Cedric spun free and ran to the wooden box. He used the height of the box to jump higher against the building, pushing off into a back flip. He imagined reaching down in midflight, taking Sven by the collar, landing on his feet behind Sven, and then snapping the vampires neck with a violent twist of his head. That was not to be.

Sven reached up, took Cedric by the collar, and pulled him down so they stood face to face. In that moment, he failed to protect his groin. Even a vampire feels pain, and Cedric's boot found its mark between Sven's legs. Buckling over, Cedric threw his knee into Sven's nose, this time breaking it. Now, he ran—twenty paces before Sven caught up again.

Blocking Cedric's punches and protecting his groin, Sven turned Cedric to face away, and began to pull his arms upwards behind his back.

Cedric cringed with pain.

Sven whispered in his ear. "Shall I break your arms?"

"If you do not cooperate, I shall break them."

Cedric decided to calm down. He would try to escape again when the opportunity was presented. If only he had worn the weapons that Adina had given to him.

"I am hungry, Cedric Martens of Linder," growled the vampire. "Normally, I would dine on your blood, but alas, Lord Domitian has other plans for you. I am to return you to Vos Castle where you will answer to the murder of Countess Marie de Vos."

"Is that so?" came a voice from behind them.

There stood Adina, standing in their path.

Sven tightened his grip on Cedric's arms, making him wince. "Back away, madam, or...," threatened Sven.

"Or what?" asked Klaas, standing behind to the right of Sven.

Sven spun around and took Cedric's neck in hand. "He is my prisoner, wanted for—"

"—treason," said Gert, standing on the street, foot propped on the curb. "Yes, we heard."

"Actually, it is murder," hissed Sven.

"Yes, we heard that, too," said Gert.

"And happy for it," said Klaas, sniffing loudly three times. "Can you smell it, brother?"

Gert smelled the air. "Yes, I can."

"The stench of vampire offends my nose," said Adina.

"If you do not back away and let us through, I shall snap his neck," warned Sven, clearly unnerved, head turning, eyes darting, trying to keep all three siblings in view.

"If you kill him, what will Domitian do to you?" asked Klaas.

Sven turned to Adina and gazed into her eyes, trying to charm her. "You will tell them to stand down and let us pass," he said to Adina. "Tell them."

Adina tilted her head and smirked at the vampire. "Let me guess...you must be Sven de Vries of Leeuwarden. You were sired by a vampire in the year seventeen twenty-three. You prefer the blood of inebriated men, as the taste of alcohol is what you miss the most. Is that so?"

Sven's jaw loosened, along with his grip on Cedric's neck.

"Now, Mister De Vries," said Adina, "you will release Cedric, for he is not your prisoner."

"He is with us," added Gert.

Sven nodded.

"Listen closely, Mister de Vries," said Adina. "We know who you are, what you are, where you live. We will find you if you mention this incident to anyone. Do you understand?"

Sven nodded.

"Very good," said Adina, lifting her hands to Klaas and Gert, who were ready to throw daggers at any moment. "Release Cedric to me."

Sven complied.

"You may go," said Adina, Cedric taking a position now beside her.

"Run," said Klaas, threatening to throw his dagger at the vampire.

At the drop of a hat, Sven was gone.

"Cedric, are you hurt?" asked Adina.

Cedric stopped rubbing his bruised arm. "No. I am quite well, but curious..."

"Cedric the Curious," said Klaas with a chuckle.

"Why did you come after me?" asked Cedric, rubbing his neck.

"One human is no match for a vampire," said Adina.

"One vampire is no match for three Meridiems," said Klaas.

"Or possibly four Meridiems," said Gert.

Adina furrowed her brow at Gert. "Let us return to the house. Clearly, there is more to discuss."

Cedric suddenly realized that all his belongings were missing. "My satchel...the sword and dagger." Flustered, Cedric started heading back to the park. "I left it by the tree...I threw it...I must find it..."

The brothers accompanied Cedric to the park while Adina retrieved the dagger with her magic. In a moment, it whirled back into her hand.

In the park, by the tree, Cedric looked all over for his satchel but found only the remnants of his food. The satchel had been taken, along with the sword.

Adina caught up to them and waited for Cedric to notice her. When he did, she presented the dagger to him.

He shook his head. "I will stop asking how and why, but I will never believe I am worthy..."

"What?" said Gert. "I can think of no one outside our family who is more worthy than you, Cedric."

"Take it," said Adina. "Returning a gift, especially one that can save your life, is folly."

"The sword was in the satchel," murmured Cedric sadly, "and the satchel was stolen. I do not deserve such gifts."

"Take it," insisted Adina.

When Cedric finally and reluctantly accepted the dagger, she revealed the sword from behind her back. "They are a set. They belong together."

Cedric should not have been surprised. He knew of Adina's magic, but the sword was inside the satchel. Still, he simply accepted it.

Seeing that he was not going to ask for an explanation, Adina explained anyway. "Your sack was untied when it was stolen. The sword simply lifted out of the satchel and returned to me. All our weapons return to us when we ask them to."

"You ask them?" said Cedric, looking at the sword, still in its sheath.

"I need not ask," said Gert. "They ask me."

Klaas laughed at his brother's comment.

Disinterested in the silliness, Adina lifted her hand, and the dagger left Cedric's loose grip and returned to Adina. She handed the dagger back to Cedric, turned, and started walking. "Cedric, come with us."

On the way back to the house, Cedric's mind raced with all that had happened. He recalled Lily and Jacob. They appeared happy together, obviously together by the way their arms were locked. He would someday find them, but for now he was content simply knowing they were alive and well.

## 15 - DECISION DAY

Cedric and the brothers took seats in the library while Adina went to a table upon which decanters of alcohol and glasses sat. The library was roomier and warmer than the secret room behind the wall of books, and Cedric preferred the spaciousness.

"Do you really want to join us and do what we do?" asked Adina, pouring Cedric a glass of cognac. Cedric knew their work was dangerous, but before he answered, Adina continued. "We do not share in your Christian faith. We are of different backgrounds and beliefs. Does that not bother you? Joining us might be the last thing you will ever do. One mistake, one miscalculation, may lead to serious injury and death. Are you so anxious to risk your life for us?"

Cedric chose not to respond so quickly. Such questions might be rhetorical, and he was learning to be as good a listener as observer. Still, he was not completely certain what they did or why they did it.

"*No* would be the sensible answer to all those questions," said Adina.

Cedric nodded. "I wish to learn exactly what you do and why you do it."

Adina smiled. "I will show you what we do and why, but first... How do *you* distinguish right from wrong, murder from killing, assassination from execution? Thou shalt not kill?"

Cedric recalled The Holly Bible, the stories it told, lessons it taught. "Sometimes there is no other option than to defend one's own life by taking another's," said Cedric, still coping with his guilt. "For example, if a thief is found breaking into one's home and is struck down and dies, there shall be no bloodguilt for killing the intruder."

"Yet, it was you who broke into the castle and into Marie's counting chamber," said Adina.

"Yes, but not to plunder." Cedric felt his emotions in his throat. His mouth went dry. "I went there to save lives. The countess had already killed so many...ten perhaps eleven orphans were dead in that chamber when I arrived. I had accessed the catacombs beneath the castle through a secret passage leading outside the castle walls. When I entered the counting chamber, Headmistress Abigail was lying on the floor, unconscious, and Countess Marie had Pierce by his throat. She was choking the life out of him. I needed to stop her. Aware of Countess Marie's compulsion to count objects, I found a clutch of coins and threw a handful so they would fall all around her. The distraction worked. She released Pierce. When she saw me, she threatened to kill all of us. I believed her. Though I defended myself and my friends, I somehow regret the choice I made." Tears began to fall. "Had she not threatened us, I would have chosen differently..."

"Breathe in and hold," said Adina, rubbing Cedric's arm. "No one is going to judge you here. Under those circumstances, you made the right choice. Exhale steadily."

After Cedric exhaled, he felt better—relieved by Adina's warm touch and words. Cedric clenched his eyes, squeezing out the last of the tears while Adina gently wiped the streams from his face with her fingers, beaming at him with seldom-seen gentleness in her colorful eyes, stirring a deeper emotion in him,. "Thank you for listening," whispered Cedric, feeling more exposed than ever. He sniffed and let out a congested chuckle. "You see...I may not be as good and kind as you had thought."

"I still think you are exactly as you appear to be, Cedric," said Adina. "You made the only sensible choice at that time.

Any of us would have done the same," she said, turning to her brothers.

"Yes, I would have done the same," said Klaas, accepting a glass of cognac from Gert.

"To murder is to kill, but to kill is not necessarily to murder," said Adina. "Motivation, intention, malice, and mercy are all defining factors. In our situation, an ancient pact binds us." She handed another glass to Gert. "This pact requires us to defend *your* enemies, Cedric." Adina sipped her cognac, observing Cedric's surprised expression. "You heard correctly. We are obligated to protect vampires in Western Europe." She lifted her glass to Cedric. "Can you drink to that disturbing reality?"

Cedric could not believe it. Why would they protect those who would kill him? How had such a pact come to be?

"I can sense your confusion," said Adina to Cedric. "It is reasonable to wonder if we have not compromised our integrity for the sake of an old perhaps irrelevant pact."

"When you say enemies, you mean Domitian and his kind?" asked Cedric.

"Precisely," replied Adina.

"A pact that protects evil is a pact of evil," thought Cedric aloud.

"Perhaps," said Gert.

"When the pact was made, it was not as much about good and evil as survival," said Klaas. "Without the pact, our family would have been cut down generations ago. The Meridiem would not exist."

"If you promised to protect Domitian, and he is trying to kill me..." Cedric was perplexed.

"It is complicated," admitted Adina.

Gert swallowed down the entire glass of cognac, coughed, and wiped his mouth on his sleeve. "I say we go to Vos Castle and speak directly to Domitian on Cedric's behalf. Surely, he will listen to reason."

Adina stared at Gert as if he were a demented fool. "Little brother, how do we convince Domitian of anything when the pact prohibits us from seeing him?" She turned to Cedric. "Even if we violated the pact, Domitian will not hear us. Hate and vengeance deafens him."

Klaas's eyes widened with an idea, and he looked to Gert for an accord. "Are you thinking as I am, younger brother?"

Gert refilled his glass and immediately drank it down. He belched and smiled at Klaas. "Are you thinking to remove Domitian's hate and vengeance?" Gert said, while pouring yet another glass of alcohol.

Cedric wondered if Gert frequently drank as much as he was drinking.

Adina wagged her finger at Klaas and Gert. "I know what you two are thinking, and it is folly."

"What are we thinking then?" slurred Gert.

"Find and restore what Domitian has lost," said Adina.

"Lucky guess," said Klaas.

"Theoretically, can you do it?" asked Gert of Adina.

"Theoretically, yes, but why would I?" replied Adina. "The countess was vile."

"The vilest," said Cedric, uncertain what they were talking about. "She murdered children."

Adina put her glass down on a side table. "Cedric, we receive assignments to remove vampires from the east who have invaded the west."

Klaas belched as he and Gert refilled their glasses. Klaas took his glass closer to the fire. "The eastern vamps are called upyr..."

"Upyrian," said Adina. "They are just one of many kinds of vampires in the east."

"Many kinds...?" wondered Cedric aloud.

"Too many," muttered Gert, "disgusting *hemo-goblins*!"

"You should slow down," said Adina to Gert, seeing that he was standing as if on a boat in rough seas.

"Did you just think that up, brother, *hemo-goblin?*" Klaas laughed at the dub. "Most of those *hemo-goblins* are rude and ugly."

"And smelly," added Gert. He lost his balance and stumbled into a shelf of books, then again into the decanters. Crystal and alcohol exploded on the floor. Still holding his glass upright, Gert frowned at the mess he made.

"Obviously, you have had too much," Adina snapped at Gert. She slowly turned back to Cedric and continued. "The vampires at Vos Castle are typical among western breeds. That particular clan is called—"

"The Royal Flemish," said Cedric, helping Gert to his feet. "Yes, I know."

"Of course you do," said Adina. "How well did you know the late master, Count Marcel Marc de Vos?"

Cedric leaned Gert against a bookshelf and turned to Adina. "Late...?" Cedric was taken aback by the inference that he was dead.

"Yes, as dead as a coffin nail," said Gert, stabilizing himself while his brother collected broken glass from the floor.

"What happened to him?" asked Cedric, offering to help Klaas.

"Assassinated," said Adina.

"Killed by his own advisor, or so we gather," said Klaas, pushing Cedric away.

Cedric swallowed. "Oh no." His recollection of Marcel was still fresh. The man appeared bigger than life, terrifyingly powerful, and seemingly invincible.

"How well do you know Domitian Augustus de' Medici?" asked Adina.

"Not very well... He was Countess Marie's closest advisor," said Cedric.

"And lover," added Adina.

A stream of memories carried Cedric back to the day he met Countess Marie. She was sitting at a fancy table counting coins in the chamber beneath Vos Castle. His chore was to replace the candles there, but Marie offered to award Cedric a gold coin if he solved her riddle, and solved it he did. He cherished that gold coin. Cedric felt extremely lucky and special when he was chosen to escort Marie to England. Cedric looked out for Marie, booking her rooms and means of travel, and being at her beck and call all hours of the day.

Cedric lifted his glass and finally took a sip of the cognac. It warmed his mouth and then his throat and stomach. He watched Klaas place broken glass on the table. "I would like to express my gratitude," said Cedric, lifting his glass of cognac. "I am grateful to you all, for risking your lives for me, saving me from my enemies in more ways than one. I owe my life to you." He turned to Adina. "Please teach me your ways. For I do wish to do what you do and will gladly risk my life for yours. I have a lot to learn, but I will learn if you will teach me."

Adina closed her eyes and breathed in deeply. She shook her head as if to disagree, but said, "Very well, you will begin your learning on the morrow." Adina stood up and moved to the entrance door.

"Good evening, dear sister," said Klaas.

"Good evening," said Adina, with a passing smirk that tantalized if not unnerved Cedric a smidgeon.

Klaas flashed a mischievous grin at Cedric. "Can you not believe it?" Klaas approached him with open arms and placed his hands on Cedric's shoulders. "I thought she would never consent to this, yet here you are!"

"Perhaps Cedric's charm is more powerful than our sister's resolve," said Gert. "She obviously fancies you, and we shall be the happier for it!" Gert joined them and all three toasted to Cedric.

## 16 - AFFIRMATION

### July 1799

Abigail entered through the catacombs directly below a castle turret. The space was circular, enclosed by stonewall foundations. Sunlight cascading down through a pentagon-shaped hole in the floor above faintly illuminated the dirt floor. During the Dark Ages, disloyal servants were dropped through the hole to perish in the dark and unforgiving maze of corridors known as the catacombs. An ordinary tree would not survive in such darkness, thought Abigail, but the deadwood tree was hardly ordinary. It was magical. With the motherly touch of a necromancer and the nourishing remains of Countess Marie, the tree would flourish. It would form connections between the incorporeal and corporeal realms—of that she was certain.

A magical tree required magical ingredients to grow and react to the *renatus*—the ritual conjuring. Abigail kept some of those ingredients in a lockbox in her bedchamber. However, many other ingredients were required to be freshly harvested from the forest. Unfortunately, Domitian and his clan were prohibited from leaving Vos Castle unless accompanied by one of Orfeo's Roman guards. Complicating matters, Abigail was never alone. Ordered to prevent her from escaping, Domitian's trusted guard, Gaétan, always kept her in view.

Gaétan Chevalier was originally from Lille, France, a Grey Musketeer serving King Louis XIV. After Gaétan foiled a republican uprising against the monarchy, and single-handedly killed four conspirators in a swordfight, Countess Marie de Vos swept in to collect Gaétan for her own. Intent on building a personal guard of gallant and skilled fighting men like Gaétan, she summarily made him a vampire, ignoring the clan's siring rule. The rule was simple. No vampire of the Royal Flemish Clan was allowed to sire a vampire without Master Count Marcel's consent. Never one to follow rules, she broke it. When King Louis's musketeer suddenly appeared at Vos Castle with a thirst for blood, Count Marcel confined Marie to the catacombs for a year and took Gaétan under his tutelage. To deter France from investigating Vos Castle, Marcel ordered all clan members to claim no knowledge of Gaétan Chevalier. It worked.

Abigail walked to the center of the space and peered up at the soft light falling from the hole in the ceiling. After a moment of basking in the diffused glow, she knelt down and placed the deadwood seed on the dirt floor and closed her eyes. She inserted her fingers into the soil and lifted a handful of it to her petite nose. She smelled fear, sadness, and human suffering. She imagined servants falling through the shaft, breaking bones on impact. If the victims had survived the fall, they would have been trapped because the entrance door was probably bolted shut, and if left open, surviving the dark labyrinth was unlikely. She let the soil funnel through her hands and turned to Gaétan, who was patiently waiting beside the doorway, a linen sack resting at his feet, a shovel leaning against the wall behind him.

"Here," said Abigail, standing up. "I will plant the seed here." She walked three paces to the right and scratched the surface with the edge of her sandal. "And the countess's remains will be buried here." She nodded to herself. "Yes, this is good."

Gaétan lifted the sack and shovel and approached the burial site. He gently placed the sack on the ground, and spaded the tool into the soil. "How deep?" he asked, his voice reverberating in the space.

"Enough to bury her reassembled remains facedown," said Abigail.

"Why facedown?"

"A tribute to the netherworld, according to my mother. Most of what I know is through observation." Abigail returned to the center of the room and scooped a hole with her hands. She placed the seed in the soil, retrieved dried herbs from a bag slung over her shoulder, and sprinkled them over the seed.

"Oh mighty Hades, son of Kronos, brother of Zeus, lord and ruler of the netherworld, I, Abigail van Ness of Hoeilaart, of the House of **Brajerean, humbly summon thee.** Oh mighty Hades, please hear me and accept my offering of my soul to thee, bestowed to thee, early and yours, yours and early, for the provisional return of Countess Marie de Vos. I beseech thee, her soul borrowed, my soul promised, both souls returned to thee, yours and early, early and yours, fleeting tenure, both souls returned to thee."

She lifted a small pouch, opened it, and poured blue powder over the seed. She gently breathed into a rising blue plume, causing it to expand and roil and take form of a man holding a forked staff, whose size dwarfed Gaétan. The figure of blue dust became more and more defined until the features of its face and hands and the curls in its long hair and beard were undeniably that of Hades.

Gaétan took a step back from the spectacle, but Abigail remained steadfast.

The god's eyes glowed cobalt blue and it looked down on Abigail with an almost fatherly admiration just before bursting into a miasma of dust.

"What was that?" whispered Gaétan.

"The affirmation."

"I was told the countess saved you from the villagers, and that is why you agreed to resurrect her?"

She wanted to tell Gaétan that Marie had killed her father, and the last thing she wanted was to resurrect her. Her brother Pierce was now guardian of all the world's magic conveniently stowed inside an old leather satchel. He and it must be protected. Domitian agreed not to hunt Pierce down if she resurrected Countess Marie. She pulled her thoughts together and pointed at the burial ground. "We must hurry. Will you please shovel?"

Gaétan positioned the spade in the soil and scooped out dirt at a quickened pace. In a few minutes, he had excavated a grave deep enough to bury the body.

Abigail knelt beside Gaétan at the grave's edge. He gently retrieved Marie's body parts from the sack and handed them to Abigail. Marie's body was a bit stiff and needed some adjusting. Abigail gently placed the body in the grave, straightened the shriveled legs and positioned the arms to the sides of her body. Then, Abigail properly placed the severed hands to the wrists. When Gaétan handed the head to Abigail, she brushed back the hair with her fingers and wiped the shriveled face clean of blood specks. She then carefully placed it facedown at the severed neck. Abigail fished out herbs from her bag and sprinkled them over the wrists and neck.

Gaétan took the shovel in hand. Abigail backed away from the grave and nodded for Gaétan to backfill over the body. In a minute, the grave was a mound of dirt.

Abigail looked over at Gaétan, who was staring at her. She had mostly ignored him, acknowledging him only when he spoke to her or if she needed something from him. He was a handsome man, and under different circumstances she might have fallen for him.

Gaétan smiled at her.

Gaétan was quite tall, as tall as her brother Pierce. His hands were large, but clean and proportioned, neither pudgy nor fat, and his fingernails were short and rounded, not long and pointed like those of so many other vampires. He wore a variation of his uniform when he was a member of the Grey

Musketeers. When Abigail asked why he wore the old musketeer fashion, he said that he preferred it to anything else. His attire was slightly different from the King's issue. Instead of the official blue cassocks, he wore a black one, lined with blue velvet instead of red, and edged with gold instead of silver embroidery. The rest of his clothes were in tones of grey and brown except for his black tricorn hat to which a plume of crow's feathers was attached.

"We should go," said Abigail, feeling awkward from all his gawking and recent talkativeness. She hated the beauty spell her mother secretly casted upon her. It was not supposed to last forever, but it was obviously still there, distracting most everyone. "What are you looking at?" shouted Abigail at Gaétan, who was now smiling oddly at her.

"You," he said simply. "I had always noticed you, but from afar. Now, after so much time spent with you, your beauty is even greater than I thought."

"May we go?" muttered Abigail, forcing herself not to lash out at the spell-blinded vampire.

## 17 - DELICIOUSLY DIABOLICAL

Fourteen days after arriving at Vos Castle and seizing everything, Orfeo had failed to recognize the importance of Sir Michael and Abigail to Domitian. Orfeo's focus was plunder, placing a guard at the counting chamber where the castle's wealth was stored. He positioned the rest of his guards on the castle's walls to monitor access to and from its keep. Orfeo needed to return to Rome and wanted to restrict Domitian and his clan from stealing *his* wealth and fleeing *his* realm. Problem was Orfeo's guards were unable to be everywhere and watch everyone at all times, and so Domitian was able to evade the Roman guards, moving in and out of the castle's walls with little risk of being seen.

After Orfeo left the castle, Domitian returned to the catacombs to pay Sir Michael a visit. No longer chained, Michael sat comfortably in a chair, reading a book, when Domitian arrived. Domitian placed his hand on his guard's shoulder and nodded.

The guard unlocked the dungeon's door and pushed it open.

"Sir Michael," whispered Domitian. "Please, come with me."

Michael reluctantly put down his book, lifted to his feet, and stretched.

"Do not get any ideas, my dark knight," whispered Domitian as Michael came through the doorway into the corridor. Domitian placed his hand on the hilt of his sword and pushed Michael in the opposite direction of the counting chamber.

They traveled deeper into the catacombs until reaching a clearing directly below one of the towers. They went through a narrow passageway to the main staircase. Noticing a Roman guard passing by at the top, they waited for him to move on. When it was clear, they quickly ascended to the top of the tower where Domitian let Sir Michael into his chambers and locked the door behind them.

Domitian's chambers had previously belonged to the former master, Count Marcel Marc de Vos. The room was completely refurbished to Domitian's taste, and Michael turned full circle to view it for the first time since meeting his late master there.

Domitian observed Sir Michael's gaze and physical condition. He was still formidable in his famished state, feeding occasionally on goat's blood to keep at bay the frenzy.

"Please, Sir Michael," said Domitian softly, hand held out toward a chair, "sit with me by the fire." Domitian waited for Michael to take his seat beside the inglenook and join him nearest a pile of firewood and an iron poker. "Too many ears, thus we must speak softly. I believe you frequently counseled Count Marcel here in this room," said Domitian, gazing over to the box containing the ashes of the late master. "You probably sat here gazing into those deadly flames exactly as you are now. If only these walls could talk, eh, my dark knight? What would they say of your meetings with Marcel?" Domitian placed wood on the fire and stoked the flames with the poker. He imagined Count Marcel sitting with Michael, his trusted advisor—and assassin. Despite the dangers of working with a man as deceitful as Sir Michael was, Domitian needed to eliminate Orfeo and believed Michael to be—at that moment—the only one capable of masterminding a fail-safe scheme.

"I wish to discuss a very important matter concerning us," began Domitian. "Fourteen days ago, Orfeo and his henchmen arrived here to do exactly what you predicted he would do." Domitian began to tremble with anger. "That man!" The angst in his whisper was scarcely audible but clear to see. "He seized everything—my castle, my wealth, my power! It sickens me to think that...that he is now our..." Domitian pressed his lips together and forced out the last word. "...master." He fell back into his chair, as if exhausted by the frustration. "Well, what do you have to say to that?"

Michael's eyes slowly found Domitian's, and he managed with some effort a tremulous smirk. "I told you so."

Domitian sat up, anger giving way to humor at Michael's unexpected response. "And so you did, Sir Michael, and that is why I brought you here. I need your advice. I know your past, and obviously your service to Count Marcel. However grateful I am to you for killing him, *you*, Sir Michael, are shrewd and would not think twice to turncoat again if it suited you. True?"

Michael slowly shook his head. "Untrue. I would think twice, if not thrice..."

Domitian chuckled. "Are you capable of unconditional and everlastingly loyalty? Perhaps you are only loyal for as long as it serves you. I might even believe that killing Marcel was a sort of higher loyalty, to end his suffering for the good of the clan. My dark knight, you are deliciously diabolical and corruptibly complex. Your loyalty to me need not be eternal—nay! I need you only to help make a certain individual disappear from our lives. When that happens, we part ways. What say you?"

Though Michael's eyes drooped with fatigue, making Domitian feel exhausted just by looking at them, his words waited like bats before dusk. After an extended silence that tried Domitian's patience, the words finally came. "You would ask a traitor for counsel...?"

A chill of discomfort poured over Domitian like iced water. "Is that a question or comment, my dark knight?" Domitian reminded himself that he was the stronger of the two, and that he should be wary of Michael's reputation while using him to get what he wanted. "I...I am no fool, Sir Michael. I know who you are, what you have done, what you are capable of doing. I can only imagine how difficult it was for you to kill Count Marcel—as close as you were to him. He was a father to you, yes? Still, you showed great cunning, preparation, and courage to end him; and by doing so, a new chapter has begun. Do you know who the main characters are?" Domitian paused for effect, wondering if the dark knight would eventually capitulate. "They are you and me and our arch nemesis Orfeo of Roma. Unless we defeat him, I fear neither of us will live to read another chapter."

"Why should I care?" asked Michael, annoyed. "I have no reason to live, and certainly no reason to help you."

"Ah, but I think you do, my dark knight. You see, I know what you want."

"To be left alone?" grumbled Sir Michael.

Domitian laughed and began to feel like the clever one. "Oh my, how dreadfully silly you can be. You want to live long enough to realize your dream, do you not? I can help you attain it. I will allow you to pursue your dream of godly magical powers, if you give me what I want." Domitian waited for Michael to respond, but the man was a statue. "How are you able to just sit there like a rock when I tell you such things? I know how you fancy witchcraft. I for one cannot understand it. Witches are filthy. They do not rule the world. Vampires with such powers do not rule the world. Aside from honoring Countess Marie's wishes to return from the depths of Hades, I for one abhor the—the—necromantic hocus-pocus—but if it can return Marie back to me, so be it." Domitian was beginning to find Michael's deadpan face amusing. A smile lifted his ears. "The only thing missing from your face of stone is feces of bird!" chortled Domitian, with a quiet but hearty laugh, leaning his chair back on two legs. "You are like a brooding statue—an irritating effigy, my dark knight."

Michael tore his eyes away from the fire and growled at Domitian. "Do not call me that."

Domitian settled down and smiled politely. "Well then, finally... I was beginning to think you were dead."

"Obviously, Gerda extracted information from Abigail's mind and shared it with you. What else did she tell you?"

Domitian put on a serious face. "Something about a satchel of magic, which sounds like a sack of dung to me, and Abigail, of course, knows where it is." Domitian noticed Michael's drooping posture lift slightly. "Sir Michael, after Abigail resurrects Countess Marie, I will have no use for her. She is no doubt a fetching witch—"

"I may have use for her..."

"Splendid," said Domitian. "Then she shall be yours after I am done with her and we have dispatched the enemy."

Michael turned back to the fire. "If I were to help you, what assurances have you to offer?"

"You have my word. I shall guarantee your safe passage out of Europe."

"Banishment, you mean."

Domitian chuckled. "Be that as it may, it is for your own good to leave Europe. Just as you had fled England, you will flee again to start another life. Take Abigail with you. However, I shall require equal assurance that you will never return to destroy us with your godly powers." After a moment of reflection, Domitian continued. "Your focus on Orfeo will allow me to focus on Countess Marie."

Michael rubbed his temples and sighed. "Very well, I will provide counsel, but you must follow my every instruction or we shall have no agreement."

Domitian snapped his fingers several times with delight. "Agreed. I was right to count on you. To start off our alliance on solid footing, I wish to extend my sincerest apology for the shackles and rats. However, I was emotional, and when I discovered you were withholding information from me, I became distrusting and vindictive. Can you blame me...? Now, let us devise a plan to be rid of that greedy swine!"

He squinted at Domitian. "I suppose you told him of your scheme to sell orphans to the east."

Domitian struggled to maintain a smile. "Yes, I told him. It bought me time."

"And time is what you are going to need," said Michael. "When Marcel was leader of the League, many outside this clan were less enthusiastic. However, a common enemy from the east empowered him and an unlikely alliance with an ancient society ensured his power."

"Ancient society?" asked Domitian.

"The Meridiem."

Domitian leaned back in his chair. Queen Žofie had already told him of the families of sorcery. "Do they really exist?"

"They do."

"But they are all witches, are they not? I hate witches."

Sir Michael stroked his beard. "You must swear never to discuss openly or reveal the existence of the Meridiem."

"Very well, but I shall have you know that secrets are not so easily kept."

"I shall have you know that helping you is not so easily palatable. Swear to take what I tell you, show you, and teach you to your grave."

Domitian signed. "You have my word. Please, tell me about these *mermaidens*."

"Meridiems...are a lineage of sorcerers that can be traced back to the age of myth."

"Sir Michael, if this is your idea of cutting to the chase, I would hate to experience the scenic route."

"They are specialized assassins. We pay them to eradicate upyrians who enter the west illegally."

"Ludicrous! Witches are incapable!"

"They are more capable than we are," said Michael.

Domitian sneered at the thought. "Who better than us to eradicate ugly upyrians?" Domitian looked for signs of agreement on Michael's face.

"Upyrian are vampires, but they are unlike us, profoundly different, which makes them quite challenging even for us to fend off. Surely, you must know that."

"Of course I do. They perform magic tricks! I am also told they cannot hover as we do when consuming child's blood— not that I would know anything about that... Anyway, what is your point, Sir Michael?"

"I had hoped you would know the point by now."

Domitian sprung to his feet. "What do you mean by that? Do you mean to insult me? Am I expected to read your mind, bend it perhaps?" Domitian paced and sat back down in a huff. "The point escapes me."

"As much as you disliked Count Marcel, he established a very important and powerful relationship with the Meridiem. Only he and Lucius of Rome were able to summon them." Michael lowered his voice. "Since you are master of this clan, you have the right to summon them, not only the right but also the means."

Domitian frowned. "I am no longer master of this clan."

"No one else knows. Orfeo will not arrive in Rome for another two days."

"Presuming you are correct," said Domitian, pinching his chin in thought. "The next move is to summon these...*merrymen*?"

"Meridiem—"

"How?"

"There is only one way, and you must have payment and instructions ready."

Domitian massaged displeasure from his temples. "I hate witches. I hate upyrians even more. I hate Orfeo the most. I will follow your instructions to the letter. When may we begin?"

"Tonight."

# 18 - *LUNABELLUM*

At Josephus's house in Amsterdam, Adina, Klaas, Gert, and Cedric met in the parlor for dessert after enjoying a delicious dinner. Cedric took a chair and Adina placed an old, thick, leather-bound book on his lap and sat down in a chair beside him.

"Do you know what a ledger is?" asked Adina.

"No," said Cedric, opening the book and turning pages.

"You are holding one. All our money transactions are entered into this ledger, which is very useful when you travel with brothers who spend money like thieves."

Cedric kept turning pages but all were blank. "I see nothing," said Cedric.

"Ledger of Fortune," said Adina to the book as if it were listening, "may I introduce Cedric Martens of Linder. He is our new bookkeeper. Reveal your pages to him." She turned to Cedric. "Now, look."

No sooner had she said to look did lines begin to appear, forming columns and rows. Cedric turned the pages and saw numbers and dates and notes.

"All moneys received—coins, promissory notes, objects of value, such as gemstones—will be accounted for in this ledger. Do you understand?"

Cedric nodded. "Yes."

Adina took back the book and flashed a half smile at Cedric. "When you are done for the day, you will return the ledger to me. You will inform me of any problems. You will give to me any money or items of value to lock away. Have you any questions?"

"I do," said Cedric. "May I see the ledger again, please?" Adina handed it back to him, and when he turned the pages, he saw that they were blank, but after a few restless heartbeats, all entries darkened on the pages until fully legible. "How is it done?"

"Really, Cedric?" said Adina. "You should know by now..."

"I know it is magic, but I want to know how the magic works."

Adina scoffed at Cedric. "If it was ordinary and explainable, it would not be magic."

Gert approached Adina as she was about to leave the room. "Sister, have we any new assignments?"

She shook her head and exited the room with the ledger.

"It is possible that Domitian cannot summon us," said Klaas to Gert, "or is unaware of us, or has no need for us."

"Domitian and Orfeo as well," said Gert, turning to Cedric with a curious smile. "Cedric, do you know who Orfeo is?"

"No," Cedric said, shaking his head.

"Can you describe Domitian, his appearance?" asked Klaas.

Domitian was usually with Countess Marie, but Cedric caught glimpses of him only when he was walking away or turning a corner, never straight on. "He was average height...wavy, light brown hair. He was usually well-dressed and in the company of Countess Marie. I never saw his eyes or heard his voice, though."

Adina reentered the room.

"How many assignments did you say we have, sister?" asked Gert.

"One left," said Adina.

Gert looked over at Klaas. "What if that is the last assignment?"

"Then we shall be released of this burden," said Klaas.

"Not as long as the pact exists," said Adina.

The brothers nodded reluctantly as if the pact were something heavy to bear.

"What is the pact, exactly?" asked Cedric.

Klaas put down his glass. "The pact is an agreement, an essential part of the truce. We are bound by the League to defend our border from the child-eating vampires of the east."

"Horrible *hemo-goblins,* all of them," muttered Gert.

"Are the assignments written?" asked Cedric.

"With quill and ink," said Gert.

"How do we receive them?" asked Cedric. "By air," said Klaas.

"A very large bird," added Gert, "like the one you had seen, Cedric. Do you remember...?"

Cedric remembered. It was a gray raven, a very large gray raven that seemed to disappear when he turned away for just a moment.

"We and our collaborators receive them as well," said Klaas.

"Collaborators such as Mister Bertonelli?" asked Cedric.

"Precisely," said Klaas.

"Are we witches?" asked Cedric.

Adina cleared her throat.

"Is not magic and witchcraft the same?" The question had been on Cedric's mind since Pierce shot a ball of light out of his hands.

"Witchcraft can include mystical magic," said Adina.

"Or trickery," said Gert.

"Or nothing at all," said Klaas.

"We prefer sorcery to describe our magic," said Adina.

"Others call it wizardry," added Klaas.

"We are one of two surviving families whose lineage dates back to the age of myth," said Adina, "when magical beasts and immortals roamed the earth. Witches are generally individuals belonging to a coven of related or unrelated individuals whose ideology is based in younger religious concepts, such as one god, one devil, heaven, and hell. Nature can be a part of their rituals as well. Our ideology is much older, and we do not call our family a coven."

"So...sorcerers are not witches?" said Cedric, still uncertain of the difference.

"They are not so easily distinguishable and many would argue that they are one in the same," said Adina. "I believe your friend Abigail van Ness calls herself a witch. She may be; however, her family descends from the House of Brajerean. Thus, we consider her to be a sorceress."

"She lost her family," said Gert.

"Thanks to Marie de Vos, Abigail is orphaned," said Adina. "We know her story."

Cedric searched for commonality with sorcerers, whose multi-theistic beliefs conflicted with his. Yet, he was neither threatened by their magic nor by their beliefs. He felt strangely comfortable and compatible. He knew not why, and summed it up to the will of God. So, it was established that the siblings and he were different but complimentary. His family was not descended from mythology, but their faith was not exactly shallow in history. He was not a swordsman of extraordinary skill. He grew up on a farm. Yet, despite all that, there he was—haunted by tragedy, hunted by vampires, protected by sorcerers, sitting in a mansion in Amsterdam, sipping liqueur, and eating cake.

"Adina," said Cedric. "Concerning the very large delivery bird..."

Adina laughed. "It is a gray corvus. Before Count Marcel of Flanders and Lord Lucius of Rome were assassinated, we received our assignments through them. They summoned the gray corvus to deliver their assignments to us."

"How does it work, the summoning part?" asked Cedric.

"A specific chant from a manuscript must be read aloud within thirty-six heartbeats, eighteen beats before midnight and after midnight. It is my understanding that the manuscript is only legible during that time and under those conditions."

"What happens as a result of the chant?" asked Cedric.

"When the corvus is summoned, it will fly to meet the assignor. There, it will pluck out a quill with which the assignor must use to sign the assignments, which are then given to the corvus to deliver to us."

Gert lifted a finger. "It has worked without fail for centuries."

Cedric was beginning to understand what they did. They were being paid by vampires to kill rival vampires. He struggled to make sense of everything and categorize what the siblings were doing against his scale of morals. "Are we assassins?"

"Yes, Cedric," said Adina. "We must not sweeten the sourness of what we do."

"I prefer mercenaries to assassins," said Gert.

"We are paid by the League to exterminate the eastern threat," said Klaas.

"Why?" asked Cedric.

The brothers turned to Adina, who was smiling at Cedric. "Three centuries ago, sorcerers and vampires went to war. That war is known as the *Lunabellum*." Adina raised her hands. The scars on her palms began to glow blue as she drew the shape of infinity in the air. She lowered her hands and the symbols remained suspended. She gently blew the glowing images to a corner of the room where, upon impact with the walls, they shattered into smoke and sparkles. "Open your minds and you will see the images," said Adina.

Miraculously, the sparkles and smoke swirled together to form a cloudy image of a different time and place, inside what appeared to be a church. Inside the church, people were fighting, running, jumping, flying, swinging iron blades. There were two young women, identical twins, firing energy—red, blue, and green shards of burning light—from their hands and eyes. The energy shards exploded on impact, fending off a swarm of vampires that were steadily flowing into the church through broken windows and doorways.

"Vampires had been killing humans for as long as anyone can remember," said Adina, her voice loud and clear inside Cedric's mind. "After the upyrian in the east developed a taste for children, they murdered an entire family of Laecian sorcerers and began to invade the west, taking children there and even killing western vampires and taking over their lairs. Elders of the Laecian families met with elders of the Meridiem and Brajerean families. After three days of discussion and debate, the families signed a declaration of war against the upyrian. Not surprisingly, the western vampire clans—even those that hated the upyrian—remained neutral to the sorcerers' cause.

"The *Lunabellum* was fought mostly at night, though we hunted upyrian at all hours. We were formidable, but the upyrian were physically stronger and outnumbered us ten to one. A year into the war, all Laecian sorcerers were either killed or captured by the upyrian. I escaped capture by changing into a raven, but as I took flight, an arrow impaled my chest. Mortally wounded, I fell over Poland and died. Luckily, my body was found by a group of Meridiem sorcerers who recognized my face. They took me to their home wherein a Meridiem necromancer lived.

"While the necromancer argued with her family to resurrect me, Meridiem elders met with the western vampire leaders, begging them to join the war, to fight beside them. They refused at first, but when the upyrian started to kill more vampires and take over their territories, an agreement between Meridiem and vampire was finally reached."

Adina abruptly went silent as the imagery suddenly changed from vivid colors to hues of gray. The scene changed, showing her sister Žofie pushing Adina out of harm's way, pleading with her to flee as Žofie fended off the upyrian hordes.

"No," whispered Adina, frightened. "How can this be? Everyone look away and block her out!" Her face pruned with determination to stop the image. "Stop it! Stop it! Do not listen to her!"

Yet, everyone continued to stare at the image of Queen Žofie as she meddled with their minds.

# 19 - I SEE YOU

The brothers, Adina, and Cedric were spellbound by the imagery that had changed from Adina to Queen Žofie. Then, another woman's voice entered their minds—a voice very much like Adina's but with a heavier eastern accent.

"After I save my sister's life," the woman said, "upyrian took me beneath the streets of Moscow. They tortured me there, bled me for days to weaken me, until one day I was taken to the king. He wanted to see me, the twin sister, Adina's sister."

As much as Cedric tried to look away, the images were so fascinating that his eyes were hopelessly attracted to them.

The image changed to another location and the colors returned, more saturated than before. Now, Žofie was lying naked at the feet of an imposing man—his blond hair tied back, his beard long and braided, rings on every finger, scepter in hand. He eased off his throne of gold and blue velvet, kneeling beside Žofie. He took her hand in his and kissed it while other upyrian watched in the background.

"The beautiful and powerful sorceress, Žofie," said the man in a brusque vibrato. "I am Rurik, king of the upyrian. Are you not honored to meet me?"

Cedric tried to block the voices and haunting imagery as Adina was urging everyone to do, but even she could not look away.

"Where am I?" murmured Žofie in the image. "Where is my family?"

Rurik glanced over at rows of glowing eyes in the shadows. "Your family is over there."

Žofie looked fearfully left and right. She struggled to get up, but her legs would not move.

A huge grin wrinkled Rurik's temples.

"My legs," whispered Žofie.

Rurik laughed, and everyone else laughed with him. "Please accept my apology, but my guards fear that you will use your powers to escape, so they broke your spine. You are paralyzed."

Žofie began hyperventilating, too weak to use magic to defend herself, realizing there was no escape.

"Fear not, my child. You will walk again, after you demonstrate shape-shifting powers, yes?"

"No," said Žofie. "Even if I wanted...I am too weak. The others will come for me."

"Others? Do you mean other sorcerers, or...your sister?" He smirked as if his comment was a joke. "Your sister is dead, and the remaining sorcerers are signing a pact with western vampires." He chuckled quietly. "I know it is difficult to believe, but all true. Lunabellum will end, no more fighting, at least for now."

"Impossible!" Žofie tried to drag herself away, using just her arms. No use, she was too weak and in pain.

Rurik continued. "Soon, you will understand what it is to be upyrian. You will be stronger, faster, more powerful than ever before."

"No, please," were the last words Žofie murmured before he penetrated her neck with his terribly long fangs, draining her to the brink of death.

The next scene was of the vampire's throne, perched atop a glistening heap of gold and silver pieces. Žofie lounged, one leg draped over the throne's ornate arm, Rurik's scepter in hand, and a dazzling tiara perched upon her head. Her robe was of white fur, lined with red velvet, the only garment partially covering her naked body. She was looking at something, something in front of her, which became increasingly clear to Cedric that she was viewing them in the same way he was viewing her—an image both suspended in air and in mind.

Adina whispered something in Latin, desperately trying to terminate the image, but nothing was working. Žofie was somehow channeling through Adina, mind-meddling with her.

Žofie licked her plump lips and smiled brightly. "Sister, it is long time. You look...surprised." Her eyes drifted to Cedric. "What a strong and beautiful boy you appear to be. Cedric is your name, yes? Now I see why Countess Marie chose you to accompany her to England. You think you are safe with my sister and those two idiots beside her? Look at them, poor little men, confused and cowering." A giggle escaped her crazed smile. "They cannot protect you from me." Žofie rose from her throne, exposing a portion of her lithe body, and extended the end of her scepter at Adina. "*Sestra*...my sweet twin. Now, I see you, all of you. I know where you are." Žofie laughed, her stomach muscles rippling. "You know the truth, sister. All those centuries ago...I saved you. How do you thank me for saving you? You abandon me to be tortured and enslaved by Rurik the very handsome but not-so-smart upyrian king. You call yourself Meridiem and you kill my kindred— upyrian. Yet, after all you do to betray me, sister, I still love you. I will prove my love to you by saving you yet again. I am coming for you. Soon, you will see me and my world through blue-and-green *upyrian* eyes."

Water suddenly flowed over Adina's head, and the imagery vanished. Adina looked up at Cedric, standing over her with an empty pitcher in hand.

Cedric was not sure if tears or water from the pitcher was streaming down her face until he noticed her trembling lips. She lowered herself to the floor. He knelt beside her and set the pitcher down. He turned to the brothers. They looked befuddled and fearful. Adina fell against Cedric, flushing emotions from her eyes.

Cedric's inclination to hold, protect, and console only added to the confusion of his standing in this secret fellowship. What was going through Adina's mind? Obviously she was shaken and probably as fearful and bewildered as her brothers appeared to be. Cedric wanted to know. He looked over to Gert and Klaas again. They were distracted, whispering, debating, and discussing what to do next. Cedric brushed her tears away.

Then, abruptly, she pushed herself away from Cedric and put on a stoic face. She went to the door and paused before opening it.

Cedric watched her as she seemed to waver before finally letting herself out. A hand on his shoulder prevented Cedric's heart from chasing Adina's fading footsteps. It was Klaas.

"Stay focused on the priorities," said Klaas to Cedric, as if cautioning the boy's heart from pursuing dreams into the sky when they needed him to be on the ground with them. "Rest well."

"Do not worry for Adina," said Gert, a bit of defensiveness in his eyes.

The brothers exited the room, leaving Cedric alone to ponder Queen Žofie, her sister Adina, and his place in all of that.

The next morning, Cedric and the siblings met in the kitchen where a man and a woman were preparing breakfast. Francois was setting the dining table in the next room. After the strange and terrifying imagery from the night before, everyone appeared weary, especially Gert, who was rubbing away the effect of too much cognac from his temples.

They were seated at the dining table and served a bounty of food, more than they could possibly eat, especially when their appetites seemed to have gone missing. As they slowly and reluctantly ate, Cedric was beginning to feel less fatigued and noticed everyone except Gert sitting straighter, as if they too were feeling better. After a sip of tea, Cedric wanted to break the silence and dare discuss last night's incident.

"So...where is Mr. Bertonelli?" asked Cedric.

"He went to Italy," said Klaas.

Cedric turned to Adina. "Concerning last night—"

"What you saw is what *she* wanted you to see," said Adina. "We must not allow her to distract us, manipulate us... Do you understand?"

Cedric nodded and finished his tea, wondering if Adina was already being manipulated by Žofie.

"Will you be ready tonight?" said Adina to Gert, loud enough to make him wince.

"Yes, sister," muttered Gert, clenching his eyelids. "My head hurts..."

"Please look after your brother," Adina said to Klaas.

"Is he not your brother as well, sister?" Klaas responded, spreading strawberry jam on his toast. "He is no child. He can look after his own alcohol sickness."

"I will be fit and ready by sundown," promised Gert, pushing back his chair and warily standing. "Please, excuse me." Just like that, he left the room.

"May I ask a general question?" said Cedric, finishing a remnant of his toast. "Where do the Meridiem—your ancestors—come from?"

Klaas lifted his cup of tea and fell back in his chair. "The Meridiem are believed to originate out of the north, Norway and Sweden," said Klaas. "Over time, our ancestors migrated to places such as Denmark, Britain, Poland, and America."

"Our mark is the stave," said Adina, revealing her palms, a faint scar on each one in the shape of half a snowflake.

"What is the significance of the stave?" asked Cedric.

"The power of the Meridiem flows through it," said Adina. "Two halves make a whole. When I bring my hands together,

I can draw upon various types of powers. Magic in my hands, so to speak."

Cedric turned to Klaas. "Do you have scars as well?"

"Not that I am aware," said Klaas.

"Do you have magical powers as well?"

"Yes," said Klaas. "However, my powers are unlike Adina's. My powers enhance my blade skills, coordination, and reflexes. Adina can enhance my powers. We three siblings are well practiced in sharing powers. No others in our extended families are quite as compatible."

"There are other sorcerer families," said Adina. "From the south came the Brajerean. They spread from Italy to Spain, France, Belgium, Switzerland, and Holland. Their symbol is *stjerne med åtte ben*—star with eight points."

Cedric recalled such a scar on his friend Pierce van Fleming's palms.

"And the Laecian came from Africa," said Klaas. "Their symbol was a triangle within a circle. They migrated east into Arabia and Persia and northward into Turkey and Eastern Europe. Some believe a group of Laecians still exist in Asia..."

"Yes, but it is more likely that the Laecian bloodline is ended," said Adina. "Now, there are only two families remaining—the Brajerean and the Meridiem." Adina placed her napkin on the table and got up. "We may need to postpone the assignment if Gert is unwell."

"How can I help?" asked Cedric.

"You will keep the ledger," said Adina, turning away and leaving the dining room.

## 20 - THE GRAY CORVUS

Nearing midnight, Domitian heated a stick of red wax over a candle flame and dripped a few drops onto two scrolls of rag-paper. As Domitian pressed his seal into the wax, Sir Michael opened a very old manuscript to a string marker. He set the manuscript in front of Domitian and instructed him: "Milord, you are to read these words aloud from start to finish in the space of thirty-six heartbeats. I will track the time—" He went to a tall pendulum clock hanging on the wall and opened its door. After restarting the pendulum, he lifted his pocket watch and set the time on the clock. "You see, milord, each swing of the pendulum equates to one second, and one second is approximately one heartbeat."

Domitian smiled merrily. "Are we not becoming splendid friends?" Domitian looked down at the manuscript, scratched his head, and flashed Michael a worried face. "How am I to read this? It...it is faded beyond legibility."

"At this moment, you are not to read it, milord. Simply follow each sentence as if you are reading at the normal rate by which you read. This is to give you an idea of how fast you must read within the given time period."

"Yes, but the words—"

"The words are faded now but will become legible when it is time to read aloud. Trust me, and please do not ask how."

"What? Become legible—but how?"

Sir Michael sighed, looked at the time, and gazed out the window at the waxing moon. "A few minutes until midnight... Shall we practice, milord?"

Domitian placed his finger beneath the first faded word and squinted. "*Magni vulpes corvum vo...vocare nocte*, something, *rursus detost...*or is it—?"

"Please, milord," said Michael anxiously. "Do not attempt to read the words."

"Yes, of course, forgive me." Domitian placed his finger on the first faded word again.

"I will announce the remaining time as you go." Michael said as he turned to the clock and raised a finger of readiness. "Ready? And...begin," said Michael, pointing his finger at Domitian.

Domitian started moving his finger along each sentence as if reading them.

Michael counted the swings of the pendulum and sounded off the remaining time in five-second intervals. "Thirty seconds...twenty-five...twenty...fifteen...ten...five, four, three, two, and finished."

Domitian shook his head, disappointed. "I know what we are trying to do, but I feel the fool... For whence the time comes, I fear the words will be no more discernible than they now are."

"Trust me," said Michael, confidently. "You will be able to read every word of it. I ask that you stay focused on the first sentence and watch for the change. The change will occur exactly eighteen heartbeats of midnight."

"Whose heartbeats?" blurted Domitian with a nervous chuckle. "My heart is full stop."

Michael continued. "Also, you will need to sign your name to the agreements after the corvus arrives. Any deviation will foil the process. On two occasions, Count Marcel tried to change the progression by skipping a step. As a result, the documents failed to be delivered."

Domitian repositioned the inkwell closer and searched for a quill.

Sir Michael noticed him. "The corvus will produce a quill for you to use, milord. Please, relax."

Domitian felt like a child, a stupid child, expecting miracles to solve very serious issues. Skepticism overwhelmed him as he stared down at the dingy pages of the manuscript—not a single sentence completely readable.

"One minute more," said Michael. "Focus on the first sentence, please."

"What if midnight has already come and gone?"

Michael shifted his attention from the clock to the manuscript. "Any moment now..."

As if someone was performing a magic trick, the grimy pages started to lighten and the faded words started to darken. Greater contrast between rag and ink made the script look as if it had been written new that very day.

Sir Michael tapped his finger on the table. "When you are able to read aloud, please do so and quickly."

Amazed at how legible the manuscript now was Domitian started to read the words aloud.

Michael timed him, whispering, "Thirty-five seconds...thirty seconds...twenty-five seconds...twenty seconds...fifteen seconds..."

As the time approached ten seconds, the pages darkened and the words began to fade. Domitian read faster: "*Supplicantum jurat in inferno, quod verum et modius aequalis nuntium continet notitia. Quod si falsum est, et fallax indicium, supplicanti, supplicanti, et maledictæ reliquiæ ad mortem intempestivam, & horribile. Potest autem pati supplicanti mille desolatum. Hoc est foedus.*"

"...three, two, and finished."

Domitian sat back in his chair. "How was that?"

"We shall soon see."

Concern fell over Domitian's face. "I was so intent on reading aloud within the time limit that I had not fully translated the Latin until after I had uttered the last words. I recall a warning. I the supplicant shall be cursed if information in the request provided by me to the Meridiem is false and deceptive, something to that effect."

Sir Michael raised his hand, "Quiet, please." He turned his ear to the window.

"Is it true? Will I be cursed to die miserably?"

Sir Michael ignored Domitian, focusing on the open window.

"What is it?" whispered Domitian, springing to his feet. "Is it coming? Is it near?" Domitian listened closely and then heard it, too—a lone bird in the distance. He wanted to go to the window to see it.

"We should stand clear," suggested Michael.

"Yes, of course." Domitian laced his hands together and rested his chin on his knuckles.

As if the bird had been flying in circles, assessing, scrutinizing, it finally touched down on the windowsill.

Domitian covered his gaping mouth and blinked in disbelief, for he had never seen such a bird.

The gray corvus stood as tall as a child of ten years. Its feathers shimmered like polished pewter. It turned its head this way and that, observing Michael and Domitian with human-like curiosity. Then, without warning, it plunged its beak into its wing, plucked a feather out, and dropped it on the floor.

Michael cautiously retrieved the quill. He handed the feather to Domitian and backed away from the animal.

Domitian could not believe the size of the quill. It was longer than his entire arm, perhaps even his leg.

Sir Michael pointed to the documents. "Quickly, sign them, please."

The bird chortled and clucked like a chicken and cleared its throat like a person all at once, and then it spoke in a female's voice. "*Signum concordia placet. Contractus placet.*"

Michael pointed to the documents.

"Yes, yes, I heard it," said Domitian as he dipped the quill into the ink.

After Domitian signed the documents, Sir Michael rolled them and slid them into a leather tube, then capped and secured the tube with twine. Very slowly and smoothly, Michael approached the bird with the package, loosely resting on both of his outstretched hands.

The corvus leaned forward and accepted the tube in its beak. It transferred the tube to its foot, followed by what sounded like a soft chuckle. Then it hopped off the sill and took to wing outside.

With the massive quill still in his grasp, Domitian rushed to the window to watch the bird fly northward. When he could no longer see it, he turned to observe the feather. "Well, at least I have—" but Domitian held no quill. It was as if it had evaporated into nothing. He turned his hands over and back and checked the floor but saw no feather. "What trickery is this?"

"There are no reasonable explanations, milord. We simply do our part, and trust that others will do theirs. Now, whence your documents are received by them, they will have no choice but to perform their part. You will know they have completed the assignment when your promissory note with their seal is returned to the depository."

Domitian grinned and rubbed his hands together. "I would love to see Orfeo's face when those Meridiems show up."

"Milord, I recommend that we speak those names no more. The society is secret, and in this case the invaders are not really from the eastern realms."

"Right you are, Sir Michael. Thank you."

"Have you contacted the queen?"

"I have."

"How, may I ask, are you able to contact her so easily, assuming she is in Russia?"

"Not through an oversized crow, I can assure you of that!" Domitian wanted not to reveal the magical images, so he lied. "We communicate with messengers...a relay of messengers Countess Marie had established years ago. That is how she was able to negotiate with the queen. Why do you ask?"

"Curious is all."

"She and I are interested in trade, and that is all. I for one prefer to focus on the countess's resurrection, which reminds me...I need an update on her progress."

Sir Michael offered a half-smile. "Seems that my work here is done. If there is nothing more, I shall prepare my leave."

"Do you still intend to take Abigail with you?"

"Yes." Michael nodded and sighed. "I suppose I can stay until she is released to me. Will that be all, milord?"

"For now, yes, Sir Michael. My guard will take you to your chamber. Sorry to keep you locked up, old friend, but appearances must be maintained." Domitian watched as Michael opened the door and the guard outside received him. The guard bowed and closed the door. Domitian sat down at the table, exhausted but pleased that his scheme was finally in motion. He would send a message to Orfeo to join him at a meeting with Queen Žofie near Brussels. The Meridiem will destroy Orfeo and his guards, and the queen will collect her sister and destroy the Meridiem. After Countess Marie was returned from the dead, Domitian intended to rebuild his Flemish Royal Clan and lead the west to a new era.

# 21 – THE ONE THAT GOT AWAY

The Fortune siblings boarded a carriage at sunset and moved slowly through the streets of Amsterdam toward their next assignment.

"We are moving too slowly," grumbled Adina.

Klaas promptly tapped the butt of his sword against the ceiling and shouted. "Mister Witt! Faster, please!"

Two snaps of the whip and the carriage lurched forward.

Adina peered out the rear window. "Was he asleep in his chamber?" she asked anyone who might know the answer.

"Who, sister?" asked Gert, looking well-rested.

"You know who..." murmured Adina.

Gert chuckled "If you mean Cedric the Curious, he was felling trees when we left the house."

An hour later, the carriage stopped in front of a lone house beside a creek. It was a two-story building. The light of the waxing moon revealed a tired and leaning structure, plaster cracking, paint peeling, windows broken, and shutters dangling from bent hinges. Devoid of human occupancy and care, every ledge and crevice was reclaimed by nature in all its forms.

Mr. Witt opened the door to let them out.

Gert sniffed the air.

"I can smell them, too," murmured Klaas, screwing up his nose.

The siblings exited the carriage and checked their weapons. After reaffirming strategies and contingencies and Mr. Witt's backup plan, they took deep breaths and stepped onto the property. Quietly approaching the house, they stopped near the front door. After a moment of listening, smelling, and looking, they tried the door but it was locked. They moved around the house in search of another way in.

A door at the back of the house was ajar. Klaas cautiously pushed the door open and entered the house with weapons ready, followed by Gert and Adina.

Adina whispered, "*Oculi accendatur.*" A soft blue glow from their eyes illuminated wherever they looked. After searching the ground floor and finding no evidence of upyrians, they regrouped at the foot of a staircase in the entryway.

Gert pointed down and waved his hand, meaning "no basement," which was not unusual for a house built so near a levy. Klaas pointed up and nodded. He ascended the stairs, staying close to the wall to minimize pops and squeaks and the dreaded structural collapse. Gert and Adina followed in his footsteps successfully to the second floor. The hallway split right and left. Klaas signaled for Adina to wait near the top of the stairs while Gert went left and he went right to investigate. If one was attacked, the other would immediately assist, and Adina was between them to support as needed.

With weapons ready, Gert gently pushed the first door open and peered inside. His glowing eyes illuminated a soggy mess on the floor from a leaking roof and a crumbling ceiling. Otherwise, the room was empty. Klaas did the same. Room by room, the brothers investigated and spot-checked each other until reaching the last doors. Both doors were closed and latched. That was unfortunate because unlatching them was going to be noisy. Though they expected the upyrian to be sleeping, too much noise might wake them up.

Klaas and Gert turned to Adina to coordinate. Adina reached out with her hand and closed her eyes. Though she might not have detected anyone behind the doors, some upyrians used counter-spells to avert detection. Gert turned back to Klaas and signaled that he would open his door first. Concerned for what his brother might find, Klaas moved toward Gert, stepping on a damp section of floor that suddenly gave way, engulfing his leg up to his knee. All at once, the doors at both ends of the hallway burst opened.

Two upyrians immediately attacked Klaas, but he was ready for them, running one through the gut with his sword and coaxing the other to jump on him and his wooden stake, impaling the upyrian through its heart.

Gert defended himself by quickly beheading one upyrian and running his stake through the other's eye.

Two more upyrians jumped on Klaas. He decapitated the first one—head rolling toward Adina, who was waving her hands and chanting spells to protect her brothers.

Klaas lifted his leg out of the hole and was back on his feet, hacking at a hissing female upyrian. Her head fell. A upyrian dodged Klaas's weapons and went straight at Adina. She threw up a field of energy and readied her dagger. The upyrian leapt into a horizontal dive and turned into a bat, evading Adina's sword. It circled her head, staying clear of her force field and dagger, as if playing with her, observing her.

Adina hollered, "*Papilio rete!*" The force field evaporated and a net of red light formed in her hand. She swung and cast the net at the bat, but the creature flew out of range. As the bat retreated down the stairwell, she threw the net after it and held on. She felt the line tighten and shake. "I have you now," she muttered and began pulling the red line in.

After killing the last of his attackers, Gert ran to help Adina. He took hold of the line, now sizzling and popping, and pulled with her. The line turned brighter red as the tugging became difficult. Klaas quickly moved past them and down the stairwell, sword and dagger in hands. When the rope went limp, Adina and Gert retrieved the net to find a small hole in the weave. She waved her hand to end the spell, but the net remained alit. Suddenly, the line lifted and wrapped around Adina's neck like a snake.

Gert took hold of the glowing noose, trying to remove it from his sister's neck. "Klaas!" he hollered. "Come quickly!"

Klaas returned to find Adina choking on the floor and Gert desperately trying to remove the constricting energy from her neck.

Klaas began to chant, "*Prohibere omnes magicae.*"

Gert began to hyperventilate.

Adina began to lose consciousness.

Klaas dropped to his knees beside her. He placed his hand on her head and whispered in her ear, "*Prohibere omnes magicae. Prohibere omnes magicae. Prohibere omnes magicae.*"

As Klaas continued chanting, Gert joined in, chanting the same words. It was working. The noose and net faded away.

Klaas placed his finger on the side of her neck. Gert looked up at his brother, waiting, waiting...

"She lives," sighed Klaas.

Gert took Adina's hand in his and rubbed it. "Sister, wake up. Adina, can you hear me?"

Adina nodded.

Adina leaned against Klaas and took Gert's hand.

"That was close," said Klaas.

"Thank you," whispered Adina. "I was stupid, careless... The bat?"

"Escaped through a broken window..." said Klaas.

"I think we should go," urged Gert.

Adina nodded, and the brothers helped her out of the house.

In the carriage, the siblings discussed the problem of letting one get away.

"It was a former sorcerer," said Adina. "For a brief moment, it conjoined with me, but instead of receiving power from the netherworld to make us stronger, it took power from me, to weaken me."

"I do not understand," said Gert. "How is that possible?"

"It *is* possible. Žofie is capable, though that was not Žofie. Until recently, I have managed to block my sister's intrusions, but I fear she has found a way in through others." Adina shivered. "I fear the worst is coming. She is coming. She wants war, and she wants the west."

"She wants you," said Gert.

"She is coming for all of us," said Adina.

"She is a threat," said Klaas, "and I do not take kindly to threats."

Adina rested her hand on Klaas's shoulder. "Brothers, we must notify all the families. They must know that Žofie is channeling our powers, and she is coming. They must close their minds to her and open their minds to us, to give us strength. There is more..."

"What more?" asked Gert.

"We received a new assignment last night," said Adina.

"From whom?" asked Klaas.

"Domitian," answered Adina.

"Is it genuine?" asked Gert. "Timing seems to coincide with increased Žofie activities. How can we know it is not a trap?"

"Domitian's signature and seals are on the documents, and Sir Michael assisted him," said Adina. "Sir Michael has never double-crossed us."

"Duly noted; however, he betrayed his own master," said Klaas, leaving everyone with an uneasy feeling.

## 22 - THE ENCOUNTER

Cedric woke to thumping at his door. He slid out of bed and stumbled forward, unlatched the door locks, and cracked the door open a few inches. He was suddenly pushed back by Adina, followed by Gert and Klaas, brimming with weapons.

"*Candelis lumine,*" said Adina, instantly lighting all the candles in the room. "Please forgive our intrusion, Cedric. We have important news that cannot wait."

Cedric leaned against a bedpost, embarrassed to be seen in his nightshirt. At least it was clean. Still trying to get his mind out of bed, he rubbed his eyes.

"Tonight, as we were about to complete our assignment, one of them got away," muttered Adina. "It saw my brothers. It knows what they look like."

"Upyrian?" asked Cedric.

"Yes," said Adina, sighing.

"Klaas and Gert were born in secrecy. Their anonymity has always been our advantage."

"*You* have been our advantage, sister," said Gert.

Cedric's groggy eyes found the brothers. "Are you not the Fabulous Fortune Brothers? Everyone knows who you are, what you look like."

"We hide in the open," said Klaas. "No one knows who we really are or what we really do."

"How did one get away?" asked Cedric, trying to understand the weight of the matter.

"Something has changed," whispered Adina, eyes drifting upward in thought. "Tonight, it used my powers against me somehow, to weaken me."

"How?" asked Cedric.

"My sister must be behind it," said Adina. "Only she knows how to conjoin and channel powers with others. She and I used to do it—during the Lunabellum, we combined our powers and conjured the netherworld, attaining powers so dense and feral that no ordinary sorcerer dare touch it. Such power will corrupt, destroy, and inflict misery upon the world. Žofie and I accessed only a fraction of the whole, and only when absolutely necessary."

Gert stepped forward. "Back to the reason we awakened you—"

"Right...," said Adina, sighing. "We came to ask for your help, Cedric."

"Will you fight with us?" asked Klaas.

Cedric thought for a moment. Just made a bookkeeper, he had yet to enter anything in the ledger, and now they were asking him to fight, which was what he wanted to do all along. He nodded. "Yes, of course, but what is this really about?"

"Guess," said Klaas.

"It is about my sister," said Adina.

Cedric noticed another wrinkle of concern on her face. "You once told me that I am not a fighter," said Cedric to Adina.

"Yes," said Gert, "that is true in the sense of how we fight."

"You will need to be trained," said Klaas.

"Are you ready for that, Cedric?" asked Adina. "Please decline if you are unsure, for the dangers are very real."

"I am ready," said Cedric. "When do we begin?"

"Tomorrow evening," said Klaas.

"Where is the next assignment?" asked Cedric.

"Sonian Forest," said Adina.

Cedric gulped dryly. He had nearly died in that forest—in nearby Vos Castle, too.

"The location is in an abandoned barn in a field beside the forest," said Adina.

The only barn near a forest that Cedric painfully recalled included a farmhouse and its mutilated occupants. His stomach churned.

"Are you all right, Cedric?" asked Adina.

"Yes, yes," he assured, feeling lightheaded. "Half asleep, is all."

Adina placed the back of her hand on his forehead and on the back of his neck—all motherly responses that confused Cedric. When she removed her hand, disturbing memories of the Sonian Forest and Vos Castle prickled his skin. He never intended to return to those places. "How long will the training last?" asked Cedric.

"Three days," said Klaas.

"Only three days?" asked Cedric, feeling uneasy. "Is that sufficient time?"

"It will have to be," said Klaas.

"The better question is, will you survive it?" said Gert.

"Fret not, Master Cedric," said Klaas. "You will receive in three days what others can only hope to receive in a lifetime."

Cedric nodded once, shaking off those horrible memories, rubbing his smooth face. "When are we to leave?" asked Cedric.

"Mister Witt will be here at first light. It is all arranged. So, rest up and be ready to go in a few hours."

"Good evening," said Klaas, moving toward the door.

"Thank you, Cedric," said Gert, following Klaas into the hallway.

Adina stayed behind. She turned to Cedric and smiled. It was a profound smile—of uncertainty, concern, and a glint of desire Cedric thought he imagined. He felt silly, almost pathetic to think that this young goddess would be interested in him, an orphaned farm boy, homeless and unremarkable. Yet, he continued to relish the possibility and searched his feelings. Was it just admiration he felt for her? Did she feel something more for him? Perhaps he was growing on her, and she fancied him more now than last week and the week before that. He blinked a few times, cracked his elbow with a stretch, and expected nothing more than a question or lecture on the dangers of what the Meridiems do.

When she closed the door and leaned back against it, his heart quickened.

Cedric's most intimate moments might be summed up with a few timid kisses he and Lily shared. He was sixteen. She was fifteen. Innocent pecks on the lips and cheek, as fleeting as their sweet acquaintance turned out to be. Now, his eyes were locked onto a strong and stunning young woman, nineteen years of beauty, a goddess if ever there was one...

*Ridiculous,* said the crotchety voice in his head. *Just look at you, boy!*

*Look at her!* said the woman's voice. *What could she possibly want from you, other than to fight and die protecting her precious Meridiem?*

Adina locked the door. Cedric stiffened, not knowing what to do or say, as she methodically removed her gloves and then her cloak, letting each article of clothing fall to the floor. She unbuckled her intricate weapon's belt on which her ornate sword and rows of daggers hung, and gently let it all down on top of her rumpled cloak.

Cedric blinked again, expecting this illusion to vanish. Yet, there she remained, removing pins from her hair, letting her blonde locks fall over her shoulders. He was a virgin, not exactly schooled in matters of sexual intimacy, though he had seen plenty of farm animals mating. When he was six years of age, he saw his parents kissing passionately. He remembered how they held each other, protectively, gently, tilting heads, pressing lips for an uncomfortably long time. He blushed and turned away. Now, Cedric of eighteen years was blushing again, same as before, but this time he fought the urges and voices in his head telling him to shy away.

Having made the first move, she waited for Cedric to make the next.

He slowly narrowed the space between them, approaching cautiously, like a wildcat fearful of upsetting its dangerous mate.

She placed her hands on his chest and slid them up onto his shoulders, pulling him closer until her bosoms pressed against him.

Cedric took her in his arms.

They awkwardly bumped noses, recovering by tilting and locking lips—plump, luscious, malleable—sliding pillows of flesh, probing tongues, nibbling teeth. They gracefully moved their embrace from the door to the bed, from vertical to horizontal.

Cedric untied and removed her stay.

She lifted off Cedric's nightshirt and slid her hands down over his well-defined chest and rippled stomach.

He helped her hike up her dress, and she straddled him like a bull. Engorged with desire, he ached in ways he never imagined.

She took back her lips and rotated, placing her hands on the tops of his feet, kissing his thighs, exposing Cedric to her erotic mysteries, caressing, suckling, stroking, tasting, and moaning, ceding to ever-growing waves of bliss.

When Cedric thought he had finished experiencing a piece of heaven, Adina rolled onto her back and guided Cedric on top and into her. She pulled her knees back, guiding him toward a much higher plateau of rapture. Sweating and panting, gliding and thrusting, quicker and firmer, Cedric had never felt so incredibly powerful and vulnerable all at once. If he died that instant, all would be as it should. He heard himself groaning, felt the rushing and tightening and the slowing and tensing as he approached his apex.

Cedric reached down with his free hand and latched onto Adina's thigh, as every muscle in his body tensed. He opened his eyes just before they drifted up into his head, catching a glimpse of Adina's eyes affixed on him, witnessing this man, this new man, bursting out like fireworks.

He collapsed on her, completely drained.

Her hands rubbed his back and she whispered in his ear, "You are a man of many skills."

Cedric wanted the moment to last forever.

"Come, let us freshen up and go to sleep," whispered Adina.

After they sponged themselves clean and got back into bed together, Cedric expected to wake up beside Adina in a few hours, but that was not to be. He woke up alone as usual, but more mystified than ever before.

## 23 - IMMORTAL BEAUTY

A The journey back to Ghent was swift, and Cedric could do little more than follow and affix his blissful gaze on Adina's back, remembering the night before and wondering why she said little more than good day to him since they left Amsterdam. Cedric followed the siblings along a barely visible path overgrown by ferns and grasses to a gate woven of thick vines, attached to a wall of large trees growing so close together that not even a cat would fit among them. Inside the wall of trees, they continued on through the lush estate gardens, relieved to see that everything, including the house, was as serene and pristine as ever.

After leaving their horses with the stableman, they entered the house to a waft of hunger-teasing aromas.

"*Grootmoeder!*" said Gert to his grandmother Lidia, who was descending the stairs.

"Welcome home, my children!" said Lidia, accepting kisses and embraces. Her smile soon faded as the serious faces on Klaas, Adina, and Cedric told of something amiss. "What is the matter?"

"We must notify the family," said Adina, placing her hand in Lidia's.

"Is it Žofie?" said Lidia, as if she already knew of the matter. "She is causing quite a rift. The elders are already talking."

"We need to conjoin powers, summon the netherworld...," said Adina.

Lidia shook her head in disagreement. "That is far too risky."

"Sister," said Gert, "Cedric's training. We have little time to waste."

Lidia smiled at Cedric. "Welcome home, Cedric dear."

Cedric was pleasantly surprised by the way she welcomed him. "Thank you for having me," said Cedric.

"Nonsense, my boy," said Lidia. "You are not a guest. You are as close to family as a friend can be. May the gods smile upon you. She turned to Adina, whispered in her ear, and left.

"Adina," said Cedric, "may I have a word with you?"

Adina nodded. "Brother, I will walk Cedric to his room."

Gert nodded. "I will come for you shortly, Cedric. Please be ready to begin your training."

Adina led Cedric up the stairs and into a long and winding corridor. When no one else was in sight, Cedric took Adina's hand.

She pulled it away and stopped.

Cedric felt awkward and somehow ashamed. Had he done something to disappoint her? "I do not understand," whispered Cedric. "Can you please help me understand, the meaning of last night?"

After a long pause, Adina began walking again and Cedric paced with her.

"I apologize, Cedric. I have not been myself of late. Last night was...well, it was a mistake of sorts, my mistake—"

"Mistake?"

"I acted impulsively and inappropriately. I was not myself. Perhaps my sister is responsible—"

"Or perhaps she is a convenient excuse," quipped Cedric, surprised by his tone. "I apologize..."

Adina stopped beside a door. "Do not apologize. You have done nothing wrong."

Cedric closed his eyes and clenched his fists, trying to manage his emotions.

Adina placed her hand on the door latch and opened it.

Cedric placed his bag in the bedchamber and turned to her. The unfortunate realization that last night might not have been as special to her as it was to him began to tear at his insides.

"You are right, Cedric. I have no excuses for last night. My devotion is to the Meridiem. I swore by it, and I faltered. I have betrayed myself."

"Why? How? I saw only happiness on your face last night."

"There is so much more to why and how. I...I am not ready to explain it. I was happy, yes, but also afraid and..."

"If you want me to leave, I will go, but please explain why. Please."

"Klaas and Gert are not my brothers."

Cedric nodded. He knew that. Žofie's vision depicted how the twin sisters were separated and Adina received a lethal arrow. The Meridiems found her, resurrected her, and Adina was reborn a Meridiem.

"They are my progeny—my grandchildren—the twelfth generation of my lineage."

Cedric's jaw dropped. "What?"

"After my resurrection, I was married to a Meridiem sorcerer, Cedric. I gave birth to six children. They married and had children of their own. My husband died, my children married and died, my grandchildren married and died, and I lived on."

"Klaas and Gert are...," murmured Cedric, trying to believe the unbelievable.

"It is easier to play the role of sister because we appear to be so close in age. However, the reality is that I am the eldest member of our family, and many of them are of my bloodline. As those I loved died and continued to die, my heart continued to be broken. Someday Klaas and Gert will die, and their children will die, and their children, and I will watch it all happen, helpless to stop it."

Cedric fell against the wall.

"I never meant to hurt you, Cedric. You are an extraordinarily kind, honest, and courageous young man. You deserve someone who will cherish and compliment those virtues, someone with whom to grow old together. I cannot be that someone. I am unnatural. I can never grow old with you."

Cedric had heard of Adina's immortal beauty but had thought it was a term of endearment, not fact.

Approaching footsteps interrupted them. It was Gert.

Cedric was still processing Adina's story, disbelieving but wanting to believe it. She looked nineteen. He recalled the image of her sister Žofie and the *Lunabellum*. "Gert," said Cedric, slowly turning away from Adina. "When was the Lunabellum? How long ago was it?"

Gert glanced upward in thought and crossed his arms. "More than two hundred years ago. Why?"

Cedric nodded and sighed, skeptical as ever. Magic and illusion were one in the same—trickery of the mind. What was he to believe? The images of the *Lunabellum*, of Adina and Žofie fighting side-by-side, might have been created with mirrors, lenses, and lighting.

"Sister, are you going to join us in the white room?"

Adina looked at Cedric, not at his face but at his chest. "That depends on him."

Cedric was not giving up, not on Adina, not on this family. He felt in his heart that magic and miracles existed, that love was the most powerful magic of all, and somehow, someway, regardless of her age and the pain of inevitable loss, Adina would allow herself to fall in love again.

"Yes, I am ready," said Cedric.

## 24 - THE WHITE ROOM

Cedric had not felt so laden with sadness and loss since the Black Death claimed his family, but this time his misery was different. It was about Adina, possibly a living and breathing goddess. He felt as if he was dying of thirst within sight of a river too far to reach. How might he train while feeling so miserable that even the voices in his head had nothing more to say?

A hand patted him on the back. It was Klaas, smiling at him, the look of confidence. Cedric saw Gert, reflecting his brother's expectations. After all they had done for him, how could he leave now? Adina or no, it was time he bore the weight of his heart and reframe matters at hand. His father had told him on many occasions that words and actions established a man's reputation, and reputation established a man's worth. What would be his worth if he quitted or failed now?

By the time they arrived at the door of the so-called white room, which Cedric felt was located at the back of the enormous house, Cedric was doing his best to put Adina out of mind. He noticed the ironclad door. It was tall and wide, wide enough to accommodate a horse and carriage. There must have been twenty small dragon heads randomly attached to the door panels, each one unique in color, shape, and face. After pressing, twisting, and pulling various heads, and knocking rhythmically on the door as Klaas always had, the sounds of bolts and latches began to slide, clink, and clatter until silence came and Klaas placed a finger on the door as he had clearly done so many times before and gently pushed it inward.

After that somewhat entertaining door-opening event, a twinge of dissatisfaction followed when Cedric saw that the room was empty with a row of very tall windows. Other than the blue sky, he saw no vistas or trees through those panes. Truth was he was expecting something more, much more—a mythical land or the surface of the moon, not a room devoid of even a single piece of furniture. It was just a big white room.

Cedric followed the brothers to the center of the void and noticed the ceiling, four levels high, thought Cedric, and not entirely flat nor architecturally sculpted, but arbitrarily irregular. The walls were not entirely straight either, and the floor slanted this way and that. Why was the white room built so terribly askew? He began to notice faint gray lines on the walls, about as wide as his hand, parallel lines creating maze-like patterns. Similar patterns on the floor and ceiling added intrigue to an otherwise sterile echo chamber.

Gert and Klaas went to the windows and noisily closed the tall shutters to darken the room.

Slowly, as Cedric's eyes adjusted to the dim, the lines on the floor, ceiling, and walls grew more pronounced, brighter as if alit.

"Cedric." Klaas's voice reverberated in the massive space. "This is the white room. This is where we train. It appears to be empty, but soon you will find that it is...well, let us show you."

With a dazzling smile, Gert approached Klaas, wooden flask in hand. Cedric immediately wondered where Gert had gotten the flask. He saw no table or niche, no collection of containers or hidden doors. He must have brought it. Klaas accepted the bottle and lifted it to his lips, but instead of drinking, he inhaled the contents. When his lungs had their fill, Klaas handed the flask to Cedric and flashed a dazzling smile at him.

Cedric examined the flagon. A cork was tied to its neck with twine, and it felt completely empty. He peered down into it and shook it gently but no liquid sloshed. He sniffed but smelled nothing.

"Go on, Cedric," said Gert. "Breathe it in."

"Is it empty?" asked Cedric.

"Good question," said Gert, still smiling as if enjoying an inaudible limerick.

Cedric had no reason to distrust them. They had always been kind to him and never steered him wrong, at least not to his knowledge. He lifted the bottle to his lips and tilted it, expecting something to pour out, but nothing came. He tilted it more and more until he felt something flowing over his bottom lip. It was air, only heavier and textured with tiny particles, but not dusty. It flowed softly and filled his mouth with the floral sweetness of honeybee pollen. He closed his mouth, cheeks bulging, and looked at the brothers, who were both smiling and nodding their approval at him. He tried to swallow the sweetness but his esophagus closed each time.

"You must breathe it in," said Gert, still smiling glowingly.

Cedric did just that. He inhaled all that was in his mouth. A feeling of warmth filled his chest and his heartbeat began to decelerate, not in an alarming way but in a way that made him feel relaxed and joyful. Then, a burst of energy rushed through his body, into his limbs and into his head. His vision became perfectly focused, and the room no longer appeared dim but as bright as the brightest day of summer. He turned to Gert and Klaas and saw that they had physically changed. Their hair and skin tone were now sterling metallic. Their eyes turned a deep magenta, and they were amusing to see with their giddy childish smiles. Cedric noticed that he, too, was uncontrollably happy about nothing more than standing in an empty room with the glistening and grinning brothers.

Wondering if he was undergoing physical changes, too, Cedric observed his hands. They seemed larger and stronger. He felt his arm muscles growing larger and denser, his clothes becoming tighter. He smelled his hands and the air—all the scents of a meadow after a rain filled his nose. He was growing in height as well as width. He touched his face, which was covered in hair. He had a full beard! It was soft and thick, and his mustache extended at the ends. He turned and saw that the room was changing as well.

The lines on the floor, ceiling, and walls were extending outward, creating a winding labyrinth of corridors around him. He turned to the brothers, but they were no longer there. *Where did they go?* He saw stairs forming ahead, leading down through the slanting floor, which was now covered by soil and grass. Another set of stairs was climbing up through the clouds as the sky replaced the ceiling.

"Gert, Klaas?" said Cedric, his voice no longer hollow but muted, like he was talking in a thick fog. He listened closely for their voices but heard only the slow and steady beating of his heart. He took a few cautious steps away from the stairs in hope of finding the siblings, but saw that the corridors continued as far as he could see. Blue, green, and gold shards of light appeared impossibly curved instead of straight. A few fireflies spiraled up from the stairwell. He surmised that something very interesting was going on down there and his curiosity carried him forward. Excited to experience the world below, he quickly descended at least three flights, perhaps four, into a forest of indescribable abundance.

Everything was aglow and pulsating with vivid textures and colors. Plants of all shapes, sizes, and colors were swaying in the absence of wind. Colorful insects of every imaginable color and shape—some with human-like faces, blinking eyes, smiling lips—were hopping, crawling, and buzzing among thousands of blooming flowers. And the reptiles, especially the enormous one laying a few paces distant, slumbered lazily in the lush, balmy forest.

The fascinating reptile was bigger than a horse, head resting on its long tail that was coiled around its body. Its skin was scaled much like a snake's but in shiny tones of bronze outlined in blue-green patina. As wondrous as everything appeared, and as happy as Cedric felt, a stitch of fear pricked his psyche and quickened his lazy heartbeat, causing him to back away from the enormous creature. Before turning to run, Cedric tripped and fell noisily on his rear. He looked to see what had tripped him, but the ground was smooth and level.

The dragon opened its eyes, lifted its enormous head, and snorted warm, stale air toward Cedric. Then, it inhaled. It took in so much air so quickly that a wind blew past Cedric in the direction of the beast's flaring nostrils. Cedric clambered to his feet and retreated into the dense forest, crouching behind a large tree. *Is that a dragon, and is it coming for me?* he wondered as the voices in his head urged him to run until he found the brothers and was let out of this very dangerous white room of nightmares.

He heard nothing and told the voices to quiet down so he might concentrate. As he settled into a calm moment, the ground quaked. Leaves fell and the flying and fluttering critters and birds squawked and buzzed frantically as the ground shook again and again, each time louder and faster. It was coming.

Trees cracked and buckled from the monster's weight as it pushed close to the tree behind which Cedric cowered. He closed his eyes, trying not to panic. *What would a fox do when chased by dogs? I'm not a fox and that is no dog. That is a dragon, just as I imagined it to be. Where are Gert and Klaas? What was in that wooden flask?*

A blast of malodorous warm air blew past both sides of the tree, followed by an eerie stillness and then cool air flowing the other way.

Like the reptile, Cedric inhaled deeply as well. He sprung forward, using the tree to shield him from the dragon. He ran swiftly past glowing trees, shrubs, and ferns, over shimmering creatures swimming in winding streams, beneath butterflies, birds, and fireflies, until he was certain the dragon was far behind. After catching his breath, he quietly circled back to where the stairs had been, and that was when he heard the swooshing rhythm of wings. He looked up and saw a bluish-yellow light through the tree canopy. The light was fire, and it was bolting down directly at him. Cedric ran for cover beside a large rock as flames and intense heat slammed to the ground and spread out, singeing everything it touched. The dragon's wings drummed up enough wind to fan small flames into a wildfire. Cedric felt the heat, which started to flood the forest. He had to get out of there. He sprinted in the direction of the stairs. Another stream of fire struck the ground beside him. He veered away and ran from tree to tree like a hectic squirrel.

Off track now, Cedric heard tree branches snapping as something huge was coming. He jumped into a stream and ran along its shallow, colorful water. Suddenly, he stopped in his tracks at another threatening sight. Rising out of the stream in front of him was a man and a woman, tridents in hand. They were unlike anyone or anything he had ever before seen. Their skin was pale green. Their hair was long and straight and white as milk. They wore no clothes, and the woman's breasts were smooth, white orbs with no nipples. As these armed water creatures continued to rise, Cedric saw no legs. They were like eels from the waist down, lifting up on monstrous tails and slithering in Cedric's direction.

No time to guess their motives, Cedric retreated out of the stream and into the forest, toward a cottage in a clearing. He recognized it—the home of Elida, the blind seer. He ran to the cottage and frantically knocked at the door, eyes darting to see if anything was following him. When the door opened, seemingly on its own, he saw Queen Žofie sitting on a throne beside the inglenook, one leg exposed and dangling over the chair's arm. He turned away and saw the serpents with human-like torsos entering the clearing, while the dragon noisily approached from the opposite direction.

Surrounded and without any weapons. Cedric needed a way out, or the means to fight back. A sharp pain caused him to shake. He expected to find Žofie at his neck, but it was something else, either a devilish creature or the devil himself—two twisted horns rising out of its head, yellow cat eyes, a long, black chin beard, and red skin with symbol-shaped scars—all matching depictions of Satan in Cedric's copy of The Holy Bible. Heart racing, energy flowing, no time left to gawk at the devil, Cedric swiftly kicked him in the crotch and struck him on the nose with the meat of his palm. He ran into the clearing. The dragon was already filling its lungs.

In anticipation of fire, Cedric ran to the serpents, ducking and sliding behind them just as the fiery breath of the dragon incinerated everything near him, including the eel-like people who almost smashed Cedric with their long and thick eel tails as they squirmed in searing pain. Their hair was singed completely off and their skin blistered. Cedric seized their tridents, still hot to the touch but bearable, and as the dragon inhaled, drawing a wind through the forest, Cedric stepped out in front of the beast and threw a weapon as hard as he could at its flaring nostril. It missed the nostril but punctured an eye.

The dragon reeled back, opened its mouth, and let out a fiery screech. It clawed at the trident until it removed it. Then it shook its great head, throwing up flames in all directions and dripping molten liquid from its nose. Cedric tried to dodge the fire, but the half-blinded beast spewed flames directly at him.

He felt his entire body heat up until his skin blistered and charred, his insides boiled, and everything faded to black.

"Easy, Cedric," said a familiar voice. Cedric opened his eyes, wondering if he was dead, and saw Gert. He was smiling brightly, eyes still glowing with shades of magenta. Behind him stood Klaas, and beside Klaas stood Adina. Adina was also smiling as if she were the happiest woman on earth.

"Where are we?" asked Cedric, strangely no longer saddened by his feelings for Adina. He felt better than ever.

"I already told you, we are in the white room," said Klaas, sounding as cheerful as ever. "You were quite good, you know?"

"You almost survived," said Adina, a chuckle escaping her lips.

Cedric smiled as well, finding this whole experience extraordinarily enjoyable.

Gert and Klaas helped him to his feet. Carefully assessing his physical condition, Cedric was surprised to find no burns or injuries of any kind. "Was any of it real?"

"Yes and no," said Adina. "The potion you took and the elements of the white room work together to simulate situations—your greatest fears made as real as we can make them. When I add my own ingredients to the recipe, we make a dish as unpredictable as anything you might encounter in the real world."

"Can I die or become injured here?" asked Cedric with a chuckle.

Adina and the brothers just laughed.

Cedric laughed as well, not understanding why. "May we do it again?"

"We have only just begun," said Adina. "Prepare yourself. We will work together in subsequent simulations."

Instantly, Cedric found himself in a different setting. This time, he was armed with a sword and shield, and he was standing inside an old building, a church by the looks of the architecture. There was a stained-glass rose window at one end, a domed apse at the other, and twin rows of towering pillars sprouting ribs that flared upward to support the gothic ceiling vaults. He heard footsteps and turned to find Klaas, Gert, and Adina there. The siblings took the lead. When Cedric stepped clumsily and noisily forward, Adina placed her finger over her lips to shush him.

Not much time had passed before the first upyrians showed their ugly faces. They were quite hideous to behold, nothing like the beautiful Queen Žofie, or even the handsome vampires of Vos Castle. They resembled hellish demons with skin so transparent they revealed the inner workings of their physiology. Their eyes were black, and their hands were bony with fingernails that were more like talons. They moved quickly, but so did Klaas and Gert. Adina was casting spells and using sorcery to aid her brothers. Cedric felt the magic as he watched it work. A field of energy bubbled around him. Cedric reached out to touch it, but his fingers passed through as if nothing was there.

A upyrian leaped from the altar at Cedric, but it bounced off the protective bubble of energy. It came at him again, and Cedric stood his ground, expecting magic to repel the attack—not this time. The upyr took Cedric down to the floor, its hand threatening to break Cedric's neck, its menacing fangs plunging into his cheek. Cedric instinctually took hold of the upyrian's arms, and with all his strength pushed and kicked it off him. Cedric rolled over and onto his feet just as the upyrian sprang back at him again. This time, Cedric took hold of its garments and fell back to the floor, planting his feet on its abdomen, and flipping it over onto its back. Swiveling around, Cedric attacked with astonishing speed, pouncing on the upyrian and plunging the stake into its chest.

After that scenario ended with everyone intact and all upyrians destroyed, they ran another simulation and then another. On the third day of simulations, Cedric and the siblings left the white room and went into the gardens behind the house. There, they sparred with swords, shields, daggers, and wooden stakes. Cedric learned how to fight with only his bare hands.

"Cedric, as you learned, there are limitations to the magic we use," said Adina. "The energy of protection might work only once or twice. You cannot rely on it. Your strength and speed will quickly fade."

"That is why it is important to vanquish the enemy as efficiently as possible," said Gert.

"What is the fasted way to kill a vampire?" asked Klaas.

"Removal of the head," said Cedric.

"If you are not in a position to behead the enemy, what is another method?" asked Klaas.

"Piercing the heart with wood," said Cedric.

"Yes," said Klaas. "If you are not in position to kill efficiently, what can you do to gain the upper hand and enable the kill?"

"A dagger into the brain through the eye, nose, or ear."

"What if you have no blades?" asked Klaas.

"Just about any object can be used as a weapon. A tree branch or hammer can be used to wound. Wounds can disable the enemy long enough to either escape or kill."

"Other less efficient means if necessary are...?" asked Gert.

"Fire," said Cedric.

"And what are efficient ways to kill men like us?" asked Gert.

"Severing the head or major artery in the neck," whispered Cedric, extremely bothered to say it. "Other methods include fatal wounds to vital organs and suffocation whether by water or choking. Poisons or potions are seldom used but can be effective in special circumstances when the enemy is too well guarded." Cedric paused. "When would we ever kill a person?"

"In a war among people and in self-defense," said Adina. "Any other questions?"

After only three days of intense and uncompromised training, Cedric not only gained specific knowledge but also instincts, reflexes, and moves necessary to kill efficiently. The magic contained in the white room enabled him to focus and practice to perfection his deadly skills. He no longer wanted to leave the siblings. He wanted to help them defend the west from intruding upyrians. He felt that his survival also depended on becoming a part of their fellowship, as the question of how to manage Domitian's vengeance had yet to be answered. As to why the Meridiem might allow him to join their fellowship was still unclear to Cedric.

"I do have a question," said Cedric to Adina. "Why me? You turned me away but then changed your mind." He turned to Klaas and Gert. "You came to my rescue in Brussels. How was it that you were there to foil my abductors? Why did you ask me to travel with you to Amsterdam? I am completely grateful to you for helping me out of several dangerous situations, and I care not to offend with such questions. I just want to understand."

Klaas laughed. "We need someone like you, someone good and honest."

"Are good an honest people so uncommon?" asked Cedric.

"They are," said Gert. "And might I add that you exceeded my expectations in the white room. I saw a fighter inside you. We just needed to bring him out."

"Thank you," said Cedric, scratching his head. "Yet, I cannot produce magic. I do not come from a bloodline of sorcerers, at least not to my knowledge. Before my training, I was a liability to you."

"Cedric," said Adina, "you are not yet a Meridiem. You are not yet confirmed. However, my brothers are convinced that you will change the future to benefit all good people in need. And unless you are with us, your destiny is gravely jeopardized."

Cedric noticed sudden displeasure on Klaas and Gert faces, as if Adina had carelessly revealed a very important secret or clarified that he was still not one of them.

"They believe that you are—I suppose—a prophet," added Adina to the further dismay of her brothers.

Cedric sneered at the notion. "I am no prophet. God has not chosen me to save or lead or represent anyone." Cedric clutched his crucifix hanging from his neck.

"Are you sure?" asked Adina. "What if your God meant for you to meet my brothers when you were lost in the field, and to meet Elida when you were sick in the forest? What if your God led Klaas and Gert to Brussels to rescue you? Are you positive that your God did not empower you to defeat the countess and rescue your friends?"

"I believe there is more to you than you realize," said Gert to Cedric.

"Time will tell," said Elida. "You are our friend, Cedric. We have revealed many of our secrets to you, placed a great deal of trust in you. Do you wish to be a sworn member of our fellowship?"

There was much that Cedric wanted to think about and not much time to think. Everything was moving so quickly and the voices in his head were doing their best to discourage him.

*Don't join them! They will get us all killed. They are unlike us. They are Godless. They are of a dying age. Let them die with their myths! Run while you still can.*

"Yes," said Cedric. "I wish to join your fellow."

"Very well," said Adina. "Gert, go with him. Explain our covenant, codes, and duties. Prepare him for the ceremony...tonight."

"Not to worry," said Gert to Cedric. "The ceremony is just a formality. I consider you to be one of us already."

## 25 - FORMALITIES

Nearing midnight, Adina and the brothers came to Cedric's bedchamber. Cedric heard Klaas' rhythmic knock at the door. It was time.

Cedric opened the door and saw that each of the siblings wore their weapons and held a candle in hand. None were smiling.

"Identify yourself," said Adina to Cedric.

"I am Cedric Martens of Linder."

"Brethren, do you recognize this man to be Cedric Martens of Linder?"

"Yes," said Klaas and Gert together.

"Cedric Martens of Linder, are you ready to be confirmed and to die?" asked Adina.

"Yes, I am ready."

"Follow us," said Adina.

Cedric stepped into the corridor behind the siblings. He noticed that all the candle sconces on the walls had been extinguished, creating a dark passageway, no end in view. They moved excruciatingly slow, extending the time to walk a hundred paces to the balcony. There, the siblings stood around Cedric and Adina blindfolded him.

Though hoodwinked, Cedric trusted his friends.

They led him into a room wherein smoldering herbs twitched his nose. He heard a door close behind him followed by chanting in a foreign tongue from all sides. Then he heard swords unsheathing and detected Adina in front of him, Gert to his right and slightly behind, and Klaas to his left and slightly behind.

"Cedric Martens of Linder," said Adina softly. "Destiny has drawn a circle in which we stand together as friends. Tonight we form a smaller inner-circle representing a sacred and secret fellowship. Cedric Martens of Linder, do you wish to stand within the inner-circle, knowing full well that should you be confirmed, you will be bound by the fellowship's sacred covenant, codes, and duties until death, and should you be rejected your throat shall be cut and your heart shall be impaled this very night?"

Cedric reached for his cross pendant. "Yes, I accept the consequences and request to be confirmed while still upholding my faith in God."

Adina nodded. "Do you make this request knowing full well the consequences of deceit and betrayal, that if you are confirmed and later you willfully disobey any part of the fellowship's sacred covenant, codes, or duties, or deceive and betray your fellow Meridiem that your vision and hearing will be removed by searing hot pokers, your tongue, hands, and feet will be severed by dull rusty blades, and your disabled body will be left naked in the middle of nowhere to suffer until Death collects you? Do you accept the consequences of deceit and betrayal?"

"I do," said Cedric.

"Are you prepared to die for the Meridiem?"

"I am," said Cedric.

"You have experienced family and friendship, death and desertion, desire and desolation, darkness and deceit. Those experiences have shaped you into a worthy candidate. Cedric Martens of Linder, the Meridiem will hear you."

"I, Cedric Martens of Linder, stand before you, humbled and honored, to solemnly promise and swear my loyalty and trust, my body and ability, my sword and shield, without hesitation or trickery but with honesty and God in mind and heart, to the fellowship of Meridiem. My earnest vow is unconditional with penalty of death as described if I willfully disobey any part of the sacred covenant, codes, and duties, or deceive and betray your trust. With utmost humility, I await your decision."

"Brother Klaas Bezuidenhout of the House of Meridiem," said Adina.

Klaas tilted his sword, resting the blade on Cedric's shoulder.

"Do you confirm Cedric Martens of Linder? If no, cut his throat now."

Cedric felt the sharpness of Klaas' sword against his neck.

"I confirm Cedric Martens of Linder," said Klaas. His weapon remained on Cedric's shoulder.

Adina asked the same of Gert and he too rested his sword on Cedric's shoulder, cutting edge against his skin.

"I confirm Cedric Martens of Linder," said Gert.

Adina removed Cedric's blindfold.

He let go of his crucifix and stared back into Adina's piercing eyes.

She tilted her sword up until the point touched his chest.

With two swords on his shoulders and against his neck, and the tip of another pointing to his heart, a sense of helplessness grew, as Adina had yet to cast her vote. Her expression appeared serious even menacing to Cedric, and he began to wonder if the night they had shared together might be cause for his rejection. *Why is she leaning into her sword?*

"Cedric Martens of Linder," Adina finally said, "your request is confirmed." She withdrew her sword and sheathed it. Her brothers withdrew theirs as well.

Cedric glanced over at Gert and saw a smile forming on his face.

"Congratulations, Cedric," said Klaas.

Gert pointed to an iron shield in which folded clothes, dark like the kind the brothers wore, rested face down on a table. "You will look like one of us, too," said Gert to Cedric.

## 26 - THE MISSING INGREDIENTS

Lounging on the late Countess Marie de Vos's bed, Domitian remembered how he and Marie had conspired to overthrow Count Marcel Marc de Vos, primarily due to his ill-conceived faith in false prophecy, claiming that the ridiculous Englishman Pierce van Fleming would succeed him. The sounds of footsteps interrupted Domitian's bitter thoughts. He planted his eyes on the door. When the footsteps stopped outside, he muttered, "Enter."

The latch lifted, the door opened, and Abigail entered the bedchamber, Gaétan behind her.

"Abby," said Domitian, sitting up against the headboard. "Come here. Tell me of your progress." Domitian signaled Gaétan to wait outside with the flip of his wrist.

Abigail approached the bed until she was standing an arm's length away.

Domitian patted the bed with his hand. "Sit with me."

After a brief hesitation, Abigail eased up onto the corner of the bed, her left side facing Domitian.

Domitian noticed her weakened state, her inability to levitate. Still, she was undoubtedly beautiful even though her beauty was the lingering effect of a witch's spell. "You are almost as weak as you are stunning, Abby," said Domitian, taking in her lovely profile. "Your new gown—thanks to Marie's wardrobe—suits you. Is it comfortable? I am certain you appreciate a bit of freedom as well."

"Yes, thank you."

Domitian twitched his nose. "So, when can we do the..." He wagged his finger as if trying to conjure the word from thin air.

"*Renatus?*" offered Abigail.

He pointed at her and smiled. "Yes, *that.* I cannot wait to see her again." Domitian suddenly grimaced with sadness. "I really do miss her, you know?" He sighed. "I need her back, you see, and soon. I am drowning in problems. I need her to rescue me from them. Do you understand? I need her back and without delay!"

"The tree is not ready, milord, and I need a few more ingredients."

"More ingredients, what ingredients...?" A wave of suspicion fell over him. "I shall remind you that we have an agreement, Abby. Break it and you know what will become of your brother. I will cleanse the earth of his existence!"

"I understand," said Abigail calmly, "but I will need a few more ingredients if you wish to begin the *renatus* a few days sooner. Will you allow me to collect them in the forest?"

Domitian wanted to refuse her request. He distrusted her. She had deceived the clan by magically stealing the oracle's identity and then manipulating Marcel with her trumped-up prophesy. There was also Abigail's loathing of Marie. However, despite his distrust, he needed her. He needed a necromancer. Reality suddenly reminded him that he was no longer master of Vos Castle, thanks to Orfeo. Domitian's eyes widened and his lips curled into a grin. "Abby, take me to Marie's resting place." He lifted off the bed and onto his feet. "I wish to see the tree, to see how tall it has grown."

"The tree is as tall as you, milord," said Abigail.

"If it has grown as tall as me in a week, it should be twice as tall in two weeks. Thus, in a week's time, the tree will be tall enough for you to perform the *renatus.*"

Abigail shook her head. "I am afraid—"

Domitian hurled himself at Abigail, knocking her across the room and into Marie's armoire. "You should be afraid!"

growled Domitian, struggling to control the volume of his temper. He brushed off his sleeves with the back of his hands and straightened his waistcoat. "You will do it, Abby. You will resurrect the countess when I say to. Is that understood?"

Abigail slowly sat up and leaned against the armoire. "She might return as a hideous monster—"

"Monster?" scoffed Domitian. "Hideous? Was she not hideous before? Hideously scheming..." He stared at Abigail for a time and sniffed her scent from the air. He smelled fear and dread, a desperate woman trying to protect her worthless brother. Despite how annoyed Domitian was of Abigail, he would not allow her to deter him from his goal. "What are those missing ingredients?"

Abigail rubbed a sore spot on her shoulder, appearing to take mental inventory. "One sterile brown frog, female."

"A what...a frog...a sterile frog?"

"Yes, female, milord."

"Are you insane?" His eyes fluttered with bother. "What more...?"

"One fire newt and one stag beetle..."

"Male or female?"

"Either, milord."

"Revolting... Why do you need them?"

"I cannot provide reasons for everything that is required, milord. I can only hope to emulate my mother's methods."

"And I can only trust that those disgusting ingredients are as necessary as you believe them to be." He shook his head, arguing against his better judgment that it was all a sham. But what if those ingredients were absolutely necessary? "Very well... As before, you will be escorted by Gaétan and me into the forest, and perhaps we shall pay Elida a visit—learn what she thinks of your ingredients." Domitian sensed Abigail's mood shift. "What is the matter, hmm? Does Elida make you nervous? What will you say to her? Will you apologize for how badly you treated her?"

"I am pleased to know she is alive and well, milord."

"Is that all? Admit it. You planned to kill her and you failed."

"I never planned to kill her, milord. I merely placed a spell on her while I borrowed her identity. She was supposed to sleep until I removed the spell."

"Your spell had little effect on her, but fearing for her life, she pretended to be dead, which reminds me to remind you... The reason you are still alive is because Marie wanted it that way. She wanted you to bring her back, and we have an agreement concerning your brother. You will resurrect my countess and I will not hunt down your brother."

"I will keep my promise, milord. I will do everything in my necromantic powers to bring her back."

Domitian glanced at the doorway. "Gaétan!" When the guard stepped into the chamber, Domitian pointed at him. "Close the door and come here."

The guard bowed and did as he was told.

Domitian's eyes moved from Gaétan to Abigail and back to Gaétan. "We will go to the tree, and then we will go to the forest.

Gaétan scratched his head. "Permission to—"

"Yes, yes, speak," said Domitian, agitatedly.

"Forgive me, milord," said Gaétan. "Orfeo's guards will not let us pass. They watch the castle's walls at all hours..."

Domitian shrugged dismissively. "I have left the castle many times since Orfeo's visit. I know of all the secret ways in, out, and around the castle." His eyes shifted quickly to Abigail. "Marie revealed all of them to me."

Suddenly, a noise from the corridor drew everyone's attention. All three focused on the door. Domitian touched Gaétan's shoulder and whispered, "When last were our Roman friends in the catacombs?"

"Not for several days," whispered Gaétan. "The guard outside the counting chamber often abandons his post."

Domitian levitated and glided to the door. He lowered to his feet and listened intently. He had heard those scratching noises many times before. It was obvious to him now—they were nothing more than rodents. He opened the door and peered outside and saw rats—dozens of them—scurrying through the corridor, running ahead of something. Fleeing, but from what? Domitian focused his senses and smelled them. Roman guards, possibly two of them. He quickly and quietly closed the door.

"Rats?" asked Gaétan.

"Extra-large," whispered Domitian urgently. His eyes turned to the armoire. He rushed to it and waved for Abigail and the guard to join him. Domitian slid the countess's clothes to the side and frantically felt around the insides of the furniture—"Where is it? Where is it?"—until, finally, locating latches along the lower edge of a panel. After two clicks, he pushed the rear panel up and then down into a large hole in the wall. He crawled through the hole and turned to help the others. The latch on the bedchamber door was slowly lifting as Abigail joined Domitian. After Gaétan got his massive body through the hole, Domitian quickly and quietly slid the clothes in front of the secret entrance and secured the rear panel in place just as the bedchamber door swung open.

Domitian heard the guards searching the room, opening the armoire doors, but the rear panel remained in place.

It was believed that the catacombs dulled the vampires' super-senses, and vengeful spirits were to blame. Domitian simply believed that the Roman guards were daft, not good at their jobs, easily duped. After all, he had left the castle and returned without being noticed by them, though he knew almost every secret way in and out of the castle.

Domitian continued through the tunnel with the others close behind. Soon, they came to a small room. It was dark inside, but they could sense the space and one another in it. Domitian gently unlatched a door and pulled it open. The other side of the door was just as dim. They went through the doorway and into a corridor, continuing through a twisting maze of narrow passageways until arriving at another corridor near the room in which the deadwood tree had been planted.

"Magnificent," whispered Domitian, arms out, quickly approaching the tree. "Oh, just look at it. It is taller than any of us." He turned to Abigail, gleaming with joy, but his expression changed to concern and sadness when he saw Marie's grave. A layer of green moss covered the grave mound. Domitian went to it, kneeled, and stroked the moss with his hands. "Hello, my sweet. I am here, longing for you. After I gather a few more ingredients, Abby will return you to me, just as you said she would. Soon, my love, we shall again embrace." Domitian stood up and backed away from the grave. "I will lead us out," he said to Gaétan. "Stay behind Abigail." He pointed his finger at Gaétan's face. "Watch her closely."

"Yes, milord," said Gaétan.

"All right," said Domitian, straightening his waist jacket. "Follow me."

## 27 – THEY IGNORED THE WARNINGS

### August 1799

At midnight, five upyrians swiftly crossed the Russian border into Belarus. All on horseback, all former sorcerers from the House of Laecian, they had become members of Queen Žofie's royal guard when the queen became ruler of all Russian vampires. Still capable of conjuring magic and shape-shifting, though to a lesser scale than when they were human, they were able to easily take the form of a rat or bat.

Perched upon a ledge of an orthodox cathedral, a white gargoyle crouched and surveyed the city of Saint Petersburg. In an alleyway below, in the darkest of night shadows, two upyrian guards waited beside three horses. When the street was clear of humans, the gargoyle took wing and glided to the alley. When it touched down, the gargoyle instantly shifted into Queen Žofie.

"My queen," whispered Damir, bowing his head.

His sister followed suit.

Damir and his sister Tatiana were the queen's most trusted guards. First cousins to Žofie, Damir and Tatiana were of Laecian lineage as well, conjurers of dark magic, and fierce fighters. The sibling guards seldom left Žofie's side. Their sworn duty was to protect her with their lives. Without a word,

Žofie took the reins of her charmed horse from Tatiana. They mounted up and rode west.

A few miles southwest of Polotsk, Belarus, the five upyrian guards arrived at a small farming community south of the Daugava River. In the Dark Ages, this sleepy enclave was a thriving village. Over time, multiple invasions and plagues reduced the village to ruins. Only a few vacated hovels remained. Moreover, people of the outer realms believed that God had forsaken the land—that it was exceedingly dangerous even to gallop through on fresh horses.

Recently, the village was repopulated by four families that emigrated from Siberia, eager to settle in a new land. They met no resistance when they arrived and ignored the superstitions that frightened others away. In fact, they were grateful for the isolation because no one bothered them, and the landlord—whoever that was—never came. They should have heeded the warnings, however. The seclusion and collection of hovels provided the perfect hideout for occasional upyrian rogues. On this occasion, the official envoy of five, traveling a day ahead of Queen Žofie, were sniffing out the surroundings for enemy vampires and the potential ambush before approaching the human inhabitants.

Little more than a knock at each door and an invitation to enter their homes, without as much as a whimper of protest from any of them, all four families—save three children—were drained of their blood. The children were entranced and tied to their beds—a gift to Žofie upon her arrival the next evening.

After Queen Žofie, Damir, and Tatiana arrived the next night, joining their envoy, they spent the evening feasting on the children, arguing how best to defeat the western vampires.

"In order to kill them all, we must build armies in the west, right under their noses," said Tatiana, drunk on child's blood. "We must not allow any to survive."

Žofie walked to the inglenook to feel the heat of the fire. The warmth was unnecessary for her survival or even comfort. She was upyrian, not human. Yet, the colors and flickering shapes of the flames mesmerized her now as they had when she was a little girl.

"I may not want to kill them all," said Damir. "Some are quite agreeable to look at."

"Yet, too stupid to tolerate!" sneered Tatiana.

"I agree with Tatiana," said a guard who resembled a demon—long hook nose, boils on his face, thinning hair, eyes of a goat. "We must kill them all."

"While we select the strongest, they select the prettiest," said another.

"Regardless," said Tatiana, "they will kill us if we do not kill them."

Žofie held out her hand to the fire, recalling her first year as a upyrian...

*Two hundred years ago, a harsh winter froze everything exposed to the blizzards, livestock and even humans where they stood. A young upyrian princess, Žofie was still discovering what it meant to be a Russian-born vampire. One night, Žofie decided to undress and leave the subterranean domain of King Rurik to wander the streets of Saint Petersburg, glimmering white, the wind mercilessly blowing her light brown hair in all directions. She continued to walk, completely naked, beyond the city's walls, toward the woods, then wending through a crystalline forest, across a solidified river, to a hill of snow. She wanted to know how it felt to be encapsulated in ice, what would happen to her. Would she freeze to death? She dug herself into the snow and fell asleep. When she awoke the next evening inside her cocoon of ice and snow, the chill had stiffened her but not entirely. She dug herself out, retraced her tracks back to the city, back to the lair beneath the streets, returning to her bedchamber and the comfort of her wooden coffin.*

"How many children is this?" asked a guard, jolting Žofie from her retrospection.

"My stomach is bulging with blood," said another.

"Mine as well," said Damir, looking at the boy on the table as if he were leftovers.

"Finish him," ordered Žofie. "We must leave soon. It is not safe here."

At nightfall, all eight upyrians mounted their horses and left the decimated village, moving southwest into Poland. They road swiftly for days, stopping only to rest their charmed horses. They traveled through Czechia, stopping briefly to feed on unsuspecting college students in Prague.

After arriving in the Black Forest, near Freiburg, they slowed to a trot, following a commonly traveled path through the pines.

"How much farther?" asked Tatiana.

"A mile or so," replied Damir.

Suddenly, the last guard in their lineup was knocked off his horse.

Damir was riding in front of Žofie with Tatiana behind her. By the time they turned to see what had happened, everyone was being attacked from above.

"Vampires!" hissed Damir.

"In the trees," said Tatiana.

"Shift now," growled Žofie.

Instantly, all the upyrians changed into bats, fluttering up into the trees, searching for the vampires. When all the enemy vampires were located, the upyrians shifted back and dropped from the sky, swords in hand, on the confused vampires. Heads and bodies fell to the ground. All but one vampire was killed. That vampire quickly mounted the nearest horse and fled.

Tatiana mounted up and fell into pursuit. Distance between the racing horses remained constant. Realizing that the vampire might get away, Tatiana stood up on her saddle, and leapt forward just before changing into a common crow, the largest shape into which she could shift and an animal that was faster than a galloping horse. When she caught up to the vampire, she shifted back to her upyrian form, dropped herself on the vampire, took hold of his head, and paralyzed him with a quick twist of the neck.

Tatiana returned to the group on her horse with the immobilized vampire draped across the other horse. A guard inspected the vampire while Žofie greeted Tatiana with open arms.

After kissing cheeks and hugging, Žofie whispered in Tatiana's ear. "We lost Vladimir."

Tatiana closed her eyes and nodded, accepting the loss of someone she admired.

"This vampire lives," said the guard, poking at the captive.

"Good work," said Žofie to Tatiana. "Please tell me we are almost there, Damir."

"There," said Damir, peering through the forest. "The cave is at the base of that crag."

"Perfect," said Žofie. "Bring the vampire."

Cautiously, Damir led them through dense woods to an opening beside a steep hill. "We will leave our horses here." He drew his sword and entered the cave. Two other guards joined him with weapons drawn. Farther in, Damir sniffed the air. "Do you smell it?"

"Vampires," whispered a guard.

"They were here," grumbled Damir. "Did they know we were coming, or was the ambush by chance? All clear inside," said Damir from the opening of the cave. He stared at the vampire, flat on his back on the ground. "I have questions for him."

"Bring the vampire inside," said Žofie, walking into the cave, stopping beside Damir. "After your questions, we will give thanks to Kronos."

"Yes, my queen."

After all the upyrians were inside the cave, sitting in a circle, staring at the vampire, Tatiana leaned forward and touched the vampire's clothing and woven necklace. She sat back down and nodded to her brother whose questions were answered with silence.

"I think I know of his kind," said Tatiana. "There is a little-known group of vampires, not a true clan, but more like an assemblage of young rogues from both east and west that live in the Black Forest. Most are exiled from their former clans. I thought it was only a weird folktale. They are said to live in the trees like monkeys. They feed mostly on the blood of forest animals. All of them wear necklaces made of holly. This one wears such a necklace." She peered into the vampire's eyes, pressing into his mind. "Are you der baum dämon?" She repeated her question three times but the vampire refused to answer.

"Prepare the crucifix," ordered Žofie.

That evening, the guards constructed a cross from branches they cut. They installed it in the ground upside down, stripped the vampire naked, and lashed him to the cross head down. They flayed his arms, draining his blood into excavated troughs. The blood formed oily puddles, and when the puddles were near full, Žofie ordered her upyrian guards to dip their cups in the blood.

Damir brought Žofie a cupful of the vampire's blood and stood beside her.

Žofie rose to her feet and held her cup out in both hands. "Comrades, on this night, we honor our fallen, Vladimir

Mikhailov." She smiled sweetly at the upside-down vampire, still trickling blood into puddles. "Pity this child cannot know what it is to be upyrian. If only we could change it, fix it. Then this child might see truth as we do. At least it can participate in this very important upyrian tradition." Her eyes drifted upward and she lifted her cup higher. "We drink in honor of Kronos, divine progeny of the primordial deities. Kronos, who castrated his own father and devoured his own children to control fate, prevent betrayal, and preserve the rule of order. In honor of Kronos and our fallen comrade, we devour our enemies and their children." She lowered the cup to her mouth, but before she drank, she glanced over at the grimacing vampire. "What is your name, child? You need not keep secrets from me. Your tree dwelling friends are all dead. Speak before it is too late."

The vampire moved his eyes to meet Žofie's. "Der baum dämon called me Flämisch."

"And your former name?" asked Žofie. "From which clan are you?"

The vampire looked away.

Žofie laughed at him. "Look at yourself, hanging and bleeding. No need to protect anyone but yourself, child. Tell me who you are and perhaps I will be merciful."

The vampire refocused his eyes on Žofie. "I know who you are, queen. I exiled myself from my clan because my master would have my head for failing him."

"Who is your master?"

"Before I answer your questions, will you answer a few questions of my own?"

"Ask."

"Before you kill me, tell me, why are you here? There must be good reason for the Queen of Upyrians to enter the west."

Žofie approached the upside down vampire. She crouched beside him and caressed his face with the back of her hand. "I have come for my sister."

"Who is your sister?" whispered the vampire.

"She is called Adina—blond, one green eye, one blue eye. She travels with two brothers. Do you know of her?"

The vampire's eyes widened.

"I see that you do."

"I met a woman that fits that description. She was accompanied by two men."

"Where?"

"Amsterdam."

Žofie nodded. "When?"

"A week ago."

"Describe the men."

"They appeared to be brothers, young men. They were armed with sword and daggers."

"Why were you in Amsterdam?"

"I was commanded to capture a boy. The woman and the brothers interfered. They protected him."

"So you failed to capture him."

"Yes."

"What is the boy's name?"

"Cedric Martens."

Žofie's smile grew wider, exposing her pointed canine cuspids. "Then, you are not a tree dweller after all."

"No. I had only arrived in the forest two days ago. Tonight was my initiation into de baum dämon. Our attack was unplanned."

"Tell me your name. No one here will say a word of our chance encounter or what was said. You have my word as queen."

"I...I am Sven de Vries."

"How do you do, Mister Sven de Vries?" said Žofie. "Let me guess...your tree climbing friends called you Flämisch because you are from Royal Flemish Clan. Your lair was Vos Castle. And your master was Domitian Augustus de' Medici. Because you failed to capture the boy, you cannot return to your lair, yes?"

Sven began to weep.

"Pitiful Sven, exiled and alone, that spells death to a vampire. You had hoped to find a home in the trees with those misfits." Žofie smiled at Sven. "Maybe I can use you. You know this land better than we. You know the fastest way back to your castle—of course you do. So, I offer you a choice: help guide us and live for tomorrow or refuse and die tonight. Choose now."

Sven sighed and peered into Žofie's glowing eyes. "I choose tomorrow."

Žofie stood up and backed away. She lifted her cup and the others joined her in a toast. "Za vstrechu, Mister Sven de Vries," said Žofie. After everyone took another drink of Sven's blood, Žofie turned to Tatiana. "Take him down."

## 28 - RETURN TO BRUSSELS

Cedric and the siblings stopped to spend the night at a sizeable inn in Brussels, the largest place of lodging Cedric had ever seen. The spacious stone building was at the center of an arcade, which contained numerous restaurants and shops. The inn stood three floors high and boasted a hundred guest rooms. Cedric followed the siblings to the third floor and to a door at the end of a hallway.

Klaas knocked on the door with his usual cadence: four times quickly and four times slowly. After a few patient breaths, the door opened and a tall, slender man dressed all in black bowed deeply. "Welcome back, honorable master of blades," the man said.

Klaas took off his hat and handed it to the man as he traipsed past him. "Thank you, Mister Thomas."

Adina entered, followed by Gert, who stopped to greet Thomas. "Good to see you again, Mister Thomas. You look well."

"I am, thank you, Master Gert," said Thomas, whose gaze moved to Adina. "Welcome, Madam Adina. Your room is ready."

"Thank you, Mister Thomas," said Adina, allowing Thomas to kiss her hand. She glanced back at Cedric and said, "This is Cedric Martens of Linder."

"Mister Cedric," said Thomas, "pleased to make your acquaintance. Allow me to show you to your room."

Cedric stepped into the foyer, waited for Thomas to close and lock the door, and followed him through a long hallway to a room with a green door. Thomas opened the door and let Cedric into a fabulous room with a grand view of Brussels.

"Dinner will be served at eight o'clock, Mister Cedric," said Thomas.

"Thank you, Mister Thomas," said Cedric, finding Thomas's use of title before the forename instead of the surname a bit odd. He gazed out the window at the city.

*Brussels.*

Cedric had promised his mother he would go there and make a new life. Problem was, monsters prevented him from honoring that promise, and that bothered him. The unfairness of his life bothered him.

*Why me?* he thought.

He was tired of running. He ran from the plague after it had decimated his home. He fled England with Pierce van Fleming because the police were after them for crimes he had not committed. He escaped from Vos Castle to Brussels, but the vampires chased him right out of Brussels and into Amsterdam. He yearned for a simple life, to be a farmer again, to have a family of his own. That was his dream, and Lily was supposed to be in it. He thought they would marry one day, and their farm would be next to his friend Jacob's farm, whose children would grow up with theirs. He had not expected Lily and Jacob to marry each other, but it appeared they had. It was better that way, he reminded himself. Tired or not, he was still running. His contribution to his friends' safety was to distract the monsters away from them.

And now, Cedric was back in Brussels.

As he observed the beautiful cityscape, Cedric noticed an abbey a block away. He had left three children there in the care of Abbess Maria and Sister Claudia. The children were Anna, Katarina, and a boy called Jon. He felt bad for leaving them there, but it was either that, or put them at risk of the vampires that stalked him.

The reality of being back in the dreaded realm of vampires drew him away from the window. He saw that the green door was closed and the room was spacious. Cedric never fully adjusted to the opulent lifestyle of the Fortune Brothers, but he nevertheless came to appreciate quality lodging, food, and drink. Then there was Adina, the goddess Adina. She had treated him with indifference because she wanted to protect him from her past. She was supposedly centuries old and dedicated to the Meridiem, not to mention her progeny Klaas and Gert. Despite those incredible reasons, firmly wedged between them, Cedric starved for Adina's love. He wanted nothing more than to smell the sweet perfume of her body again, to touch the silkiness of her hair, and feel the warmth of her smooth skin against his. His thoughts were of a man whose lover had left him with hope that someday she would return.

## 29 - PLANNING AN AMBUSH

Orfeo and his twelve soldiers arrived on horseback to the edge of the Sonian Forest near Vos Castle. They encountered no troubles along the way and fed well on random vagabonds. From the edge of the forest, he sent one soldier to the castle to announce his arrival, and to affirm it was safe and secure to enter. After the man returned with good news, Orfeo led his procession to the castle.

Inside the castle walls, Orfeo was greeted by the six soldiers he had left behind to guard the castle—all of them dropping to their knees.

"Master Orfeo," said one of his guards, "welcome back."

Orfeo smirked. "I take it Domitian and his flock behaved themselves."

"There have been no incidences, master. Everything is in order."

"And the wealth in the counting chamber?"

"Just as you had left it. All there and untouched."

"Excellent. Any issues with nosy humans?"

"None, master. Domitian helped with that."

Orfeo dismounted his charmed horse and went to Domitian, who remained kneeling. "Rise, rise, everyone! You appear well, Domitian."

Domitian stood up and straightened his waistcoat. "I am, milord. I trust your journey here was enjoyable. Are you hungry? I am arranging a feast in your honor."

"I am neither hungry nor here to be honored," said Orfeo, dismounting his horse. He walked to Domitian and placed his hand on his shoulder. "Let us speak in private." The two men strolled toward the castle, Orfeo's hand still resting on Domitian's shoulder.

"Still cross for losing all this to me, Domitian?" asked Orfeo.

"No, milord. I am your faithful servant, and the Royal Flemish Clan is yours."

"Come now, Domitian. I took everything from you." Orfeo gazed around the property. "Quite frankly, I am surprised you made no attempt to take it back." Orfeo gauged Domitian's mood, which appeared level.

"I have no qualms with you, milord," said Domitian, allowing sadness to change his expression. "I am still grieving...Countess Marie..."

"I understand...and agree that she was an extraordinary woman. Do you not remember the day I met her?"

"Yes, milord. We were practicing archery outside the walls."

Orfeo laughed loudly. "She was quite displeased with you. Something about stringing up a human target in daylight was the stupidest thing she ever saw. 'Thou hast violated thy castle rules in the open,' is what I think she said, no?" Orfeo sighed. "If only she had lived. Perhaps she would be in power here."

Domitian eked a smile, knowing full well that no woman had ever ruled the clan, and like the Catholic Church, no woman ever will.

"Do you really have only ten kindred in all, Domitian, or are there others slithering about?"

"We are all that remains, milord."

"And Sir Michael Livesey...?"

"He is an unfavorable remnant, a traitor, as you know," said Domitian.

"Better to execute a traitor," said Orfeo, moving to the castle with Domitian alongside him. "I am appalled yet impressed by your relationship with the upyrian queen— appalled that you granted her—our most hated enemy—safe passage, yet, equally impressed that you had arranged to meet her. How in Hades were you able to do that?"

"Countess Marie is how, milord."

Orfeo nodded, as if agreeing to something he had known all along.

Domitian continued: "Had the late Countess Marie de Vos not befriended Queen Žofie, our meeting would not be possible. Countess Marie was quite—"

"Decapitated?" interjected Orfeo with a spiteful chuckle. He noticed Domitian's sullen face. "Oh, cheer up, Domitian! Such a strange one, you are not to appreciate the dark humor."

Domitian forced a polite laugh.

"I am curious...why and to what end had Marie developed this relationship with Queen Žofie?"

"To gain wealth and power, milord," said Domitian, openly.

"Of course...and upon the inertia of Marie's relationship with Žofie, you built yours with Marie." Orfeo stopped and turned to Domitian. "You are naturally charming, Domitian. Not much for planning, but a good conversationalist and sometimes a good negotiator. I know this much because you convinced me to support your treachery of Count Marcel. A pity most of your clan was destroyed in the process—due perhaps to your lack of planning." He laughed. "Domitian Augustus de' Medici, though you are weak, fret not, my friend. I will allow you to thrive as long as you remain loyal to me. To demonstrate my sincerity, I offer my soldiers to you. I will leave them here to serve you, and you will serve me by protecting my property. Well?"

"You are both gracious and generous, milord," said Domitian, bowing awkwardly.

"Yes, yes, I know," said Orfeo, with a flick of his finger and moving on. "Have you any questions, Domitian?"

Domitian walked faster to stay alongside him. "Yes, milord, however unrelated to your generosity."

"Speak."

"Have you formally announced your accession, milord?"

Orfeo stopped. "Why do you ask?"

"Would you not ask such a question if you were in my position, milord?"

Orfeo slapped Domitian's face. "I would never find myself in your position, Domitian... You are like a cornered rat, at risk and frightened. What difference does it make to inform or not to inform? Fact is, *you* dishonored our agreement, and so everything of yours is now mine. What more is there to know?"

"Forgive me, milord. I was only curious to know if you had announced—"

"All will know in due time."

Domitian nodded affirmatively and lowered his chin.

Orfeo cracked his neck and resumed marching through the castle. "So, Domitian, tell me about this meeting. When did you say it was?"

"Tomorrow, first hour of the snake."

"Where?"

"Two miles north as the crow flies...inside an abandoned barn. It is quite safe in the dead of night."

"Excellent! It is the perfect setting for an ambush."

"Ambush, milord?"

Orfeo smirked. "Do you really expect me to share a table with the queen of goblins? Firstly, we do not need her money. I am the richest man in Europe. Secondly, we will not sell our children to her. Thirdly, the upyrian are not to be trusted and thus not to be allowed to enter the west! Any sort of agreement with them will no doubt fail and weaken our position. So, I have brought my best soldiers to destroy the queen and any guards she may bring. Erm, do you know how many she will bring?"

"How many, milord?"

"Guards, you idiot! How many guards will she bring?"

"She would not share that information, milord, but she cannot bring so many guards as to draw unwanted attention to herself. I estimate five to eight."

"I have eighteen soldiers. How many have you to spare?"

"I can spare two soldiers, milord."

"Then we shall have twenty to her eight. Describe the barn and surrounding area."

"The barn is quite large. It stands in a field near the edge of the forest."

"Good. Whilst we meet with Žofie inside the barn, my soldiers will be in the forest waiting for my signal to attack. The queen will not survive."

"Signal, milord?"

Orfeo lifted a metal whistle dangling on a gold chain from his neck. "My soldiers can hear this from miles away."

"Milord, you do realize the queen and probably her soldiers possess magical powers. At least that is what I have been told."

Orfeo scoffed. "Exaggerations, fear tactics..."

Domitian was about to disagree but moved on. "After the upyrian council discovers your ambush, what then, milord? The truce will be broken. The Lunabellum—"

Orfeo raised his hand to silence Domitian. "War or no, it matters not. We cannot lose."

"What of the humans, milord? Will they not see us and retaliate out of fear?"

"Your concerns are noteworthy, Domitian. Let me ask you this... What is the ratio of hare to foxes? Would you say thousands to one?"

"Yes, milord."

"Like the fox, we are predators. Like the hare, humans are prey. Let them see us. Let them see that we are the predator and they are the prey."

"May I comment, milord?"

"You may."

"Unlike humans, hares cannot attack their predators. Humans, however, can and do attack vampires. We are stronger, yes, but they are many and dangerous when driven by fear."

"Strange how we tend to forget that we were once human. Do you remember your mortal life, how miserable it was? I remember how I feared everything. Now, I fear nothing. If humans attack us, we will eat them. We will kill all of them if need be. Imagine a world devoid of humans. How peaceful..."

"Milord, if there are no hares, the fox will die of starvation—*we* will die of starvation."

Orfeo scoffed. "We may suffer bouts of the frenzy and shrivel like old apples, but have you ever heard of a vampire starving to death?"

"No, milord,"

"No!" Orfeo squinted at Domitian. "Your face is covered with cynicism. You believe in the implausible, that they would someday destroy us." Orfeo laughed. "I say, let them try!"

Meanwhile, as Domitian and Orfeo prepared to discuss plans to ambush the queen, she and her guards were marching through the Sonian Forest, with Sven leading the way. They halted at the edge of the woods and peered at a barn on the other side of a field.

"There it is," said Sven to Damir, who was standing beside Žofie.

Žofie's eyes remained affixed to the barn. "Sven," asked Žofie. "Will Orfeo or Domitian bring an army?"

"Orfeo will no doubt bring soldiers," said Sven, "but not an army. I would expect a dozen of his finest guards."

"Do you think Orfeo will try to ambush me?" asked Žofie to Sven.

"Your Eminence is wise," said Sven. "It is likely Orfeo will attempt an ambush."

"They would be fools to fight us," said Žofie to Damir. "However, we will be ready for them if they do." She peered into Sven's eyes. "Wait here while we investigate the barn." She turned to one of her guards standing beside Sven. "Stay here. You know what to do."

With a snap of her finger, Žofie changed into a large bat. All but one of her guards changed into smaller bats, and together they flew across the field to the barn, leaving one behind to kill Sven.

While Žofie and her guards were investigating the barn, and Domitian and Orfeo were planning to ambush them there, the Meridiem were en route to the barn.

# 30 - BUBBLE TRICK

At approximately nine o'clock at night, Domitian, Orfeo, and twenty of their soldiers arrived at the forest's edge within view of the meeting place. Thunder clouds blacked out the moon and stars, and a warm, humid breeze rustled the trees. At the peak of alertness, still no one detected Žofie and her now five guards gathering downwind on the opposite side of the forest. The guard she had left behind to kill Sven was—yet unknown to her—killed by Sven and slowly decomposing on the ground behind her.

Žofie was listening to Orfeo—his voice on the breeze—commanding sixteen of his soldiers to stay behind and listen for his signal. She observed Domitian and Orfeo moving swiftly across the field with four soldiers. They approached the barn cautiously. When they finally entered the barn, Žofie turned to Damir and lit up her green eyes—the signal.

Damir acknowledged her, turned to their guards, and pointed to the Romans in the woods upwind. In a wink, five upyrians shifted into bats and flew toward the unsuspecting Romans. A few seconds later, they were circling over them, selecting targets. Žofie mind-melded with Damir to share his vision.

In air, and by Damir's lead, the upyrians shifted back to their original shapes and fell through the tree canopy, catching the Romans by surprise. Materializing, weapons in hand, the upyrians lopped off ten Roman heads in an instant. The remaining Romans took up weapons, but irrespective of their valor, a few minutes later, none were left standing, and all five upyrians returned to Žofie's side.

Inside the barn, Domitian and Orfeo stood beside a heavy table while each of the four soldiers stood beside one of the several thick, wooden columns supporting the structure. They waited in silence, their senses heightened.

When the tension grew too much for Domitian to bear, he turned to Orfeo and whispered, "Milord, I recommend that one soldier stand guard outside and inform us when the enemy arrives."

Orfeo stared at Domitian for a few uncomfortable seconds and then turned to one of his soldiers. He nodded to him. "Leave the door open and inform us when someone is coming—"

"Be on the watch for a beautiful woman with guards," added Domitian.

The soldier nodded and followed his orders.

Orfeo's plan was not to attack anyone peacefully entering the barn, but to attack them after they were sitting at the table, deep into negotiations, unsuspecting and defenseless.

Domitian, of course, was expecting the Meridiem assassins to attack at any moment, and his objective was to escape and return to the castle to witness the rebirth of his Countess Marie. Familiar with the old barn from previous visits, he knew exactly where to go to escape, and he was already inching toward a hole in the wall behind leaning planks of wood.

Žofie and her soldiers watched from the edge of the forest as the Fortune Brothers, Adina, and Cedric arrived on foot. A breeze erased discerning scents and even the sounds of horses, which she was certain they rode in on. The night was so dark that she was unable to make out their faces, but she knew well enough that her sister was among them. She continued to hide her thoughts and presence. Not an easy task, being so close in proximity to her sister. She turned to Damir. He gently cradled her face in his large hands and rubbed her cheeks with his thumbs. She closed her eyes and drifted to another place, evading her sister's heightened awareness.

Klaas, Gert, and Adina froze when they saw the guard outside the barn, but the guard heard them and quickly went inside. The element of surprise was lost.

Adina knelt down and retrieved a rock from the ground. Using the rock, she scratched a large circle around her in the damp ground. She stood up and her brothers joined her. When Cedric came forward, she held up her hand. Shaking her finger at him, she pointed to the barn and spoke in sign language: "Stop the runners." Cedric nodded and stepped away from the circle.

Adina turned the palms of her hands to the ground, closed her eyes, and conjured a spell. The line of the circle on the ground began to illuminate. A pale blue skin of energy formed a sphere around them. Adina turned the palms of her hands upward. The bubble lifted them off the ground and into the dark sky.

Cedric was stunned by the magic. He just shook his head and wondered if Klaas and Gert were the least bit as fearful of Adina as they all ought to be. Voices entered Cedric's head. He had not heard them for days and had hoped they would never return. He shook his head, as if trying to shake them out through his ears.

*The devil's work, this is,* muttered the crotchety voice.

*Witches and demons, they are!* said the elder female's voice. *We will die if you stay. Now is your chance. Run!*

Cedric clenched his eyes and imagined the voices falling into his mouth, him chewing them up, and swallowing them into silence. Soon, the only noise inside his body was his hungry stomach.

When the sphere of energy was higher than the barn's ridgeline, Adina turned her palms to the barn and moved in that direction.

Žofie watched with amusement. "What is she doing?" she whispered to Damir. "My sister never ceases to embarrass herself—wastes energy on floating bubble trick. That is good for me. She will be weak when I take her."

As the ball of energy and its human contents floated over the barn, Cedric took up his position outside. The boy had trained every day and had learned to wield a sword and shield and wooden stake nearly as good as the brothers. It helped that Adina used magic to enhance his strength and agility. That, too, was fascinating. Cedric was trying not to be so mesmerized by Adina's powers, distracted by her beauty and desires of her love and attention. He was managing his emotions by focusing on his training and now on his guardianship and survival. Yet, it was impossible to forget that night in his bedchamber. He continued to monitor the barn doors and the floating bubble, now descending and almost touching the roof.

Was Adina an angel or the holy daughter of God? He wondered. Was she a goddess from another world? *Hardly...all things, including her, were created by God. She must be a child of God. She must be carrying out His wishes.*

Cedric backed away from the barn to gain a larger perspective. Flashes of lightning in the distance warned of an oncoming storm.

Adina lowered the bubble over what appeared to be a low spot in the roof, suggesting a good place to break through. When they were positioned directly over it, the siblings took up their weapons and Adina ended the spell. The ball dematerialized and all three of them fell. Adina and Gert broke through the roof, landing safely on the floor. Klaas, however, was stuck on the roof, legs dangling, straddling a rafter, in pain from the impact.

"*Oculi accendatur*," said Adina. Gert and Klaas's eyes lit up so they could see in the dark, but also a faint orb of light formed between Adina's hands. She floated it up into the middle of the large room. "*Revelare.*" Five curling beams of light stretched out of the orb, each one twisting and turning until shining on Orfeo hiding behind a pile of wood and his soldiers behind columns.

No sooner had the beams evaporated into darkness did Gert attack, throwing a knife at a peeking soldier. The blade embedded into his forehead up to the handle. Stunned by having his brain pierced through, he staggered out and Gert beheaded him with his sword.

Three remaining vampire soldiers quickly converged on Gert, while Orfeo continued to hide and blow his whistle, but none of his sixteen ambushers were going to come.

"Where are they?" hissed Orfeo. The only way out was to fight his way out. He unsheathed his sword and jumped over the pile of wood into the center of the barn. Before his boots touched the floor, however, his head and body were falling in different directions by Adina's blade.

One of the three vampires broke away from Gert to attack Adina at the very moment she was reinforcing Gert's energy shield. She was vulnerable, barely managing to move out of the way of the charging vampires. Momentum carried them past her. She lifted her sword and turned to engage them. The vampire's swords clanged loudly against hers. She flicked bright energy into their faces, stunning them for an instant. She glanced over at Gert to see if he was alright. At that moment, the nearest vampire pounced on her. His hand gripped tightly around her throat, threatening to break it, his sword pointing to her stomach, but Klaas fell from the roof and threw his dagger at the same time. It impaled the vampire, causing him to pause long enough for Adina to run him through. Klaas quickly came and lopped off his head.

Adina went on the defensive as another vampire came at her.

The vampire sank its fangs into Klaas's arm just as Klaas plunged his dagger into the vampire's neck three times. The vampire released Klaas's arm. Klaas quickly pivoted, wrapping his legs around the vampire's torso, pulling its head back by the hair and slashing its neck with his dagger, severing the neck in the process.

Outside, Cedric saw movement beside the barn's wall. The figure was moving swiftly and quietly—and also saw Cedric. The man stepped away from the barn and pointed two swords at him.

Cedric came at him—sword and shield in hand—but instead of charging directly into the man's iron defenses, Cedric leapt as high as he could over him. A bent-knee landing allowed Cedric the option of lunging in any direction.

"You!" blurted Domitian in a tone that sounded almost cheery to Cedric. "Oh, I know who you are. I never forget a face, though you do look grown-up and...oh my, so terribly handsome, Cedric Martens."

Cedric had not expected to see Domitian again, nor hear him utter his name as if they were long lost friends. The boy lifted his sword and shield.

Domitian surprisingly lowered his swords and smiled. "What are you going to do, Cedric, kill me? Why? What have I ever done to you?"

"You are hunting me," said Cedric. "What have you done with my friends?"

"Friends? I have hunted no one, captured no one."

"Your men tried to capture me outside Brussels."

Domitian sneered. "I wanted to return you to the castle because that is your home."

"They were taking me against my will."

Domitian glanced back at the barn. "Now, I know who killed my guards outside Brussels. You are with them, the assassins, the Meridiem. Oh yes, I know who they are. I know what they do. They are here to kill the uglies from the east. So, you may be wondering, why am I here?"

Cedric lowered his weapon. "Who is inside the barn?"

"Who? *Who* is not important," said Domitian slowly circling around Cedric. "Countess Marie misses you, as do I," he lied.

"The countess?"

"Yes, will you not return to the castle to see her?"

"The countess is dead," said Cedric.

Domitian widened his eyes as if surprised and expecting to hear it all at once. "Dead? How can you know that? Perhaps you know how she died, *who* killed her?" No sooner had Domitian begun to grin when something in the sky caught his eye.

Cedric saw it, too—bats circling the barn. He turned to Domitian, who was now moving toward Cedric with swords raised.

Inside the barn, the siblings were catching their breath. "That was easy," said Gert, turning to a concerned Adina.

She was inspecting a body of one of their victims. She shook her head. "This is not right." Her urgent whisper seized Klaas's attention.

"Romans," murmured Gert, now seeing what Adina was thinking, and turning toward the door. "Cedric."

Cedric used his shield to block Domitian's attack.

The wind was picking up now, and the rumble of lightning in the distance announced the storm's arrival with a few large raindrops that quickly became torrential.

Domitian turned to face Cedric and immediately turned sideways to avoid a thrown knife. It came from the direction of the barn. The Fortune Brothers and Adina were coming.

Klaas threw another knife at Domitian.

Domitian blocked the swirling blade with his swords and retreated into the open field.

"Wait," said Adina to Cedric before he gave chase. She placed her hand on Cedric's chest: "*Tibi et ego dabo vobis tionum animique fortitudinem.*"

Cedric felt warmth from her hand and his clothes tightening across his chest, arms, and legs. His body was growing and tingling. He felt stronger—incredibly stronger.

Lightning struck a tree in the forest, a sizzling crack so loud that it hurt everyone's ears. Domitian was completely illuminated by the explosive bolt as he ran toward the forest at high speed.

"Go!" said Adina to Cedric. "Finish him."

Distracted by the storm and Cedric chasing after Domitian, the siblings failed to notice the bats overhead.

Five upyrians shifted into their original forms while Žofie shifted into a gargoyle and stayed aloft. The upyrians fell from the sky all around the siblings. Gert narrowly evaded two blades coming down at him like axes. Klaas received a cut on his arm. Adina would have been killed if the upyrian landing behind her had used her weapons, but she hesitated.

The brothers immediately defended themselves as three upyrians attacked Klaas, three attacked Gert, and the one nearest Adina was about to conjure a spell.

Adina waved her hand, creating a field of energy. She extended her hands, pushing the field of energy into the upyrian woman, knocking her back. Adina took her knife in hand and leapt into the air, but not quite as high as she had hoped, falling short of her would-be victim. Much of her power had been transferred to her brothers and to Cedric.

The enemy came at Adina with a magical net of red energy. Adina was still as fast as any vampire and was able to tumble-roll onto the muddy ground, evading the spreading net. Adina got up, brought her hands together palms out at the enemy, and shot two bursts of energy at the very moment that lightning struck the barn and illuminated what appeared to be a winged gargoyle circling overhead. Adina saw that the upyrian woman had been adequately stunned, and went to aid her brothers.

Blades whirred and sliced through the stormy downpour, as clashing iron and steel emitted sparks between the brothers and the upyrian attackers. Bodies twisted, elevated, ducked, and spun evasively in a deathly dance as the wind drove heavy rain at an angle and lightning tore across the sky.

When the brothers threw knives, the upyrians elicited their powers to deflect the weapons. Adina continued to help thwart upyrian magic with magic of her own, shoving the enemy with her energy, trying to keep them off-balance. Gert deeply sliced the neck of a upyrian as he lost balance, but he still managed to finish him off with a second blow.

Adina turned to look for the upyrian she had stunned, but she was no longer there. Abruptly, Adina was knocked down by the winged gargoyle. She yelped out of fear and pain from claw wounds gouged deep into her skin.

Cedric was bearing down on Domitian when he was suddenly knocked down with a tremendous blow against his shield. On his back, Cedric spun to his feet in time to block his attacker's sword with his shield.

It was Sven—armed now with the upyrian's sword which was meant to kill him.

Cedric successfully evaded Sven's attack and went on the offensive, slamming his shield against the vampire, pushing him back and cutting him with his sword. Sven jumped high to elude the assault, but Cedric matched him, and their swords clashed before they touched ground. Sven was fast, but Cedric was faster and stronger, overpowering the famished vampire until it lost footing and Cedric plunged his sword through its chest.

Sven laughed at first until realizing that Cedric's sword was unusual. It was a blood sword, with a thin strand of wood magically inserted into the blade. The poison from the wood entered Sven's heart and traveled throughout his body. Before Sven's body collapsed to the muddy earth, Cedric heard Adina scream.

He turned the moment that lightning illuminated the barn and the siblings. He plainly saw Klaas with a sword protruding from his back, fending off two upyrians while Gert was fighting two others, and Adina was being attacked by a...

"Gargoyle?" whispered Cedric to himself.

Realizing that Domitian had gotten away, and as electricity filled the air and every hair on Cedric's body stood on end, he turned back to help the Bezuidenhouts.

The gargoyle swooped down at Adina and landed on the ground, its eyes green and glowing, lips stretched and grinning. It ran at her on all fours, like a mad dog. Adina escaped the attack by changing into a large gray raven and taking flight. The gargoyle took wing behind her. They flew higher and higher until clearing the rain clouds. In the dry air above the storm, Adina continued upward, but the gargoyle was gaining on her. The creature reached out with its clawed hand just as the bird turned, leaving the gargoyle with only tail feathers in its grip.

Through the rain clouds toward earth the bird dove, its wings held tight against its sides. When the brothers came into sight, the raven targeted the enemy. She pulled out of her dive and flew into a upyrian with such force as to knock him head over heels. The raven tumbled as well, coming to rest in a rain puddle.

The gargoyle appeared from the sky and landed a few feet from the dazed raven, which was now shifting into Adina's human shape.

Gert tripped and fell flat on his back. Gert blocked Damir's blows with his sword and stabbed his leg, while Tatiana began conjuring a spell to immobilize Gert. Before she could finish, Cedric charged in, foiling the conjuring and drawing Tatiana and her brother away from Gert. Gert quickly rolled away and got to his feet, joining Cedric. Side-by-side, they fought back against the upyrian siblings. The Fortune Brothers would not relent. Fiercely parrying, they denied the upyrian time to conjure spells or generate energy to fire at them. Finally, the enemy siblings turned into bats and retreated into the sky. Gert and Cedric turned to find Klaas at the exact moment that two other upyrians conjured magic to stun him and then sink their swords into his body from both sides.

Klaas fell to his knees. Gert and Cedric went to him. Those remaining upyrians shifted into bats, too, and joined their kindred in the angry sky.

Gert went to Klaas, who was wheezing and bleeding, while Cedric desperately looked for Adina. Lightning ripped the sky open, revealing the silhouette of a gargoyle carrying Adina away. Adina appeared as a lifeless doll, arms and legs and hair dangling. When another jagged flash of light shot across the sky, Adina and the monster carrying her were almost out of view. Cedric looked in the direction they were flying—Vos Castle. He began to understand what happened. Domitian had lured the Meridiem to the barn and helped Žofie ambush and capture Adina. Now, Adina was being taken to Vos Castle because it was the nearest and safest place for Žofie to go. His heart sank at the possibility that he would never see Adina again, at least not the woman with whom he fell in love. Against the voices in his head that told him to leave this madness behind, he vowed to save Adina from her sister Žofie.

## 31 - FERN SOUP

At Elida's cottage in the Sonian Forest, Cedric dismounted his horse and helped Gert unlash Klaas from the other horse. Daybreak was nearing, the rain had finally stopped, and Cedric hoped Elida was at home and willing to help them. Gert had wanted to take Klaas back to Ghent, but the journey there and back would have cost them two days too many if Adina was at the castle and they hoped to rescue her at all. Going on their gut instincts, Cedric and Gert hoped that Elida would not only help care for Klaas but also confirm Adina's whereabouts.

Cedric saw a thin coil of smoke rising from the chimney of the cottage, a good sign that someone was home. Gert slung Klaas's arms around his neck, and Cedric helped drag him to the front door. Cedric knocked at the door and waited. He knocked again and tried to open it. He jiggled the latch and was about to kick the door in when the sounds of latch bolts sliding stiffened him.

The door creaked open just enough for Cedric to view half her face. "Madam Elida?" said Cedric, managing a partial smile. "It is I, Cedric Martens of Linder. We met a year ago, and then later again with Abigail and Pierce van Fleming. Do you remember?" The door opened more and more until Elida stood in full view. She looked as he remembered her, slightly hunched, graying nest of hair, cloudy eyes. Her green cloak was hanging on the wall beside her gnarled walking stick.

She raised her shaky hands to Cedric. Cedric allowed her to run the tips of her fingers over his face.

"I see...yes, I know you, more man than boy now." She tilted her head toward the sound of Gert struggling to support his brother's weight.

"I brought my friends," said Cedric, "Gert and his brother Klaas. We hoped you might—"

Elida stepped aside. "Gert and Klaas Bezuidenhout, the Fortune Brothers. Yes, of course, I know who they are. Come in, come in!" said Elida. "What happened?" She rushed to a cupboard, moving as if she had perfect vision.

"We were ambushed," said Gert. "My brother is injured. They took Adina."

"Lay your brother on the bed." Elida pointed to a door. "Through there." She turned to an iron pot and barked orders at Cedric. "Cedric, fill that pot with fern shoots and water from the river. Be quick."

"How many fern shoots?" asked Cedric, taking up the pot in hand.

"Half ferns, half water," said Elida, turning to join Gert and Klaas in the bedchamber.

Outside the cottage, Cedric carried the pot to the stream just as a small patch of yellowing blue sky between rainclouds peeked through the tree canopy. After gathering ferns and adding water from the stream to the pot, he started back to the cottage, passing by a vine-covered pile of rocks. Once before, those vines had ensnared him. Elida caused them to move like serpents. That was the first time he had met her and had experienced supernatural occurrences. Though he was quite sick and delirious at that time, Cedric was certain Elida was no ordinary woman.

Elida was in the bedchamber tending to Klaas when Cedric entered the cottage. Klaas had been undressed to just his undergarments. She was cleaning Klaas's wounds, slathering some sort of paste on them and applying clean strips of linen. She wiped his face with a damp cloth and placed the back of her hand on his forehead. She didn't look his way, but she sensed Cedric standing at the doorway and said: "Place the pot on the counter." Her Nordic accent reminded Cedric of their first encounter. She had given him food and told him to leave the forest before it was too late. He had always wondered what too late meant, and if he had indeed left too late.

Cedric placed the pot onto the counter and collapsed into a chair beside the inglenook. His mind wandered for a moment and the voices in his head began to speak.

*Cedric the Coward, how could you possibly expect to survive?* three disharmonious voices cackled.

"Not now," whispered Cedric, shaking his head.

Elida went to him, placing her hands over his ears as if trying to feel what Cedric was hearing.

*Who will protect you, now that your fairy witch-mother is captured?* said the crotchety voice. *She will die because of you. You are weak and—*

*Silence!* A woman's voice sliced through the naysayers, confusing Cedric.

It was Elida—her voice was in his head, too.

*How dare you interrupt us!* shouted the crotchety voice.

*Who are you?* asked the elder female.

*I said, silence!* repeated Elida with more vibrato. *Why must you discourage this young man, hmm?*

*Who are you?* asked a young voice tinged with curiosity and fear. *You do not belong here. We and the boy are one.*

Elida replied: *It is quite normal to debate ideas and actions in one's own head. It is quite the opposite to disparage, confuse, and terrify one with unfounded insults, and Cedric is no boy.*

*He is foolish. He will kill us all. He has no wizard to protect him now—*said the crotchety voice.

*He needs no wizard, though he still has one,* said Elida.

*Who? Gert? He is no wizard!*

*No, me,* said Elida.

*You? You can do nothing, old woman!*

*Yes, I am old, but I am no less a sorceress, and I will use my powers to silence you unless you agree to help him.*

*How dare you threaten us!*

*I need not to dare. I need only to do. Cedric agrees. Can you not feel him nodding?*

*But...but we are here to protect him, not to encourage him to fight and kill himself! He is no fighter. He will die. And if he dies, so shall we.*

*Better to die doing what is right than to live doing what is wrong. What say you to that?* Elida waited for an answer... *Stay or go?*

*Stay,* said the voices finally.

*In order to stay, you must encourage Cedric to do what is right, or—as his sorceress—I shall silence you all! Cedric would surely prefer the former. He is gifted, charmed, and looked upon favorably by the gods. Keep this in Cedric's mind.*

*We will support him, to encourage him when it is in our best interest,* said the voices in unison.

*Say nothing if you have nothing encouraging to say,* said Elida. After a long moment of silence, Elida placed her hand on Cedric's head and gently rubbed it. "How do you feel?"

"Tired," whispered Cedric, closing his eyes.

"Are the voices gone?"

Cedric nodded. "I cannot hear them, not for the moment." He forced his eyes to open and peered up at Elida. Her frosty eyes seemed to be focused on some distant point beyond the walls of her cozy little cottage.

"Excellent," she said and turned away. She went about her business, tending to the pot of ferns. She added ingredients, hung the pot over the fire, added wood, and stoked the flames.

Cedric closed his eyes again and fell asleep. He dreamed of happier times with his family in Linder. Nothing pleased him more than to work beside his father in the fields, tending to their crops and harvesting the bounty. He recalled his first time away from Linder. It was his fourteenth birthday. His father had borrowed two mares from a neighboring farmer. They rode until they were within view of the Sonian Forest.

218 | THE MERIDIEM

*The forest...*

He felt tethered to it by some invisible force of fate. Happier memories of his parents and little sister transitioned to the plague, suffering, death, and then the castle.

*Vos Castle...*

*A vision...*

*Sitting on a stone floor, cold and drafty, single candle, obscuring shadows, table askew in the center of a large room. On the floor, numerous purses and lockboxes, their insides spilled out like the guts of flayed carcasses, dusty and dank.* Cedric looked closer. *Legs, ankles, smooth and delicate, skin of a young woman, riding breeches that matched Adina's the night she was taken.*

*What is this...? Is this Adina? Am I seeing through her eyes?* He recognized the counting chamber beneath Vos Castle. He continued to look through her eyes for anyone else, but it was too dark to see beyond the flickering glow of a single candle.

*Cedric?* whispered a young woman's voice. *Can you hear me? Cedric?*

It *was* Adina! Unlike the annoying voices in the center of his mind, her voice came from above.

*Adina?* Cedric replied, completely surprised to hear her so clearly.

*Cedric, I thought I would never find you.*

Cedric felt instant joy and relief. She was alive! But then he thought of her sister Žofie. The siblings warned him of her powers. Could this be a trick? Could this be Žofie instead?

*How can I know it is you?* he asked, fearful and respectful of Žofie's powers and guile.

*You spent three days in the white room, training with us. How are my brothers? I could not protect them.*

Cedric wanted to tell her that Klaas was injured and Elida was helping him, but the truth might expose too much. *Are you injured, Adina?*

*No.*

*Are they guarding you?*

*Yes.*

*How many guards?* Cedric expected her to reply in tempo, but got silence. *Adina? Adina?* A lump formed in Cedric's throat.

Formerly a place of torture, all the clan's wealth was stored in the counting chamber. Cedric had both met and killed Countess Marie there. Of all the rooms in the castle, why was Adina held captive there? Why there?

*Yes, I am here,* said Adina finally. *Three guards. I have little time, Cedric. Žofie is resting, regaining strength while I am chained and exhausted. I have successfully repelled her attacks until now, but soon she will overpower me. Ask my brothers to summon the elders. Tell them what is taking place here. Tell them my sister intends to change me. They will know what to do...*

Cedric woke to busy noises in the kitchen and soft conversation between Elida and Gert. He searched for Adina's voice but was unable to communicate with her unless he was asleep. No longer tired, he noticed Gert staring at him.

"Sleep well?" said Gert.

"Give this to your brother," said Elida, handing a bowl of soup to Gert. Cedric watched Gert take the soup into the bedchamber. Elida placed another bowl of soup on the table and pointed at it while looking toward Cedric.

The stiffness and soreness of Cedric's body surprised him when he stood up. He felt old as he slowly moved to the table, took a wooden spoon in hand, and tasted the soup. It was delicious.

In the bedchamber, Gert opened Klaas's mouth and Elida placed one hand on his throat and a spoonful of soup over his lips. She blew on the soup, massaged his throat, and poured it between his barely parted lips. Encouragingly, Klaas swallowed each spoonful until the bowl of soup was empty.

Gert followed Elida out to the inglenook where Cedric stood beside the table.

"Cedric, Elida will care for Klaas while we are away," said Gert, searching for his things.

"Gert," said Cedric, moving toward the entrance door. "May I have a word with you?" Cedric led Gert outside the cottage. The chilly air was damp with mist, rising from the earth where rays of the morning sun touched the ground. Cedric turned to Gert, searching for the words. "Adina spoke to me. I saw her."

"How?" asked Gert.

"She spoke to me as I slept."

"How can you know it was not a dream?"

"I cannot know, but her words were sensible."

Gert nodded. "What did she say?"

"Adina is alive and well but imprisoned beneath Vos Castle and exhausted." He paused to remember Adina's words.

"Go on," said Gert, a fleck of anxiousness in his tone.

"She said that you must summon the elders. They will know what to do."

Gert nodded and turned back to the cottage.

Inside the house, Gert asked Elida to join him beside Klaas. Gert knelt beside the bed and stared at his brother's face. Klaas remained still, breathing steadily, eyes twitching beneath his eyelids.

"We must contact the elders," said Gert to Elida.

Elida nodded as if she knew exactly what he meant. She kneeled beside Gert and took his hand. Gert took Klaas's right hand. Cedric kneeled on the other side of the bed and took Klaas's left hand. Gert and Elida closed their eyes while Cedric observed. Gert and she remained still and silent, as if meditating, and Cedric watched closely for any signs of magic, but nothing happened. When Elida and Gert opened their eyes, they looked at each other, nodded, and stood up.

"Cedric," said Gert. "It is done."

"What is done?" asked Cedric. "I saw nothing."

"Were you expecting wind and lightening?" said Gert, shaking his head.

"Yes," replied Cedric, watching Gert exiting the bedchamber, followed by Elida.

Elida went to the kitchen, reached into a cupboard, and retrieved a small vial containing orange powder. She gave the vial to Gert. "Do you know what this is?"

Gert nodded. "Acid?"

"*Acidum*, said Elida, nodding. "Do you know what to say?"

"Yes," said Gert. "Thank you. I am indebted to you."

Cedric and Gert gathered only the items they would need to use inside the castle, their weapons and a sack of equipment.

Elida approached Cedric. "Where in the castle is Adina?"

"In the catacombs, the counting chamber..."

Elida nodded and gave Cedric a clove of garlic. "You know what to do with this."

"Madam Elida," said Cedric. "You are the clan's oracle. Can we save Adina?"

"Anything is possible, and there is still time for her, but Cedric my boy, your future fades with each passing minute."

"My future?"

"Beware the monster that seeks to devour you, Cedric."

"Monster?"

She wrinkled her brow. "It is as impure as it is unnatural— quite the abomination. Quick, my boy, time is of the essence! Take Gert to Adina, and pray that your god will protect you.

"Come, Cedric," said Gert, waiting in the doorway.

"May the gods be with you!" said Elida, to Cedric and Gert as they mounted their horses and rode off.

## 32 - BED, COFFIN, OR TOMB

At Vos Castle, Queen Žofie Cervenka and her personal guard Damir sat in a large room on the main floor. The queen placed her hands on Damir's waist. "Our journey was long and costly, but we have her now."

Domitian knocked at the opened door to the room.

Žofie glared at Domitian. "Domitian, we are exhausted. Where can we find rest in this filthy place?"

Domitian bowed deeply. "My apologies, Your Eminence. Please follow me." Domitian moved to the doorway and waited for them to pass through. When they reached the foyer, he took the lead. "This way, please. I am honored to accommodate Your Eminence here at Vos Castle. I am quite certain you will enjoy your stay in the catacombs. The draft is temperate and damp. Our guest rooms are completely safe, with double bolted timber and iron clad doors. Our spacious chambers consist of three types of resting accommodations: bed, coffin, or earthen tomb." Domitian paused, emphasizing his next point. "When your arrival date was confirmed, I immediately imported soil from Saint Petersburg. They are placed in wooden urns beside your coffins. However, if you should prefer the scrumptious luxury of silk sheets dyed in child's blood, you may indulge in a bed fit for a queen! Though the coffin and bed are undoubtedly the finest sleeping arrangements, the earthen tombs are in my humble opinion the ultimate *naturale* slumbering arrangement. Penetrating through the earthen ceiling of the tomb are roots from the original forest. I enjoy running my hands over them and—"

"Shut up, Domitian," hissed Žofie. "Just because I rest below the city in Saint Petersburg, does not mean I wish to rest below a dirty castle! Do you rest in the catacombs?" Žofie observed Domitian's face. "You do not, do you? Where do you rest?"

"Well...in my chambers, Your Eminence."

"Where are your chambers?"

"Why...in the tower—"

"I thought so. Take me there. Damir will come."

Domitian bowed. "Yes, of course, Your Eminence."

After showing Žofie and Damir to his tower chambers, Domitian slinked back into the catacombs, into the darkest tunnels leading to the base of the turret, where bright-green moss carpeted over Marie's grave. Abigail was there, sitting in a chair, reading a book. The tree was nearly twenty feet tall now, its gnarled and sparse branches nearly touching the walls. Her guard Gaétan stood like a statue, arms crossed, gazing up at the tree like a boy with thoughts of climbing it. He uncrossed his arms and bowed to Domitian. Abigail put down her book and stood up.

"Missed me?" asked Domitian with a cheerful snigger. "Are you ready yet?"

"Yes, milord," said Abigail. "I am."

Domitian's eyes widened as if surprised to hear it.

"We may begin the *renatus*," said Abigail, gazing steadily at Domitian.

Domitian could barely contain his excitement, covering his grin with his shaking hand. "I was expecting yet another excuse in favor of delay." He belched a chuckle bordering on giggle.

"Why are the upyrians here?" asked Abigail, a tone of worry in her voice. "I sensed their presence."

"They are of no concern, Abby. They will be moving on after tomorrow. I am certain of that. All that matters to me and to you is this tree and the countess," said Domitian, pointing to the mound of hairy moss. He moved beside Gaétan and waved the back of his hand toward the tree. "Go on, do what you do. Begin, please."

Abigail took in a deep breath for effect and knelt beside Marie's shallow grave to begin the *renatus*.

## 33 - THE RENATUS

Every week for a year, Abigail's mother would go into the forest to place fresh flowers on her son's grave. Because she was a necromancer, she made certain to plant a deadwood tree near his grave in case she decided to resurrect him—a decision that took a year to reach. Bringing the dead back to life had its risks. Many things could go wrong, and witchcraft was punishable by death, but she cautiously and flawlessly performed the *renatus*, resurrecting her son, Pierce. Pierce was sent away to protect him and his family from those who would kill witches. Unfortunately, a villager saw him before he had departed, setting in motion deadly consequences for Abigail's family. Resurrecting Countess Marie de Vos had its risks, too, but in a different way.

Abigail was not at risk of persecution and punishment for what she was about to do. Contrarily, the failure to perform her craft and resurrect Marie was her greatest risk. Failure would elicit Domitian's rage, causing him to renege on his end of their agreement. Another risk was botching the *renatus*, bringing Marie back in severed parts instead of fully assembled. Even a perfect resurrection was not without peril because the first order of business of a newborn revenant was to avenge his or her murderer; and in Marie's case, Cedric Martens was her killer.

Abigail did not shelter feelings for the boy, but if Cedric had not ended Marie when he did, she and her brother would have been killed. Like her mother all those years ago, Abigail decided to resurrect the dead, but in a way that would also improve her predicament. She intended to change Marie and bring back a version that would help safeguard her brother and the legacy of magic she bequeathed to him.

At noon, Žofie opened her eyes. She had been resting in Domitian's bed since arriving at the castle the night before. She reached across the bed for Damir, but found no one. He was leaning against the door, arms crossed, eyes closed. "Must you always stand while resting whenever we travel?" asked Žofie, throwing off the beddings and levitating to him.

He gazed down at her with a jaded sneer, as if the question had been asked too many times. She pressed her body to his, slid her arms around his waist, and placed her cheek on his chest. He draped his large arms over her.

"Today is the day, my faithful love," said Žofie. "I am rested. She cannot resist me, not today."

"She will try."

"She will fail. After I make her a upyrian princess, we shall take this castle."

"What of Domitian?" asked Damir.

"He will do what we tell him...or we sacrifice him and his flock to Kronos. Then, we will build our army here and crush the west. Finally, a happy ending to Lunabellum. All of Europe will belong to us."

Deep in the catacombs, Abigail knelt between the deadwood tree and Marie's grave. Tingling fingers and toes indicated energy rising from deep within the earth.

Domitian stood near Gaétan, backs against the curved foundation wall of stone and brick, biting his fingernails and anxiously watching Abigail's every move.

Abigail fretted behind a facade of confidence, as no amount of studying, recounting, or rehearsing the *renatus* produced an adequate level of certainty. Memories of her mother were incomplete, and filling those gaps with knowledge gleaned from various manuscripts on the subject of necromancy would need to be enough. If only she still possessed the satchel to which she bequeathed her brother to guard and in which the world's sorcery was contained. She might have retrieved step-by-step instructions, but Sir Michael would have stolen that satchel had she not transferred it to Pierce. She knew her brother was still alive—otherwise, the satchel would have returned to her just as she had instructed it to do.

She placed a *Mandragora* root on the floor and some kindling of leaves and twigs over the root. She held her hands over the kindling, whispered *ignium* several times, and started a flame. She gently fanned the flame into a small fire, gazed up at the deadwood tree, and started to recite incantations. After a moment, it seemed to be working. The fire burned blue and then red, and it grew in size and intensity until the flames were nearly as tall as she. Unexpectedly, fiery beetles flew upward from the red flames to the uppermost branches of the tree and burst into thousands of fireballs that fell back to earth.

Those flecks of fire on the ground began to grow and form into little people. Abigail presumed them to be Countess Marie's family members responding favorably to her request for Marie's soul to resurface. She found it interesting that the effigies were so small—about ankle high.

Colorful lines of fire spread out from the base of the tree— like roots across the floor—to Marie's grave, where gold and silver flames engulfed the mound. Abigail waited patiently, chanting over and over for Marie's soul to rise and fill her body of flesh and bone, and to walk among the living once again. She listened to her own voice as she had once listened to her mother's, trying to imitate her tone and tempo. She glanced randomly at the small effigies of fire dancing around the gnarled and sparse deadwood tree. From the corner of her eye, she saw the strangest effigy of them all, smaller than the rest. Was it a fairy or a frog, dancing upright on its hind legs?

*The tree should be alit by now,* she thought, but it remained unburned. She continued to chant but began to worry. The frog effigy suddenly hopped onto the fiery grave and sank into the soil, leaving behind a thin trail of green smoke. All the other effigies dancing around the tree submerged themselves into the grave as well—wisps of smoke marking each one.

The gold and silver fire on the grave was dwindling in size and intensity. Abigail could no longer hide her concern.

Domitian stepped forward when the room darkened for lack of firelight, and Abigail's voice wavered for lack of poise. "Is this supposed to be happening?" he asked, rubbing his chin.

Abigail nodded and nervously waved him away. She clasped her hands and chanted more fervently, but the flames were soon replaced by swirling wisps of smoke. She went to the grave and placed her hands on the mound and continued to chant as if begging Hades to release Marie's soul. Were she to fail, she feared Domitian would retaliate by hunting down her brother in America. He would banish her alongside the traitor Sir Michael. She despised Michael for assassinating their master, Count Marcel. If not for Michael, Marcel would still be alive and Domitian would not be master of the Royal Flemish Clan, and she would not be in this predicament. Abigail shook off those useless thoughts and refocused on the spell at hand. Necromancy was a precarious process, and she wanted to know if she could do it. She wanted to know if she was like her mother—if she was as powerful as she had been. Determination began to displace desperation as her focus intensified and the tingling sensation flowed throughout her body.

The grave mound was smoldering with gold and silver smoke now, lifting higher like forest ferns with coiling tips. The tree began to smolder, white smoke winding around its dry branches like phantom vines. *This was not over yet*, thought Abigail.

A wind came out of nowhere, flowing into the dry and smoky space, churning the smoke into curling puffs of dusty explosions until the top of the tree was no longer visible through coiling clouds of silver and gold. A funnel cloud stretched down to the center of the grave mound. Moss and soil lifted into the twisting smoke, forming a dusty orb halfway up the funnel. The orb of debris grew denser and denser as more soil was sucked into its form. The orb began to change geometry from spherical to cubical to cylindrical, and finally a star with five legs. From the ends of the star's legs, a head, two hands, and two feet began to form. The legs and feet lengthened too much, resembling a frog more than woman. The mixed form continued to change, amphibious, insect, woman features appearing and disappearing like ingredients in a boiling pot of stew.

Abigail was drawn to the twisting earth and smoke and developing form of flesh and bone that would become the Marie de Vos of Abigail's design. Abby moved toward the blending mass of flesh and reached out closer and closer to the suspended form. Slowly, from inside the twisting mass, an appendage of dust reached out to Abigail. It was an arm with a hand and fingers. As if pointing at Abigail, it extended an index finger. When Abigail touched fingertips, the arm retracted back inside the tornado. A red fireball grew inside the stomach of the person of dust. The brightness of the fireball was barely visible through the swirling smoke, but red flames flicked outward. Slowly, the woman of dust became a woman of fire and the likeness of Countess Marie began to shine through.

Abigail stepped back, chanting her mother's words as she had remembered them. Marie's body-of-fire descended to the floor, and the whirling fragments blew away to reveal the fiery shape, frolicking around the deadwood tree. When she was close enough to touch the tree, Marie's body placed both hands on it. At that instant, the tree erupted into flames of all colors. Marie hugged the tree and pressed herself into it, completely sinking into the tree.

The flames were brilliant but emitted neither heat nor smoke. Aromas of licorice root, sage, and leather were tainted by the stink of rancid still water. Abigail backed so far away from the burning tree that she was now standing beside Gaétan, their backs pressed against the wall. She glanced up at him and saw the reflection of fire and magic in his eyes.

Domitian's mouth hung open, eyes leaking pink tears, hands reached out as if hoping the fiery image of Marie would come out to meet his embrace.

The tree suddenly exploded. Wood chips and cinders pelted everything in the room. Darkness and silence fell over Abigail, Domitian, and Gaétan.

# 34 - ABOMINATION

Snaking through the forest along a seldom-traveled path, Cedric led Gert toward Vos Castle. They had no choice but to leave Klaas in Elida's care.

"How much farther is it?" Gert's question sounded tense to Cedric.

Cedric pointed to the edge of the forest ahead and a meadow with a steady incline beyond it. "The castle is on the other side of that meadow and hill. We will see it soon. Shall we rest here and review our plans?"

"Very well," said Gert.

"Tactics," said Cedric. "We have weapons, but they have strength, speed, and magic."

"You have a magical sword and dagger, so do I. You have been trained, and you know the layout of the castle. With surprise on our side, we will succeed. We must get inside the castle without being seen."

"The main gate through the wall is usually guarded. Guards walk the ramparts in shifts, so sections of the wall are left unguarded. We should scale the southeast section nearest the church when it is clear. Between the church and service door into the castle is about twenty paces. The church can hide us, but if new orphans are locked inside, they will be guarded by a man on one end and a woman on the other."

"Why a man and a woman?"

"The church was partitioned into two chambers—boys on one side, girls on the other."

We will need to remove the guards before they see us."

"Yes."

"Time is not on Adina's side, Cedric. Are you ready?"

Cedric nodded. "Yes."

Žofie and Damir joined two other upyrians outside the counting chamber.

"My sister, did she behave?" asked Žofie of her guards.

"Yes. No problems, Your Eminence," answered a guard.

"Excellent. Where is Domitian?"

"We have not seen him," said the other guard.

"Does not matter," said Žofie. "After my sister has joined us, we will decide what to do with this castle and all its riches." Žofie turned to Damir. "I am famished. You...?"

"Have you the strength to turn her?" asked Damir.

Žofie scowled at the question. "Even when I am tired, she is no match for me. Well, perhaps I should feed. Go. Bring food."

In the catacombs below the tower, settling smoke revealed the outcome of Abigail's *renatus*—a smoldering deadwood tree stump and a naked woman, curled in fetal position upon the grave.

Abigail felt Gaétan's hand on her shoulder. She placed her hand on his and watched as Domitian slowly approached the woman and attempted to communicate with her.

A few paces distant from Marie, Domitian dropped to his knees and fell forward onto his hands. Then, he began to sob. "Oh, thank Hades for this miracle! My countess, my love, welcome home." With his nose nearly touching the ground, Domitian inched closer to the woman who was now unfolding her legs and reaching above her head, stretching until her body was fully extended, arching, yawning, and moaning. She turned to her side to face Domitian.

He searched for the Marie he knew in her hazel eyes. "Countess Marie de Vos," whispered Domitian. "Are you in there? Do you remember me?"

Marie slowly lifted herself to a sitting position, one knee raised, squinting at Domitian as if trying to see him or remember him. Her supple lips curved into a beautiful smile, a youthful smile. Domitian turned quickly to Abigail. "Bring the robe."

Abigail looked to where Domitian had been standing and saw a neatly folded robe on the floor. She pointed at it and Gaétan delivered it to Domitian. When Gaétan returned to Abigail's side, she took hold of his muscular arm and led him to the mouth of the corridor and watched Domitian and Marie from there.

In the counting chamber, Žofie inspected a young woman. She was calm and seemingly willfully there. However, Damir had charmed her. She had no inkling of imminent death.

"Where did you find this woman?" asked Žofie, eyes beginning to pulsate.

"She was guarding the building in the courtyard."

"Children?"

"No, my queen. There was a man, but this woman was younger."

Žofie smiled, her incisors lengthening. "That is why you are my number one." Žofie went to the young woman, gently moved her hand to her face and behind her head and let down her long hair. She then took a firm hold of the woman's hair, yanked her head to the side, and sank her fangs into her neck. She let go after a few seconds, blood rhythmically spurting out.

Damir quickly placed his mouth over the wound and drank, leaving the last several heartbeats worth of blood to the guards. When the woman was completely drained, a guard removed her body from the counting chamber.

Rejuvenated and calm, Žofie moved her attention to her sister, observing her dirty skin, torn breeches and shirt, and messy blonde hair covering most of her face. As Žofie approached Adina, she glanced at a guard and a chair. The guard instantly brought the chair to her. She sat and stared down at Adina.

Adina gathered her locks from her face and shook her head at Žofie. "Stop it."

Žofie's green eyes were glowing.

"No," said Adina. "Stay out of my head." Then Adina's blue and green eyes lit up. *No, I said,* thought Adina, as her sister forced her way into her mind.

Their eyes glowed so hot and bright that the guards' eyes narrowed and looked askance.

Adina lifted her hand to block her sister's searing eyes and struggled to get her out of her mind.

Žofie levitated and floated over Adina, facedown, brown hair eerily floating out and upward as if suspended in water. She hovered over Adina, her green eyes bearing down on her like they were magnified light.

Adina moved into a sitting position with her back against the wall, eyes closed, feeling the burn against her eyelids. When she opened them again, Žofie's face was directly in front of hers. Adina tried to push her away, but her hands bounced off Žofie's field of energy.

Then, Žofie's fangs grew long and pointed, and her mouth opened wider as she moved closer to Adina. She placed one hand on Adina's forehead and the other on her chest.

Adina's arms fell to her side, numb and useless as Damir assisted Žofie with a spell of his own. Žofie tilted Adina's head, exposing the side of her neck.

*At long last, sister,* said Žofie in Adina's mind. *We are together again.*

*Get out,* said Adina, using all the strength she had left to fight back.

*Remember when we were little girls?* said Žofie. *We used our powers to float, and up we would float, to the ceiling of our bedchamber and wait for the ugly nanny. When she entered our room, we would pour our bedpan on her.*

*That was you, not me,* said Adina.

*Do you remember how badly you wanted to be a princess? The nanny told you that you were not pretty enough to be a princess. I hated her for saying that to you, and I swore that one day I would use my powers to make you a princess. That day is today.*

The tips of Žofie's fangs met Adina's neck, pricking the skin, drawing blood.

When Žofie paused for just a moment to taste a droplet of blood, Adina forced the numb-arm spell back on Damir and used her mind to push Žofie away. Damir found himself without the use of his arms, and Žofie found herself wondering how her sister was still strong enough to reject her.

As Žofie came at her again, Adina brought her hands together and with a sudden burst, emitted a sphere of energy at Žofie's face. The impact snapped Žofie's head back and launched her body into a guard on the opposite side of the room.

Damir and Tatiana waited for Žofie to spring back in utter rage, but she remained as still as death on the floor. Damir ran to Žofie, but his arms were still useless. Žofie's neck appeared to be broken. He turned to Tatiana, then Adina, whose blue and green eyes were glowing brightly.

"Her eyes!" shouted Damir. "Stop her!"

Tatiana nodded and cautiously approached Adina while Damir elicited help from the guard.

"She is alive," said the guard, his hand over her neck. "Not completely broken."

Tatiana formed an energy shield and crouched beside Adina. "Do you remember me, auntie? You used to call me Little Tata." Tatiana blew a gentle poof of energy at Adina to distract her. When Adina's eyes began to cool, Tatiana continued. "I remember you, auntie. Along with your twin sister, you were my favorite auntie. I can only imagine how powerful you truly are when you are not so weak and chained to a wall—"

"Little Tata," murmured Adina, the glow in her eyes fading. "Yes, I remember you and your brother Damir." Adina glanced over at her brother, who was gently repositioning Žofie. "How many from our family were changed?"

"Not many, auntie. Most of us were killed in the war, remember?"

Adina remembered standing beside Žofie, their last battle together. The sisters were supposed to flee the battle together, but Žofie stayed behind, trying to distract the upyrian forces so that Adina might escape. Neither escaped... "Why, Tata? Why do you protect her? She is leading you to your destruction."

Tatiana smiled. "After Rurik captured and changed your sister, she changed my brother and me. We are her children now, Laecian turned upyrian. We call ourselves Laepyrian. Once you become Laepyrian, you will see, auntie. You will serve your sister and rule the empire with us."

"Impossible. I am no longer Laecian," said Adina, closing her eyes to rest.

From a knoll in the meadow, Cedric and Gert peered at the castle. The distance to the ramparts was an archer's range away and contained several large trees and rocks behind which they might hide as they advanced.

Gert pulled Cedric back and whispered, "I see no guards, you?"

Cedric shook his head.

"I will go first." said Gert.

Cedric shook his head again and placed his hand on Gert's arm. "Let me."

Gert sighed and agreed. He slung his bag of tools over his shoulder and got behind Cedric. "Wish Klaas was here."

## 35 - THE SECOND COMING

In the cylindrical space beneath the tower, Countess Marie stood before Domitian, covered by the robe he brought for her. Abigail continued to watch them, curious to know if this version of Marie was different from the original. Perhaps she no longer craved child's blood—one of her many egregious indulgences. Perhaps she was no longer consumed by power and wealth. Perhaps she no longer needed to count things. Abigail had not intended to create an exact copy of Marie or one as perfect as the woman standing before her appeared to be. Surely, the ingredients Abigail had purposely added must have changed her in some way. Marie had not uttered a single syllable or replied to Domitian's ceaseless dribble. Abigail recalled that newborn revenants needed time to find their thoughts and voice.

Marie suddenly turned to look at Abigail, her eyes penetrating as if looking for an explanation. Abigail sensed no attempt by Marie to meddle or meld minds. Relief came when Domitian turned Marie's attention back to him.

"Is she not every moment as beautiful as ever, Abigail?" said Domitian, walking around Marie, beholding her presence with childlike wonder. "Just look at her! She is flawless." Domitian laughed. "You did it, Abigail. You most certainly did. She even smells of perfection, like fresh child's blood." He turned to Abigail with glee on his face. "You honored your end of the agreement, and so shall I. Gaétan, go and gather our kindred, including Sir Michael. Guide them here and be quick. Bring food as well, and beware those stupid upyrian. They must not know of this."

"Yes, milord," said Gaétan. His eyes briefly met Abigail's as he turned to leave.

"Master Domitian," said Abigail. "My promise to you is fulfilled. May I leave?"

Domitian finally turned away from Marie to Abigail. "Not without a proper sendoff, my sweet. Be patient. I honor my agreements, and you may go after I have officially banished you. When I do, you will be put in the charge of Sir Michael. You see, I always honor my agreements."

Abigail felt betrayed. "I am to be banished with that traitor?"

"Yes," said Domitian, returning his gaze to Marie.

"He wishes to hunt down my brother," huffed Abigail. "That was not our agreement."

"Our agreement was that neither I nor any member of my clan would hunt your brother. I am keeping my word. For neither you nor Sir Michael will be members of this clan after you are both exiled."

Abigail wanted to kill Domitian...and what of Marie? Perhaps she was completely useless to Abigail's plight. She recalled how incoherent her brother had been immediately after his resurrection. As Abigail contemplated suicide if all else failed, she turned her thoughts back to Marie. Abigail was never very good at melding or meddling with minds. She never practiced the skill, but she had never resurrected a person before either. Now was the time to use her powers—or at least try. With no idea how to do it, she searched for a way into Marie's mind. She gently swathed Marie in energy and probed her, trying to communicate telepathically. She continued as Domitian stroked the side of Marie's face with the back of his hand.

"My love, my dark perfection, my muse, returned to me..." babbled Domitian.

Abigail clenched her eyes and focused all her powers on Marie until it was hard to maintain balance. *Countess Marie, can you hear me? Countess Marie?*

In the counting chamber, after Žofie was stabilized and resting, Damir flew at Adina, fists ready to pummel her, but he stopped inches from her defiant face. He had remembered Žofie's orders. Adina was not to be harmed. She belonged to Žofie. He pointed to the doorway. "Go bring us food," he told the guard. Tatiana laughed at him, and Damir ignored her, still glaring at Adina. "I would normally kill you for harming my queen mother." He glanced over at Žofie. "As you can see, she is alive and quickly healing. You will not resist her again. For if you do, even my queen's orders will not stop me from breaking *your* neck." Damir smiled as if relishing the thought. "I see in your eyes a glimmer of hope—your comrades are coming for you. I hope so. Do you know how they will die? You will kill them when you are finally upyrian."

Adina's eyes drifted away from Damir's smug face.

When Gert and Cedric approached the castle wall, they had not yet encountered any guards. Cedric wondered if the upyrian killed Domitian or kicked him and his clan out of the castle. He led them along the base of the wall to a location nearest the church building where new arrivals were quarantined. The plan was to scale the wall and enter behind the church building. Gert opened his bag and fished out a grapple attached to a rope. He swung the grapple and let it go up and over the wall. The clanging noise was alarming. They paused and listened but heard nothing. Gert pulled on the rope until the grapple became anchored and the rope went taut. Then, he used the rope to scale the wall.

When Gert reached the rampart, he peeked over and saw no one. He pulled himself over and waved for Cedric to climb. After Cedric scaled the wall and was standing beside Gert, he led them both down a flight of steps into the courtyard and church building. No one was guarding the church building either. They quickly moved to the front door and pushed it open. A waft of devil's piss flared Cedric's nostrils and a flood of memories overwhelmed him as he entered the room.

Gert touched Cedric's shoulder, concerned.

Cedric shook it off and smiled to show he was all right. Seeing nothing inside, Gert and Cedric exited the church building and moved into the castle through a service door. Cedric kept wondering where everyone had gone as they moved quickly into the main hall and down into the catacombs. Cedric led Gert through a narrow corridor into the darkness. They listened intently but heard no one. Quietly and slowly, Cedric backed around into the light of torches leading to the counting chamber.

In the counting chamber, the upyrian guard brought an old man to Damir. "This is all I found outside the castle walls," said the guard to Damir.

"He will have to do," said Damir as he pushed the man to his knees beside Queen Žofie. While his sister entranced the man further, Damir inserted his incisors into a vein. He cupped his hand over the pulsating blood and directed the warm liquid into Žofie's mouth. She swallowed and coughed as the blood brought nourishment and accelerated healing. Soon, Žofie would be well enough to turn Adina.

## 36 - THE MONSTER

Countess Marie stood before Domitian's Royal Flemish Clan, Abigail and Sir Michael behind them.

Michael's interest fell on Abigail. Abigail glared back at him and hissed. She was neither amused nor intimidated by the man who assassinated Count Marcel, her lover and master.

Gaétan brought the church guard to Domitian. He was human, early twenties, handsome, physically strong but easily manipulated. The man had hoped to become immortal, a member of the Royal Flemish Clan.

After Domitian thoroughly entranced the human and made him to sit on the floor behind Marie, he paced between the countess and clan members standing shoulder to shoulder in an arc around them. "I see on your faces the look of astonishment," said Domitian. "I see the look of fascination and wonder at the miracle standing before you. I am as astonished as you are. Just look at her, our Countess Marie de Vos, returned to us from Hades himself. All hail Hades," said Domitian in a soft tone.

All members repeated: "Hail Hades."

"Kneel," said Domitian to the clan.

All the members kneeled, including the outcasts, Sir Michael and Abigail.

Domitian turned to Marie and dropped to one knee. "Countess Marie de Vos, we...we honor you..." Domitian's voice trailed off as a strange clicking noise grew louder. Everyone looked to the corridors for possible intruders.

A chill coiled up Abigail's spine when she heard the odd sound. Only a moment ago, Abigail had meddled with Marie's mind and discovered the perplexing likelihood that Marie was growing acutely aware of those around her, and of her uniqueness. It was as if Marie was reincarnated vampire, amphibian, and insect all in one. When Abigail had called out her name in her mind, Marie answered with clicking and buzzing noises. After several minutes of that, Marie mumbled her first coherent words: *Art thou Abby?*

There was so much about the countess that Abigail had always feared. Should she fear her more or less now? Perhaps all ought to fear her because she was undeniably different. Abigail continued to meddle with Marie's mind, gently gleaning her thoughts, trying to make sense of them. *Domitian is your nemesis,* Abigail said through her mind. *He will betray you, as he had betrayed Count Marcel Marc de Vos. Marcel was your husband, your master. Do you remember him? All in this room conspired against Marcel. Do you see the filthy man leaning against the wall beside me? That is Sir Michael Livesey. He murdered Marcel. You must kill all of them before they kill you.*

"Domitian," whispered Marie, followed by grotesque gurgling and clicking from her throat.

A few hands rose to cover gaping mouths at the sound of Marie's voice. Domitian began to weep with joy. "Yes, my dear countess. It is *I*, your faithful servant, Domitian."

"Come here," said Marie in a guttural tone bracketed by clicks and buzzing noises.

Domitian stood up and went within an arm's length of her. He lowered his head and waited.

"Look at me," said Marie as her robe began to move outward from her torso.

Domitian looked into her eyes, which were now aglow.

The robe fell to the floor to reveal Marie's naked body and four appendages growing out of her rib cage. Covered in thick black hair, the appendages grew until they were as long as her arms. Mesmerized by her bright-yellow eyes, Domitian went to her, arms open to embrace her. From the tips of her four insect legs sprouted talons, long and pointed hooks. She extended her four appendages and pulled Domitian close to her, sinking her talons into his back.

Domitian yelped in pain. "Please, my countess, you are hurting me."

A vertical crease formed on Marie's face. Along her hairline, from the top down, her face began to peel away from her skull, revealing a very different face beneath. Her mouth was much wider now, her nose just two holes in a pulsating weave of glistening muscles, and her eyes resembling those of a frog, but many times larger. When she opened her massive mouth, rows of shark-like teeth lined the top of her jaw, while the middle of the lower jaw contained a toothless space.

Crying out in fear and pain, Domitian struggled to free himself from her deathly embrace, but it was no use. Marie's thick and sticky tongue dropped out of her mouth, filling the toothless gap of her lower jaw. She wrapped her tongue around Domitian's neck and lifted him off his feet with it. As his head entered her mouth, he began to punch and claw at her, but soon his head was inside her huge mouth—his neck placed in the toothless slot of her lower jaw. He twisted his body and kicked his legs as her tongue pulled Domitian's head apart from his neck, and her jaws closed to sever it clean off. His headless body fell to the floor, and as his body began to decompose she ground his head into a pulp and swallowed it.

All six vampires were still kneeling, paralyzed with fear. Marie's monstrous frog eyes found Abigail, and she moved to her in a swaying motion, like a strange praying mantis.

Abigail forced herself to detach from Marie's mind, using her magic to block the entrancing clicks and pops the monster was emitting, which seemed to have a stunning effect on everyone there. She took Gaétan by the hand and tried to pull him away, but he resisted—entranced by the monster.

Marie stepped on a clan member, crushing his body beneath her weight as she was only a pouncing leap away from Abigail.

Abigail slapped Gaétan to rouse him.

When the monster leaped at Abigail, Gaétan unexpectedly stepped between them. He took hold of Marie's spider arm and attempted to break it, but she was too big and strong. Her talons pierced Gaétan's back and he became wrapped up in her hairy arms. Abigail attacked the monster with a wall torch, but she was knocked back by its massive amphibious foot. She looked on helplessly and horrified as the beast lifted Gaétan and inserted his head into its gaping mouth.

Right after the monster detached Gaétan's head from his body, it pursued Abigail, who was back on her feet and sprinting into the corridor.

The darkness of the labyrinth tunnels embraced her, and she knew the catacombs so well now that she ran swiftly, scraping against walls only twice before reaching the first torchlight. She stopped and listened for lurking upyrian enemies. Expecting to run into them, she lifted the torch, broke off the fire, and shaped the tip of the handle into a pointed weapon.

From behind her came footsteps and scraping body parts against the masonry walls so quickly that she had no time to react. Sir Michael plowed into her, both lying on the ground now. They scrambled back to their feet, and not a moment too soon.

Marie was coming for them, her hairy arms reaching out like a spider, her muscular tongue jutting out of her slimy mouth, sticking to the back of Abigail's head. Abigail pushed forward with all her strength, ripping out a patch of hair by the roots.

The monster reeled in its tongue and spat out the hair. With legs twice as long as human legs and thighs of a massive frog, the beast leaped forward, scraping its head on the ceiling and its body on the walls, leaving broken torch sconces, bent door handles, and debris in its wake.

Michael and Abigail ran so fast, inertia carried them past the stairs leading up and out of the catacombs. With the monster merely a leap away from trouncing them, they had little choice than to duck into the nearest chamber. At that moment, a upyrian guard stepped out to investigate the commotion just as Michael and Abigail slid into his knees, causing him to buckle to the floor.

Instantly on their feet, Abigail and Michael entered the chamber and closed the heavy door, locking it behind them. When they turned around, they found themselves in the presence of Queen Žofie, Damir, Tatiana, and Adina—shackled to the wall—behind them.

From the corridor outside, they all heard screaming, then silence, followed by popping and grinding and clicking noises.

Startled and confused, Damir and Tatiana took defensive positions in front of Žofie, whose attention remained affixed on Adina.

Sir Michael slowly but purposely moved from the entrance door to one side of the room while Abigail moved to the other.

"Stop," said Damir. "Stay where you are." His eyes drifted from Michael to Abigail then to the door, a look of wonder on his face as the strange noises outside came closer.

Abigail considered warning them of the monster, but decided to let happen what may. She glanced over at Michael. He appeared to have the same strategy: let them remain focused on the door and what was about to break through it. It would create the perfect distraction.

"It comes," said Žofie and Adina at the same time, their voices and minds connecting, their eyes drifting to the door.

The monster's entrance was exactly as Abigail had imagined it. Chunks of door, plaster, and bricks exploded into the chamber, and the Marie-monster plunged her hulking body into the counting chamber.

She was an astonishing creature, standing nearly twice as tall as anyone there. Her only recognizable features were two slender arms and the visible portion of her face, which was peeled into two halves. Her massive head was amphibious with green and glistening strands of muscle covered in pustules and oozing craters. Though her head resembled a deformed salamander or frog, her long brown hair somehow remained attached in patches to its bumpy scalp.

"This...this is my counting chamber!" said Marie. Her voice, which was studded with gurgles, pops and clicks, was an octave lower than her former voice. "Where is my delicious Abby?"

Abigail pressed herself against a wall, as if trying to sink into it, and focused on the mangled doorway behind Marie.

"More importantly, where is the boy?" Marie's huge, golden bug eyes searched the room. "Where is Master Cedric Martens?" Her eyes shifted to Damir and before anyone could react, Marie opened her massive jaws and shot her tongue out at Damir. The sticky tip slammed into his chest, crushing it. Her tongue lifted the man off his feet and pulled him toward her hairy insect arms. Tatiana shot a blast of energy at Marie and attacked her with her sword, but it was not enough to stop her from methodically removing Damir's head in her jaws.

As Marie was chewing Damir's head into a pulp and Tatiana was chopping away at Marie's massive legs, Abigail and Michael were inching toward the entranceway.

Tatiana raised her sword at the beast and shot red jagged energy through the blade at the monster, searing Marie's flesh. The creature gave a piercing scream, making everyone cringe. Instantly, the monster shot its tongue out at Tatiana, wrapping it around her neck. As Marie reeled Tatiana toward her rows of filthy teeth, Žofie turned her attention back to her sister Adina and latched onto her throat, inserting her fangs and drinking her blood, while Tatiana's head was inside the monster's drooling jaws.

Michael made a mad dash to escape, but the monster hooked a leg around his arm. Abigail seized the opportunity and rushed between the monster's legs to the doorway and out into the corridor. She ran toward the stairs and slid to an abrupt halt.

Standing at the base of the stairs were Cedric and Gert, swords drawn, ready to kill.

## 37 - THOU ART A WICKED BOY

"Headmistress Abigail," said Cedric, equally startled by the chance encounter in the catacombs.

Abigail was in a quandary. The monster would surely seek Cedric—her killer—after she killed everyone in the counting chamber. Should he be warned? She lamented. "Cedric, what are you doing here? You must leave!"

"We are here to—"

"Leave!" shouted Abigail. "Go now! Please!"

"We will not! What is happening?" insisted Cedric, standing in her way.

"My sister is in there!" blurted Gert, alarmed by the harrowing noises.

"Wait, Gert," said Cedric, using his sword to block him. "Who is in the counting chamber?"

Abigail clenched her eyes shut. "A monster is in there."

"Adina is in there," hollered Gert, pushing past them.

"It wants *you*, Cedric," cried Abigail. "You cannot defeat it. It will surely kill you."

"Me?" Cedric muttered, eyes following Gert as he crept toward the counting chamber. "Gert, wait! We must enter together."

"Come, Cedric, now!"

"You have been warned," whispered Abigail in Cedric's ear as they parted ways.

In the counting chamber, Žofie was no longer focused on Adina, who was still shackled helplessly to the wall, still alive, covering her neck wound with her hand.

Marie slowly chewed Tatiana's head into a pulp, as if savoring the flavors, eyes rolling back into her massive green head.

Žofie changed into the shape of a small dragon, taking to wing in the chamber with barely enough room to fly, scraping her wingtips against the walls.

Marie-monster twisted and turned, keeping her frog eyes on the dragon. She leaped into the air at the flying beast, trying to grab hold of it.

The dragon blew fire into the monster's hideous face. Marie squealed and clicked, then twirled and shot her tongue at the dragon. She missed and her tongue stuck to the wall.

The dragon was circling the monster, blowing fire on its outstretched tongue, when Cedric and Gert entered the chamber.

Gert skirted around the distracted monster and ran to his sister.

Cedric saw the headless bodies, the horrific monster, and the winged dragon overhead.

Gert lowered himself to Adina, removed her hand from her neck, and saw the bite marks. The severity of the bite was anyone's guess. He knew how vampires sired children. After draining the victim's blood to near death, vampire's blood was fed to the victim to initiate the change. Was Adina drained to the point of death and fed vampire's blood? Were they too late to save her? Gert leaned in and said something to Adina and she responded with a nod.

Cedric went to them and kneeled. "Gert," he said, "before you release her, we must be certain." Cedric reached into his pocket and retrieved the moldy clove of garlic Elida had given to him. He broke it open and held it to Adina's nose.

At first, she recoiled, and Cedric was instantly afraid. After she saw what it was, she leaned in and breathed in the aroma. "I like garlic when not so moldy," said Adina to Cedric.

Gert brought out the glass vial of orange powder Elida had given to him. He broke the vial over the chain at the shackle and began chanting. Then Adina joined in. A vapor formed as the shackle and chain links melted away.

"Get away from her!" shouted the dragon.

Cedric felt a surge of power enter his body and he threw a dagger at the dragon, embedding it in its chest. The dragon veered away and slammed into a wall. On the floor, the beast changed back into Žofie, whose resemblance to Adina stunned Cedric. The dagger between her bosoms nearly brought Cedric to his knees with guilt and shame for harming he—until she took hold of the dagger and slowly extracted it whilst grinning at Cedric.

Žofie extended her arm, dagger resting in the palm of her hand, blade pointing directly at Cedric. He was ready to jump out of the way if she threw it at him, but Žofie moved her aim away from Cedric, pointing it instead at Marie, who was furiously cackling, clicking, and popping, leaning against a wall, resting from serious burns received from the dragon's breath. Žofie blew on the dagger, launching it from her hand and straight into the monster's head.

Cedric was stunned to see such magic, and disappointed to see that the dagger had little effect on the monster, which was moving toward him now.

Žofie changed into a winged gargoyle and flew at Gert, but an energy field surrounding him deflected her attack. "She is mine!" growled the gargoyle just as Gert swung his sword at it, causing it to veer away nearly into the oncoming monster.

Marie roared and flailed her hairy arms, catching Žofie by her leathery wing.

Žofie instantly changed into a snake and fell onto Marie's shoulders. The snake quickly coiled around the monster's neck and began to constrict.

"Gert, take Adina to safety!" shouted Cedric. "I will distract the monster! Go!"

Marie gouged her talons into the snake's body, easily removing it. She threw the snake into her mouth, but before she could close her jaws, the reptile changed into a bat and escaped.

Marie finally noticed Cedric and took aim at him. "There you are." The monster clicked and popped and moved to Cedric, who moved away from Gert and Adina as they tried to get around the beast. "My sweet boy," the monster's guttural voice clicked. "It *is* you, Cedric Martens of Linder. Thou art a wicked boy!"

Unbelieving his ears, Cedric had little time to ponder the creature that reminded him of Countess Marie. It leaped at Cedric with astonishing agility, its spider hooks barely missing him but snagging away his shield as he dodged her attack. He tumbled to the floor and back onto his feet, running past the bat, which changed back into a gargoyle and thwarted Adina's escape by attacking Gert.

Realizing Gert's ongoing battle with the gargoyle and the dangers of a monster that could kill them all, Cedric coaxed the monster out of the counting chamber.

"Countess Marie!" shouted Cedric at the monster.

"Murderer!" rumbled Marie. It followed Cedric into the corridor. "You cannot outrun me, boy."

Cedric ran as fast as he could, leading the monster up the stairs and into the castle's grand foyer.

In the counting chamber, the gargoyle attacked Gert again and again, evading his sword and daggers, until he tripped and fell. The creature grabbed Adina's arm and lifted her with two massive flaps of her wings. Gert threw two daggers at it. Both daggers bounced off a field of energy. Gert ran to the table, jumped onto it, and leaped high enough to grab hold of Adina's ankle. The sudden weight was too much for the gargoyle to carry. Adina and Gert fell to the floor, and the gargoyle landed beside the doorway, instantly changing back to Žofie.

Žofie began to form a static ball of red energy between her hands.

Adina held her hand out just as Žofie propelled the ball of barbed light at them, but it split into two, both halves buzzing past Gert and Adina, then turning around and targeting Žofie. She threw up a shield to block the two halves and scowled before turning into a bat and escaping into the corridor.

Gert tried to pursue the bat, but Adina held onto his wrist.

"No," Adina whispered, almost entirely drained of energy.

Gert turned back to his sister and helped her up. "What happened? Her energy appeared to fail her."

"I did exactly what she was doing to me. I used her powers against her."

"Brilliant!"

"We must go help Cedric. He drew the monster out."

In the castle's foyer, Cedric faced Marie—a clicking and buzzing bloodthirsty monster. He held his sword at waist height, circling the grotesque creature. Unaware of its deadly tongue, he underestimated a safe distance. If only he still had a shield.

Without warning, its tongue shot out and hit Cedric in the middle of his chest with such force to knock his senses and sword loose. Breathless and weaponless, the thick and sticky tongue pulled him toward the monster's massive mouth—agape and slobbering pink with chunky goo.

When Cedric tried to pull away, the tongue lifted him off his feet and into the clutches of those hairy insect arms. Cedric punched and wriggled in seething pain, as two talons pressed into his back.

"Countess Marie!" yelled Cedric. "Stop!" His pleadings went unheard as the tongue repositioned around his neck and his head approached the balmy and putrid mouth. Sharp teeth scraped against his face as his head was inserted into the crux of its lower jaw. Cedric clenched his eyes and submitted to a horrible fate, perhaps a deserving one after what he had done to Countess Marie. A head for a head, a life for a life, a never-ending cycle of retaliation...

The voices in the boy's head whispered frantically, encouraging him to fight back, not to give up, confirming that he was right in defending his friends from certain death. Cedric pushed with all his strength against the bottom lip, but its tongue and talons would not yield. He kicked and punched while the upper jaw began to close like a clamshell.

Abigail entered the castle in time to see Cedric's body helplessly dangling from the monster's mouth. She saw Gert hacking at the monster's legs with his sword and Adina shooting smoky puffs of energy at it. It was soon to be too little too late for Cedric.

Instantly and instinctually, Abigail closed her eyes and reached deep into the darkest depths of her being, drawing upon her entire life, her mother's life, her father's life, her brother's life, and every life she had ever known, drawing upon all her memories and energies, and reaching down into the earth, past the depths of soil and rock and water, farther yet into super-heated magma and the realm of Hades.

In complete silence, Abigail opened her eyes and saw that everything around her had stopped, as if everyone had turned to stone. Gert's sword was inches from Marie's leg but unmoving. Adina's useless puffs of energy were suspended in mid-flight. The monster was as still as Cedric was. From the energy she gathered and stored, she relaxed and let it all rush out. Beams of white light streamed from her body into the monster's body.

"Hades, *salvare* Cedric Martens *et accipe* Marie de Vos *et me. Gratias tibi,* Hades. *Gratias tibi.*"

The castle shook and a hot wind blew up from the earth, and everyone except for Abigail remained frozen in time. Ahead of her, a faint, almost invisible shape rose up from the floor. It was a man, twice as large as the Marie-monster. It stood in the foyer for only a few blinks, but to Abigail he stood for an eternity. As the god faded back into his realm of the dead, time and motion resumed—slowly at first, so slowly that Abigail might walk around the entire foyer before Gert's sword moved nary an inch. As the energy streaming out of her body began to fade, motion sped up until all the energy in Abigail's body had expired.

Marie and Abigail collapsed to the floor. Cedric fell to the floor as well, bleeding from Marie's bite wound.

It was at that moment that Cedric saw the monster lying like a giant blob of mucous in the center of the foyer. Next, he saw Abigail, lying on her back. He crawled to her as fast as his aching body allowed, dripping and smearing blood as he went. He looked down on her beautiful face. Her eyes were open and seemingly focused on his face. She was perfectly still, and he imagined her smiling back.

"Headmistress Abigail," he whimpered, calling her by the title she held at the castle when orphaned children there served the vampires. She had watched out for him when he was a slave there. She had prepared him for the journey to England with Countess Marie de Vos. She was his friend, yes, but not the sort of friend to give her life for his. "Abigail," he said again, lifting her head, cradling her in his arms. "Why?"

Abigail was a magical being, but also a vampire. Cedric knew that. Yet, she was not decomposing like vampires normally did. She was instead gradually fading. A tear drop fell toward her face, but it fell through and splashed down on his leg. Abigail continued to fade until she completely disappeared.

Adina and Gert crouched beside him. "Cedric," said Adina softly, holding her hand over his neck wound. "The monster and Abigail have vanished."

"Vanished?" Cedric said hoarsely, trying to believe his eyes, looking for Marie's remains. "Your sister, Žofie, where is she?" asked Cedric.

"She fled," said Gert. "Her guards are all dead."

"Come, we must go," said Adina. "We must join Klaas."

## 38 - THE EPIPHANY

In Elida's cottage, Klaas felt well enough to enjoy his fern soup at the table.

Elida sat in her rocking chair beside the inglenook, ignoring the knocking at the door.

"I will see who it is," said Klaas finally, getting up from the table and gingerly moving to the door. When he opened it, Adina came forward and hugged him, causing him to yelp with pain.

Gert entered, followed by Cedric, who went directly to Elida and kneeled before her.

She placed her gnarled fingers on his head, leaned forward, and gently touched the wounds on the back of his neck. "Small wound," she murmured. "Fill that pot with nettles and ferns and water," said Elida, pointing at another pot in the kitchen.

Cedric nodded and stood up.

Elida reached out to him and smiled. "You saved her—you saved Abigail."

"She saved me."

"I cannot know all the details, but I dreamed of her agreement with Hades. She gave herself to him in exchange for Marie's soul with which to use and do as she pleased."

"Would she not eventually die and end up with Hades anyway?" asked Cedric, not really believing in the Greek mythology. "Why would Hades bother with such an agreement?"

"You forget, boy, Abigail was a vampire. Vampires can live for centuries. Her agreement was to give herself sooner rather than later. She almost faltered but then she saw you, did she not give everything to save you?"

"Yes."

"She might have fled and reneged on her agreement had you not been there. She might have left the monster behind. Can you imagine the horrors had she done that? You, boy, you are the reason she returned. You gave her the strength and will to make good on her promise, to sacrifice herself for a greater good, absolving her of her sins."

Cedric recalled Elida's words from last time: *Better to die doing what is right than to live doing what is wrong.* He nodded, understanding Abigail's decision but not feeling worthy of her sacrifice. He gazed over at Adina and her brothers—or rather, twelfth generation grandsons—still chatting as if they had not seen one another in years.

"Your heart is heavy with sadness, Cedric my boy," said Elida, cloudy eyes still staring into the fire. "Go, go collect the ingredients. A hot soup will cheer you up."

After enjoying Elida's soup and the siblings were preparing to leave, an epiphany as resounding as a bell toll convinced Cedric not to go. It started out as an idea which expanded into an opus of possibilities. He approached Elida with it. She had always been helpful, caring for Klaas, making the best soups Cedric had ever tasted. It was becoming clear to him that she would play an important role were his ideas to become real.

Cedric draped his arm over Elida's shoulder and gently moved her away from the siblings. "Madam Elida," said Cedric. "Thank you. Thank you for all you have done for me and for us."

"Been thinking, have you?" quipped Elida.

Cedric was startled again by her intuition. Was she reading his thoughts or perhaps planting them in his head? "Yes, I have been thinking...about something very interesting. Your proverb—better to die doing what is right than to live doing what is wrong—inspired my idea, that in order to live right, one must learn to do what is right."

Elida allowed a seldom-seen smile wrinkle her cheeks. She placed her hand on his chest. "Pure at heart, honest and caring, clever yet humble."

"Thank you, Madam Elida. I want to establish an academy, a place where orphans can live and learn the arts and trades."

"Why?"

"I wish to give those who have nothing the knowledge and skills to live right."

Elida chuckled. "You will need money."

"Money, I have. Good teachers, I have none."

Elida shook her head. "I have no patience for teaching."

"You have so much to offer, Madam Elida. You are the oracle from an ancient Norse family of sorcerers. And you make the most delicious soups."

Elida laughed and nodded as if she had solved a difficult riddle. "The castle, you want to establish your academy at the castle."

"Yes."

"The castle is a place of horrors and death, my boy. I thought you wanted to leave all that behind and travel as far as the ocean is wide."

"The castle is abandoned and as big as an ocean to me."

"It is not completely abandoned, Cedric. One vampire still lurks there."

Concern befell Cedric as he imagined who the lone vampire might be. He hoped it was not Sir Michael or Domitian. "Who is it?"

"Her name is—"

Adina inadvertently interrupted them. "Please forgive my intrusion. Cedric, we are ready to leave."

"Thank you," he said to Adina, still captivated by her aura, still aching and praying to be with her.

When Adina left them, Cedric turned back to Elida. "Her name...?"

"She is a relatively young vampire. I would not trust her, though. She will feed on your thoughts and on your blood if hungry enough."

"Is it Gerda?"

Elida nodded slowly.

"I know who she is. She was married to the man in the sunroom. They had a son."

"She is a mindbender."

"Can she not be reasoned with?"

"Why bother? She has no master or clan and cannot survive for long without one. I suspect she will leave to join Sir Michael Livesey if she knows what is best for her."

"Where is Sir Michael?"

"He is probably in Oostende, intent on sailing to America to seek power and fortune."

"Will you help me, Madam Elida? You are wise and kind and—my hope is that you will at most be my oracle. Besides, will it not be safer to live in the castle than to remain out here?"

Elida stared out the window, not quite focused on the brothers standing outside beside horses that had been borrowed from the castle's stables.

"This cottage has been home to me and my predecessors for centuries," said Elida. "It is written in the truce of the Lunabellum that my family shall provide oracles to the Royal Flemish Clan in exchange for their protection."

"There is no clan," said Cedric.

Elida turned to him. "I must consult with my family on the matter. I suggest that you return to the House of Meridiem in Ghent. You should discuss your lofty vision with them and elicit as many supporters as you can. You will receive my answer by messenger."

"Thank you, Madam Elida. One more question...?"

"Yes?"

"Pierce van Fleming," said Cedric. "Do you know where he is?"

"Even if I knew, his whereabouts should remain unsaid."

# 39 - THE MERIDIEM

*A*	*Year Later...*
Walking through the halls of Vos Castle, Cedric stopped to peek into a chamber through a boxed opening in the wooden door. Inside sat six children at desks, boys and girls younger than twelve years of age, raising their hands to answer Professor Dunkel's questions concerning the forces of nature. Farther down the hall, he peered into a classroom of adolescent boys and girls, studying weaponry with Professor Gert Bezuidenhout.

On the first level, Cedric sauntered past the kitchen, wherein Elida the oracle and Auntie the Fortune Brother's Aunt Dunkel were teaching two girls and two boys how to cook and bake. He tried to sneak by without being seen and failed yet again.

"Cedric Martens!" shouted Elida from the kitchen.

Cedric turned to find Elida standing in the hallway, drying her hands on her apron, Auntie peeking out from the kitchen. "Good day, Madam Elida and Auntie."

"It has been a month. Where are my new ovens?" asked Elida, obviously frustrated.

"Yes, well, I am on my way to speak to Klaas about that," said Cedric.

"Good, because the old oven is junk, and your Auntie and I are exhausted having to use magic to maintain temperature and quicken the process because we have only one broken-down oven to feed dozens of hungry little mouths. It is neither fair to us nor the students."

Cedric lowered his chin. "I understand. I will check on the ovens straight away."

Elida nodded sharply and returned to the kitchen.

Cedric climbed the stairs to the second level, down a corridor past the boys' dormitories and into the library where Klaas would surely be. It was his favorite place to relax during the day. In the center of the room, boots propped up on a heavy desk, sat Klaas. He was smoking a pipe and reading a book in the light of the morning sun. "Good day, Klaas."

Klaas closed his book and put down his pipe. "Ah, Chancellor Cedric Martens of Linder, how dost thee fair?"

"Quite well, and you?"

"Reminiscent," said Klaas somberly.

"Yes, well, hopefully teaching ways to slay monsters provides some solace."

"No, not really, but what else can I do, and what can I do you for, Chancellor Martens?"

"Elida—"

"Right...the ovens. They are on the way and very expensive."

"Can we not afford them?"

Klaas laughed. "Do you have any idea how much money is in our treasury?"

"Quite a lot," said Cedric, recalling Countess Marie's counting fetish of the castle's wealth.

"We are wealthier than the state of Flanders. We can afford to build an entire army and a fleet of warships with which to invade the east and remove every upyrian from the face of the earth if you will approve it."

"Klaas, we are not in the business of building armies and waging wars. We are a school for orphans, and we have limited means for earning money."

"In twenty years' time, Cedric, mark my word, you will have an army comprised of students—highly trained Meridiem fighters, and there will be war—war the likes of which no one has ever seen."

"I think you meant to say highly trained and skilled artisans the likes of which no one has ever seen."

Klaas chuckled. "Yes, that, too."

"Thank you for ordering the ovens, Klaas. When should we expect them?"

"When they arrive, dear friend," said Klaas, tongue in cheek.

Cedric laughed and watched Klaas lift his pipe to his mouth and puff its contents to an orange glow, blowing smoke in various geometrical shapes—square, triangle, star. It was becoming clearer to Cedric that Klaas and Gert were sorcerers in their own right. Not to the level of Adina's magic—theirs were still developing, but the more they practiced, the better they got.

Klaas gazed thoughtfully and pointed the mouthpiece of his pipe at Cedric. "I see less sadness in your eyes these days."

Cedric knew exactly what Klaas meant. He had been recovering from a broken heart. Though he pleaded with Adina to stay at the castle, she wanted no part of the academy and obviously with him. She stayed at the family home in Ghent. Cedric wrote letters to her, of course, but she never responded to any of them. Whenever he went to visit her, she was never there.

"She still cares for you, you know?" said Klaas, a glint of empathy in his eyes.

"I'd rather not know," murmured Cedric.

"Adina renewed her vows to the Meridiem and, to a life of celibacy. No one but she can change her mind, of that we all know."

"Still, the flavor lingers bitter sweetness," Cedric confessed with a sigh. "Thank you, Dean Bezuidenhout, for encouraging me not to be so...pathetic," he said, half smiling.

"Excellent! Now, I must go and meet with our newest professors: Lukas Putnam, Stephanie DuPont, and...Georgina van Bristol. They were employed when you up and left us for two weeks."

"Respite..."

"How was the weather during your respite in Ghent?"

"Have you heard anything from your sister?" asked Cedric, suddenly ashamed at himself for inquiring about Adina.

"We need you here, Cedric. You should have been here when the professors were employed."

"Yes, of course, my apologies. However, I trust your judgment in such matters."

"You are the Chancellor, Cedric. Your hands must touch all aspects of this academy. It is, after all, your creation."

"Our creation, our academy," said Cedric, amused at Klaas for acting uncharacteristically sensible and sensitive. Perhaps his role as head dean was growing on him. "I will introduce myself to them today—you have my word."

"Good! Just so you know...Lukas Putnam of Marblehead, Massachusetts—wherever that is—is a self-proclaimed warlock. He is skilled in the dark arts, but in a good way, according to my brother." Klaas puffed on his pipe and snorted smoke out of his nostrils like a dragon. "Stephanie DuPont is a seamstress from Mechelen, whose skills exceed any tailor's I have met. We should all be dressed in royal threads very soon. Now, concerning Georgina van Bristol's archery skills, shall we say all bull's-eyes? I think you will fancy her, especially her." Klaas winked and chuckled.

Cedric nodded. "And where is she from?"

"Why not ask her yourself?"

"Thank you again for employing them in my absence."

"Yes, well, please take on more of the managerial work, whilst I smoke and reminisce the tedium away." He took a dagger from his belt and tossed it behind him, without looking, at a target hanging on the wall, which was already impaled by five daggers along its edges. The sixth dagger he just flicked hit its mark dead center.

Cedric laughed. "Good day, Klaas."

"Good day, Chancellor."

The castle outside appeared much improved with a good cleaning, fresh paint, leafy vines starting up its stone walls, and a livery of flags representing Flanders and the academy's coat of arms. Cedric noticed a young instructor with five students in the courtyard. They were pushing a handcart loaded with bows, arrows, ropes, nets, and iron grapples, among other tactical equipment. Cedric was certain the instructor was Georgina. She appeared to be younger than he imagined, perhaps closer to his age, boyish-looking in an archer's uniform, knee-high boots, breeches, a black shirt, brown vest, gloves; yet she also looked undeniably feminine with dark, wavy hair tied back out of her delicate face. He stood and watched as they pushed on toward the target range.

After his rounds, Cedric found Professors Putman and DuPont in the faculty chambers, enjoying conversation over a bowl of Elida's vegetable soup. After introducing himself to them, Cedric went outside in search of the archery instructor. However, when he arrived at the archery range, no one was there. He gazed up at the sky. Birds were chirping, crows were soaring, and the forest in the distance beckoned to him.

He had strolled through the woods nearly every other day these past several months. All the horrible things that had happened to him in and around those trees no longer troubled him, and Adina was no longer in his every thought, because Cedric's focus was the Meridiem Academy of the Arts and Trades. Whether his new focus helped to bury his feelings for Adina or the heartbreak helped to pursue a new focus, he had much to be happy about. The Bezuidenhout family helped him secure the title for the castle and its surrounding lands. Cedric now owned the property and held it in trust for the academy as beneficiary. The academy was doing better than anyone had expected in its first year of operation. The cost of admittance was to study and work hard, not only to develop artisan skills and scholarly knowledge but also to participate in the maintenance of the castle and the sustenance of its budding population.

Realizing he had been inside his head discussing the academy with those internal voices which no longer disparaged him but rationally debated and helped him to make hard decisions, he came back to reality and entered the forest, wending along a deer's path and right into an unpleasant trap.

Instantly, Cedric was swooped up off his feet in a net!

His first thought was danger, followed by confusion and stupidity for letting down his guard, forgetting that the forest was not always the safest place in which to stroll. His eyes darted in all directions, looking for a way out. Seeing that he was ensnared in a net attached to a rope slung over a tree branch and tied off at the trunk, he reached for his knife just as crunching footsteps approached.

Beneath him gathered a group of children, looking up and pointing at him.

"Who is that?" asked a boy, trying to get a better look at Cedric's face.

"Is that Chancellor Martens?" asked another.

"I think it is," replied the first boy. "Yes, that is the chancellor."

"Oh no," said a woman, alarm in her voice. "Hold on, sir. We'll let you down."

Cedric saw that it was Georgina, the archery instructor, who was evidently also a traps expert.

"Thank you," said Cedric, sweating with embarrassment.

"Come, students," said Georgina. "Take hold of this rope and hold tightly."

Three boys took hold of the line as Georgina untied it from the tree.

"Hold on," repeated Georgina as she untied the last knot.

Cedric held his breath, expecting to be dropped, but the boys let him down gently to the ground.

Georgina and the students circled around him and spread open the net.

"Are you all right?" asked Georgina, extending her gloved hand to Cedric.

He took her hand and got back to his feet. After he patted off a few leaves, he looked into her eyes. They were quite large, like green pools of wondrous secrets in which to swim.

"I apologize for this...," said Georgina, looking to the net, French accent infusing the forest sounds. "I am teaching my students how to capture game such as deer and pig."

"You clearly captured me," said Cedric, feeling awkward for his choice of words. "My apologies, I should introduce myself."

"This is Chancellor Martens," a boy said to Georgina.

"And this is Professor Van Bristol," said a girl to Cedric.

"Thank you, students," said Cedric. "I have heard many good things about you, Professor van Bristol. May I accompany you at the faculty dinner tonight?"

"That would be a pleasure," said Georgina.

That night, Cedric sat beside Georgina at the dining table among the faculty. Uncle Dunkel sat at the other end of the table with Auntie, weaving tales to Gert and Klaas and their families. Elida retired to her room at the top of a tower.

Cedric was nineteen now, and more reflective than ever. Never a day passed without thoughts of his parents and sister, and of his friends Lily and Jacob who was now married and living happily together on a farm near Rotterdam. He thought of his friend Pierce van Fleming who left in haste for America nearly two years ago, and his sister Abigail—beautiful, troubled, vexed Abigail. Her sacrifice for him was as incredible as the magic that caused her and the Marie-monster to vanish before his eyes. Elida had surmised that Abigail's agreement with Hades required no trace of her or the monster's remains on earth. Then, there was Adina and the longing she left in his heart...

"Master Cedric," said Georgina, reeling him away from his thoughts. "Care for some wine?" She was holding a bottle.

Cedric blushed and nodded. "Forgive me, yes, please." He finally noticed since seating himself beside her that Georgina had let down her wavy dark hair, bundled it all to one side, exposing her neck to him. Aside from her woolen hooded cloak, which she had removed, she had exchanged her archer's clothing for an elegant burgundy dress with fitted bodice of green velvet. "Madam Georgina, please forgive me. My mind had been an endless source of distractions of late."

Georgina laughed. "I understand. You are very busy. What you have done here is miraculous. You should be proud of your accomplishment."

Cedric's eyes roamed the room. "None of this would have been possible without the support of my friends. Please, tell me something about yourself—anything at all."

"My father is Dutch. My mother is Flemish. We are dairy farmers with land near Brecht. The French tried to enlist my father in their military. He refused and joined the rebellion instead." Her face went serious, and she sighed. "The uprising was crushed and my father...he was executed."

"I am deeply sorry for your loss."

Georgina managed a half smile and took up a cup of wine with a defiant look. "The French burned down our farm, but spared the lives of my mother and brothers."

"Where did your family go?"

"We went to Ghent to stay with the Bezuidenhouts. My family is related...mother's side of my family. Klaas and Gert are distant cousins. Adina is like my fairy-god-mother," she said with a glowing smile.

Cedric stiffened. "Are you two very close?"

"Adina?"

"Yes."

"We were, but this past year, she has distanced herself from everyone except *Grootmoeder* Lidia. They traveled abroad. After returning two months ago, I spoke with her. She suggested that I come here—that you were in need of teachers. With my mother's and brothers' blessings, here I am."

Cedric fear of a growing satisfaction that perhaps Adina was not ignoring him motivated his desire for Georgina's company. "I know from firsthand experience that you are an expert trapper."

Georgina blushed. "I apologize for this morning, Chancellor Cedric—"

"You are obviously a master of the bow as well. I am not so bad myself."

"Are you?"

"Indeed."

"Care to demonstrate your skills tomorrow morning, Chancellor?"

"I am still not used to that title. Would you mind calling me by my given name? I would very much like to match skills at the archery range with you. However, I have business to attend to on the morrow—the day after, perhaps?"

"Agreed," said Georgina, beaming.

Cedric and Georgina told of tales over four cups of wine before retiring their separate ways for the evening, and Cedric never felt more optimistic about the near future.

## 40 - TRUTH

The next morning, Cedric received a cabriolet from the stable master. He got in the buggy, released the brake, and tapped the two black stallions into motion. Students waved at Cedric as he continued on through the barbican and main gate and across the new bridge over the moat, which had been excavated and refilled with water from a natural spring. He turned back to view the castle and the young shade trees planted along its wall. A new sign above the gate shone brightly:

**Meridiem Academy**
✳ of the ✳
**Arts and Trades**

Farther out were the academy's row crops tended to by students under the tutelage of knowledgeable farming instructors. Beyond the crops were the pastures whereon the academy's cows and sheep grazed.

Cedric traveled swiftly in the fair weather and arrived in Brussels by noon. He drove to the abbey in the city's center and parked beside a stable. As he made way to the abbey's entrance, sounds of children playing drifted nearer. His only thought was for the three children he had left at the abbey over a year ago.

He entered a vestibule of three hallways and heard footsteps. It was Abbess Maria Theresa, coincidently turning a corner and walking toward Cedric. She smiled when she saw him, lifting her hands in a way that reminded Cedric of the holy mother.

"Mister Martens, what a pleasant surprise!" said Maria.

"Abbess Maria," said Cedric, taking her hands in his.

"Are you here to see your children, Mister Martens?"

"Yes," said Cedric, feeling especially happy to fulfill his promise—that he would return for them.

"They will be so pleased to see you."

"Abbess Maria, I wish to take them home with me today."

"Oh?"

"Yes, I have returned from my journey and will not be leaving again." Cedric knew the church viewed Vos Castle in the darkest of ills. "I have established an academy, a school for orphans, south of here. I call it Meridiem Academy of the Arts and Trades. I would like for you to direct children to the academy if you have no room for them here."

"That is an interesting name...Meridiem, is it?"

"Yes."

"Does this academy serve God, Mister Martens? Does it have a church in which to worship and receive communion?"

"Yes, of course, Abbess Maria...and the children will be cared for and taught useful trade skills."

Maria smiled and brought her hands together. "Preparing them to leave will take some time. Would you like to wait or come for them later?"

"I will wait. Thank you, Abbess Maria."

Two hours later, Cedric was in the receiving room, sitting at a table beside an inglenook when all three children entered like a flock of kid goats, jumping on Cedric, pushing him to the floor. They had grown quite a bit since the last time he had see them.

"Cedric, Cedric!" they kept shouting his name. "Are you going to take us home? All of us?" Anna, Katarina, and Jon were now ten years of age.

"All right, now, you are all too heavy. Please let me up." The kids kept holding onto Cedric as he struggled to get to his feet.

"Mister Martens," said the abbess, a wooden box resting on the floor at her ankle. "Here are their belongings, Mister Martens. You will need to sign for their release."

"Yes, of course," said Cedric. He turned to the kids. "Please take that box to the foyer and wait for me there."

After signing release forms and leaving the abbess a sizeable cash donation, Cedric loaded the wooden box and the excited children into the buggy and started off in a direction he never dreamed of wanting to go. Yet, he could not stop from smiling, and the children could not stop from singing songs the entire way.

Passing by a windmill and nearing the castle, memories of his friend Pierce van Fleming and his sister Abigail came to mind. They had saved these children's lives. Cedric missed them very much. If not for Pierce, Cedric might still be in England or worse yet, dead. If not for Pierce's sister Abigail, he would have lost his head to a hideous monster! Knowing that Abigail was forever gone, Cedric wondered if Pierce was still alive and well. "Will I ever see him again?" mused Cedric, his voice drowned out by the children's singing.

Back at the castle, the first person to greet Cedric was Georgina. In anticipation of his arrival and archery match, she had been shooting arrows at makeshift hay bales on a cart in the courtyard.

After Cedric helped the children out of the buggy, Georgina came to them. "Are these our new students?" she asked, imparting twinkling smiles to each child.

Cedric laughed. "They are!"

Georgina knelt down and smiled at the smallest girl.

Cedric nudged her forward.

"What is your name?" asked Georgina.

"Anna," whispered the girl.

Georgina enticed Anna to come closer with outstretched arms. Anna went to her, and Georgina embraced her warmly.

While Georgina was charming the children, Cedric was scanning the courtyard. He noticed a woman standing between the church and the castle. She was staring back at him, eyes reflecting the setting sun.

Georgina turned to see what Cedric was looking at. "I saw her earlier. Who is she?" asked Georgina, holding Anna's and Katarina's hands.

Katarina pointed at the woman. "That is Gerda!" she said cheerfully.

"Gerda!" shouted the boy, waving his hand.

Cedric also knew who Gerda was—a vampire, the clan's mindbender. She was believed to have fled to Europe with Sir Michael Livesey. A chill blew down Cedric's back as Gerda stood there in the growing shadows of dusk, waving back at the children.

"Georgina," said Cedric, "would you kindly take the children to their bedchambers? Their rooms are all ready for them, each one with their name above the door."

"Certainly," said Georgina.

"Children," said Cedric. "Go with Georgina. I will bring your box of things later."

"Come, children, follow me," said Georgina.

Cedric kept an eye on Gerda while someone entered the courtyard on a large black horse. Cedric needed to talk to Gerda. He feared that one day vampires might return to the castle, which was why he had sealed off the catacombs. The last thing he needed were vampires living beneath the school.

As Cedric took a step toward Gerda, a familiar voice caught him by surprise.

"Cedric!"

With eyes on Gerda who seemed to be in no hurry to leave, Cedric waved a finger at her, signaling for her to wait. When Gerda nodded and leaned against the church wall, he turned to address the rider who had already dismounted on the opposite side of the horse.

The rider led the animal by the reins to Cedric, finally revealing herself.

"Adina?" blurted Cedric, feeling mixed by her unannounced visit.

Adina removed her gloves and looked around the courtyard at children playing nearby, and then at Gerda, who was still leaning against the church. She quickly turned to Cedric and her eyes alarmingly darted back at Gerda.

"I saw her," said Cedric, looking at Gerda again. The vampire was standing there for all to see, not exactly threatening. "I will speak to her."

Adina wrinkled her brow as if a vampire in their midst should not be acceptable by any stretch. "And I came to speak to you, Cedric."

Cedric assumed that she came to see her brothers. "Yes, yes, of course. Shall we go indoors?"

"May we speak outdoors...privately?" she said as children approached them, pointing at the beautiful Belgium black horse.

Cedric nodded. "Yes of course." He took the reins from her, waved the children away, and led the horse and Adina to the rose garden north of the castle. Cedric lashed the horse to a post and escorted Adina along a gravel path between the rose bushes where no one could eavesdrop. Near the center of the garden, Cedric stopped and waited anxiously for Adina to speak. He had not seen or corresponded with her in a year. He remembered how he had asked her to take residence at the castle, to develop a curriculum and head up an academic department of her own, but she declined. He still believed that she wanted nothing more than to avoid him.

"The castle is beautiful," she said with a happy sigh. "I remember how menacing it used to look. I am impressed, and very proud of your accomplishments here, Cedric."

"Thank you," he said, trying to look past her beauty, her golden hair in random strands of thinly braided locks. Her huntsman attire beneath a cloak revealed enough of her womanly figure to breach Cedric's emotional fortifications.

Adina's eyes, those stunning eyes, drifted back to Cedric. "How are you getting along?"

Cedric crossed and uncrossed his arms, feeling uncomfortably awkward in her presence. "I have been very busy. There is still much to do. Your cousin Georgina joined our faculty, by your recommendation—thank you. She is delightful. And your brothers and their families...well, without them, little if anything here would get done."

"You are the reason my brothers are here. I am very happy for you, Cedric. Your academy will continue to flourish. It must." Her gaze trailed off as if listening to whispers on the breeze. After a moment, she licked her plump lips and steadied her gaze on a red rose. "The roses are quite beautiful, are they not?"

Cedric saw that something was troubling her. He was becoming troubled himself and wondered if something horrible had happened. "Adina, what is it?"

"Everything, nothing, the future," Adina said softly, concern etched into her face. "This past year, I isolated myself from everyone in Ghent except Lidia. She and I traveled north to Elida's family home and stayed there for eight months. There, Lidia finally told me everything. Apparently, on more than one occasion, she conjoined her powers with Elida's. Together they saw your future." Adina turned to Cedric and peered deeply into his eyes. "Before Lidia revealed her vision of the future to me, she made me promise to listen to her every word. She made me promise not to react hastily by body, thought, or voice, that I instead remain calm and quiet. I ask the same of you, Cedric."

His worries mounted, but nothing was going to prevent him from listening to what she had to say. "I promise."

She nodded and squinted as if peering into his mind. "Truth has a way of rising to the surface even when it is immersed beneath layers of denial. Lidia saw the truth in you, and I denied it. After *that* night—

Cedric's only regret from that night was the likelihood of never experiencing another like it with Adina again.

"—I felt that I had betrayed the Meridiem and myself, but I was mistaken. Lidia explained all of it, from the time you first met my brothers. They were meant to protect you. You were meant to defeat the countess. Even that night, our night, was meant to be."

Cedric wanted to ask if leaving him was also meant to be, but he pursed his lips.

"Cedric, leaving you was necessary," said Adina as if hearing his thoughts. She paused to notice a butterfly and pulled back her hair. "It was Lidia's idea to leave Ghent without telling anyone. That too was necessary in order to prepare for the future. I listened to her, just as you are listening to me now. Though I wanted to refute her prophetic visions, I held my tongue. And with each passing day, Lidia's visions became my visions, her truth became my truth. As I continued to change in both body and thought, I gave birth to a child—our child, Cedric."

He felt as if the ground had dropped out beneath him. His mouth went dry, and his heart palpitated. The voices in his head offered no counsel. Had he heard her correctly?

*Our child?*

"Cedric, aside from Lidia, and a few of Elida's closest family members in the far north, no one else knows, not even my brothers. For the safety of our child, no one else must know he exists. Do you understand?"

Cedric nodded, feeling nauseous and confused and elated and worried all at once.

"Our son is being nursed by Elida's granddaughter, Camilla, who also gave birth recently. After my visit here, I will return to the north to be with our son."

"Will you take me with you to see him—?"

Adina raised her finger across her lips. She gently placed her hand on Cedric's flushed face, calming him with her eyes wistful with cautious optimism, drawn-up brows, trembling lips—like a beautiful, ancient tree preparing to succumb to the tempest of ages.

Shades of dusk darkened the sky and shadows grew longer against the fading light, as their gazes lingered like dreams, wondrous, magical dreams. At that moment, nothing else mattered—not Gerda, leering at them from the edge of the garden, or Georgina, gazing down on them from a castle window.

Nothing else mattered...

# EPILOGUE I - *BALCLUTHE*

## May 1799

A fter the battle at Vos Castle, Pierce van Fleming fled to Oostende, leaving three children rescued from the castle in Cedric's care.

ırd the merchant ship *Balcluthe,* Commander Jonathan Crowley checked the manifest and had his second-in-command, Mister Douglas, take final inventory of the cargo while the crew set the sails for departure. Crowley's responsibility for ship, crew, and cargo included eight passengers: a middle-aged man from Kentucky, a family of four from Holland, a couple from Belgium, and one Pierce van Fleming from god-knows-where.

All passengers, except Pierce, were assigned modest private cabins. There were no such accommodations available when Pierce booked passage merely a day before departure. Crowley had originally refused Pierce, citing no vacancy, but a profound change of mind (and Pierce's generous fare of gold pieces) caused him to offer up a hammock on the starboard side of the crew's berth, two decks down. Anxious to flee Europe and his enemies, Pierce was thankful.

Aboard *Balcluthe* nearly two months later, to make uncomfortable accommodations more uncomfortable, Pierce had not fed. To cope with his extreme fasting, he slept deeply and continually, waking only twice—once when a storm ejected him from his hammock and again when the metallic smell of blood roused his vampire eyes open. Ordinarily, sounds and smells would not have stirred him, but he had not yet perfected the hibernation-like state of dormancy—and he was hungry, hungry for the blood oozing from a sailor's hand wound.

As difficult as it was for most vampires to resist fresh human blood, Pierce was the exception, or at least he strived to be. He was undoubtedly different, but how so and why were beyond his understanding.

When the scheming vampire Countess Marie de Vos made Pierce a blood-feeding immortal, he was already twice born, though unaware of it at the time. He had no recollection of his childhood, that his biological mother had magically resurrected him from the dead.

His sister Abigail—also a vampire progeny of the evil countess—restored Pierce's childhood memories to reveal their supernatural lineage: a necromancer mother and sorcerer father. Despite the magical branches of their family tree and Pierce's uncanny love of humanity—he still needed blood to thrive. That was the problem. What he had done and wanted to do to get his fill of human blood weighed heavily on his conscience.

Luckily for the injured sailor, the cook dressed his wound with strips of canvas dipped in rum and vinegar. Pierce corked his nostrils with his fingertips. Nothing smelled more revolting than vinegar to him. It smelled worse than raw garlic and onions mashed together. Despite the odor, he feared the sweet undercurrent of blood might awaken the frenzy in him.

The frenzy was a maddening and uncontrollable urge to feed. Owing to Pierce's ability to achieve a deep and prolonged sleep, the frenzy had not yet invaded his sanity, and he was determined not to let it.

Pierce turned away and gazed out through a brass porthole at the glowing sliver of dawn on the horizon. The Atlantic Ocean appeared as flat and as vast as the western plains of America that Pierce had read about. A faint silhouette of a schooner to the northeast with billowing triangles of fabric among three raked masts seemed to appear out of nowhere. As it came into focus, it looked to be Caribbean. Pierce felt it was a good omen that soon the transatlantic voyage would conclude and his new life in the New World would finally begin. All that mattered was getting there, and not killing anyone before then.

He closed the scuttle cover and listened to the mended sailor and cook exit the cabin together. He listened to and smelled the day crew snoring in their hammocks on the port side of the spacious and smelly berth. They hung in rows, like aging meat, bodies and blood enticing him to indulge. It was borderline overwhelming. He needed space devoid of such distractions, of his cursed blood-cravings, regrets and fears, and those damned voices gurgling up from his hollow stomach:

*Why suffer? Accept us for what we are—a predator of the highest order. Be the hunter. Kill and be nourished! Go on. Do it!*

*No!* said a defiant voice.

*Why no? Why act the shepherd, watching over people as if they were sheep? Really, how long must we continue this preposterous charade? What we need is a bellyful of blood!*

*What we need is for you to shut it!* retorted another.

A cacophony of jumbled dissonance followed. After the mêlée and bellyaching faded to a bearable instant, Pierce quickly refocused. He repeated in his mind: *Must sleep, must sleep for the duration...until we arrive in Virginia.*

In the dankness of the crewmen's berth, the deep sleep Pierce had been struggling to pull off finally came, and just moments before the day crew woke.

In the depths of his slumber, Pierce drifted face-up over field and flock into a space of whiteness and then on toward the darkest edge of existence. From there, he teetered in a dormant state. No physical or mental anguish with which to contend, only a sublime hush in a timeless void. But it was not to last. Pierce would not sleep until finally rising to the clambering of dropping anchors in Virginia.

No.

He would instead rise three hours later to blood-curdling mayhem, suffering, and murder at sea.

## EPILOGUE II - *BRUJA DEL MAR*

A boatswain noticed reflections of daybreak off something shiny in the distance. Nearsighted to a fault, he would not have seen the pirate ship, let alone the reflection of the boy's spyglass had it not been polished. The boatswain was astute enough to report the sighting to Chief Mate Douglas, who then conveyed the information to Commander Crowley.

Briar pipe jutting from his gray, chest-length beard, smoke-coils eddying skyward, Crowley was every bit as old and tired as he appeared to be. From the pocket of his indigo-blue frockcoat, he retrieved a monocular through which he saw the schooner to the northeast. From the side of his mouth, he spoke with little inflection and just enough volume for Douglas to hear. "Privateer...Bermuda-rigged...American flag, good, good." He turned to Douglas, whose skin appeared as blotchy and sore as his own. "Keep an eye on her, Mister Douglas. Sound the bell if needed. I'll be doing my rounds."

"Aye, sir."

As Crowley approached the deck ladder, he gazed at the forward cabin occupied by the wealthy Dutch couple and their twin daughters of eighteen. The girls had been the subject of libido-driven conversation amongst the crew since Oostende. Crowley reprimanded a sailor for openly expressing his erotic fantasies of the sisters and mutinous piracy all in one breath.

After his walkabout on the main deck, Crowley went below to the crew's berth, a room spanning the width of the hull and with a community table at its center. An oil lamp was mounted to a post beside the table and scuttlebutt. He peered through the dim at his day crew, snoring and swaying in concert to the creaking and groaning of the old vessel. Then his eyes found Pierce suspended in his hammock like a giant cocoon on the opposite side of the berth.

Crowley had come into an agreement with Pierce not to disturb him, no matter how dead he appeared to be. Furthermore, he agreed only to wake Pierce if sinking of the ship was certain. Crowley might have questioned the unusual agreement if Pierce had not paid with coin and entranced him. Be that as it may, Crowley's second-in-command, Chief Mate Douglas, received concern from the crew on several occasions that Pierce had not wakened, not even once to eat or drink or to use the chamber pot—let alone the beakhead where the crew did their business. To which Commander Crowley replied, "None of that is necessary for a man who sleeps like a snake in winter. Do not disturb the man. That is an order! Comply and you shall be rewarded."

The commander put Pierce out of mind and went up to the gun deck, a room containing eight cannons—short barrel carronades. He hoped the guns would always remain silent, at least until after his retirement the following year.

Aboard the black schooner, Captain Nora Burns stood beside the wheelhouse, resting her gloved hand on the hilt of her rapier while Lieutenant Diego summoned all swabs on deck. The crew was a mixed lot, comprised of Spanish, Mexican, African, and U.S. nationals. All were fleeing prosecution, if not for crimes committed in their former towns, then for those committed under Captain Burns' command.

In a span of three years, Nora's notoriety had reached fabled status, especially among the young Spanish sailors whose sensational descriptions of her stirred the imagination of people everywhere. Cunning, stunning, and armed, few knew of her old salt temperament. Images of a more heroic figure evolved in the minds of those who had never seen her, even from a distance.

In truth, Nora stylized her attire after her father's royal navy uniforms, but in darker shades of brown, burgundy, and blue. She preferred thigh-high cavalier boots, popular among American frontiersmen, and her favorite hats were tricornes made of shark's skin under which her locks hung like frayed ropes. Unlike Diego's cutlass, her shortened rapier was spectacularly ornate with a patina many believed to be bloodstains. She concealed daggers and single-shot pistols—strapped to her thighs, tucked inside her boots, sewn inside her tricorne. Arguments to whether her eyes were sea blue, kelp green, or color-changing to match her stormy moods often escalated to improbable bets, personal insults, and brawls among impassioned drunks. Her fearless reputation might be traced back to the first Spanish gunship she had sunk after plundering it of gold, silver, and supplies, which made her the ire of the Spanish throne. The humiliated Spanish admiralty labeled her *bruja del mar* (Sea Witch) and hunted her. The captain who captured the Sea Witch would not only receive a fortune in bounty but also military advancement and fame.

Nora laughed whenever she heard the name Sea Witch. If she was truly a witch, she would have used her powers to restore her father's life. But witches, demons, and God in heaven were as real as mermaids to her. Nora's faith was reserved for her crew on the schooner she named *Vengeance*, and no crewman dare spoke of mutiny or of the bounty on her head, lest he fancied a long walk on a short plank.

From the gun deck, Master Crowley heard the bell. The tone pierced his ears, making him cringe. On the upper deck of the *Balcluthe*, Chief Mate Douglas set a course with the wind to gain headway. Crowley noticed the schooner closing the gap despite their new course.

"Sir," said Douglas to Crowley with a steady tone, "pirates, sir."

Crowley gulped to moisten his throat and leveled his monocular.

Douglas leveled his. "Twenty canons and forty men or so, sir," said Douglas.

In his twenty years at sea, Crowley had encountered pirates only once, and that was off the coast of Haiti when he commanded a formidable gunship. The *Balcluthe* was no match for a fully armed pirate ship, and he knew it.

"I estimate canon range within the hour," added Douglas.

The commander lowered his spyglass and nodded. "Notify the crew and ready the cannons, but leave the gun-ports shuttered."

"Aye, sir."

"Confine the passengers to their quarters until further notice."

"Understood, sir."

Crowley looked through his monocular again at the schooner and saw Nora Burns standing beside her lieutenant and navigator. "God help us," muttered Crowley to himself.

*Vengeance* came at *Balcluthe* with the sun and wind in her favor. She fired across *Balcluthe*'s bow, raising concern among the passengers who were confined to their berths.

When *Vengeance* turned hard port and came alongside *Balcluthe*'s starboard side with guns aimed and ready, Mr. Douglas turned to Crowley. "Orders, sir?"

Crowley knew a week's worth of stale provisions alone would not appease pirates. The ship and women probably would though.

"Orders, sir?" repeated Douglas with a heightened tone of urgency. "Commander?"

Crowley nodded. "Come about thirty degrees starboard."

"Come about thirty degrees starboard!" shouted Douglas.

*Balcluthe*'s bow swung to the right, aligning her starboard side to the oncoming *Vengeance.*

Open gun-ports, Mister Douglas."

"Aye, sir! Open gun-ports!" barked Douglas. He listened to his order echo down into the gun deck and leaned out to confirm all ports had opened.

"Fire when ready," said Crowley

Douglas waited for Vengeance to come aside. When the ships were within range, he gave the order: "All guns, fire!"

Captain Burns had presumed the *Balcluthe* was helpless until the thunder of colonnades rattled her schooner with ten-pound balls.

Burns regained footing and belted out her orders. "All guns, fire! Blast those bastards to hell!"

Sangrenel injured two of *Balcluthe*'s crewmen and damaged her equipment on the upper deck. A few carefully placed cannonballs punctured through her side, one leaving a gaping hole just above Pierce's hammock. It would have taken off his head had it been a few inches lower. And if he were awake, he would have seen *Vengeance* through the jagged opening.

In his hibernation-like state, Pierce saw a tiny white light suspended in darkness, expanding in size as he floated toward it. The closer he got, the larger it became, until he was moving through a cavernous tunnel into a plane of luminescence. He turned to see what appeared to be a black spot from whence he came, diminishing in size as he continued on. Then, the old leather satchel that had materialized when he embarked in Oostende reappeared. Suspended in space, it orbited him, slowly at first and then accelerating until it became a contiguous ring of colors. He held up his hands to shade his eyes and noticed the eight-leg-star-shaped birthmarks on his palms swelling and glowing. He felt warmth from inside his chest spreading throughout his body, followed by ringing in his ears, tingling in his limbs, and breathing as if it mattered, as if his heart was vigorously pumping oxygenated blood throughout his body and he was a living, breathing, human being again.

Then the muted sounds of violence entered the void, and the satchel vanished as suddenly as it had appeared. The smell of salt and wood and gunpowder roused him.

When *Vengeance* came alongside again, planks extended from the gunwale and pirates ran across them, weapons in hand, leaping onto the *Balcluthe* in waves of terror.

Pierce smelled blood, heard sounds of skirmish, and saw Elijah Scott staring back at him.

"Mister Fleming," shouted Elijah. "Wake up, sir! We are being attacked!"

"Attacked?" mumbled Pierce in a confused stupor.

"Yes, Mister Fleming! Pirates! Please get up! We must protect the women, if not ourselves."

Noticing the sea through the damaged hull and realizing they were not in Virginia and were indeed in serious trouble, Pierce rolled out of his hammock and took in the sea breeze blowing in. "Women?" whispered Pierce, attempting to ignore the blood trickling down Elijah's temple.

"Yes, the Dutch girls and their mother. They are here." Elijah looked to where they huddled beside the scuttlebutt. Pierce's incisors ached for flesh as they grew longer. The sensation of fangs puncturing skin, sliding through moist tissue into a bulging artery was incredibly sublime.

He shook off the desire and pinched his nose. "Their father, where is he?"

"Dead," said Elijah, his concerned eyes turned up to the ceiling. "I fought his killer on the main deck."

Pierce heard men climbing down the ladder. There was no time to dither. They had to move. Pierce led them down, deep into the bowels of the ship. It was the space along the ship's keel. It contained knee-deep bilge water that stunk of rot and tar. Discarded supplies such as old barrels, wood planks, glue, oil, and canvas collected there like a dump site. A few of the barrels were cut in half, floating in the grimy water.

"I can't see a thing," said one of the girls while her sister whimpered.

Pierce saw everything, but in hues of red. His night vision was better than an owl's. He was grateful for the stench of the bilge and focused on it instead of the girls. Still, the agony of extreme hunger was unremitting. His stomach grumbled: *Look at these people, blinded in the darkness, their hearts racing with fear. Oh, what a feast! Start with the man, drain him to death. Then feast on the mother. Save the young ones for dessert.*

Pierce's incisors were like daggers, ready to extract blood through a groove behind each fang. He kept swallowing and fighting for control of his appetite. But it was no use. The frenzy was coming.

As Pierce moved like a panther toward Elijah, the ship trembled violently. Everybody except Pierce fell into the bilge. Rancid water splashed on Pierce's face and he regained his senses.

"Is everybody all right?" shouted Elijah.

"Yes," said the girls in unison as they helped each other up.

"Thank you," said the mother as Elijah lent her a hand.

"Mister Fleming! Are you all right, sir?" shouted Elijah, reaching blindly for Pierce.

"Yes, Mister Scott," said Pierce. He splashed the water onto his face and shook his head. A moment of calm came over him. "Mister Scott, grab hold of my coat, and everybody else stay close. I shall lead you to some barrels in which you must hide." Pierce led them to the far end of the room, where Elijah helped the women into half-barrels. He placed the other half over them like a stew pot.

"Madam, what is your surname?" said Pierce to the woman.

"Margaret Berlinger, sir," said the mother in a feeble voice. "Thank you, sir, thank you."

"Missus Berlinger, stay calm and stay here until one of the crewmen comes for you. Respond to no one unless they call you by name. Do you understand?"

"Yes, sir. Thank you, sir. God bless you, sir."

Pierce turned to Elijah. "Mister Scott, you will remain here."

"Oh no, Mister Fleming. I would rather die fighting on deck."

"Very well," muttered Pierce, already making his way to the ladder.

Elijah followed closely behind Pierce as they climbed steps and ladders toward the battle. Before reaching the main deck, two pirates sprang at them. Pierce was ready. He shoved Elijah out of harm's way and took hold of the pirate's wrist, breaking it, confiscating his sword, and running both pirates through with it.

"Keep going, Mister Scott," said Pierce to Elijah. "Up the ladder to the main deck. I will be right behind you." As Elijah started up the ladder, Pierce went to the nearest pirate and tried in vain to suck blood from his wound. Realizing more blood awaited him on deck, he quickly ascended the ladder behind Elijah.

On the main deck, Pierce quickly assessed the battle. Master Crowley and First Mate Douglas were back-to-back, surrounded by pirates and fighting them off. Their odds were dire. *Vengeance* and *Balcluthe* were tracking side-by-side, locked in battle, hulls bumping and scraping. For the *Balcluthe* to get away, Pierce would have to cripple *Vengeance* and hope *Balcluthe*'s crew defeated the remaining pirates.

"Mister Fleming!" shouted Elijah.

Pierce turned to see Elijah with two swords he had obviously purloined. Elijah tossed one to Pierce. Pierce turned to help Crowley, mortally injuring two pirates, then grabbing another and pulling him behind the aft mast where Pierce sank his teeth into his neck and gulped down a pint of blood before shoving the pirate overboard. With renewed energy and clarity, Pierce leapt aboard the *Vengeance.*

He was welcomed by gunfire followed by stupefying pain. Pirates came at him from all sides. Bullets and blades riddled his body. Then, as he staggered backward, a single bullet entered his brain through the center of his forehead.

# EPILOGUE III - *VENGEANCE*

When Pierce regained consciousness, he saw the sky framed by faces. A woman's face, an English face, upside down directly above his. He tried to move but was paralyzed and immobilized.

"What to do with him?" asked a sailor in an Irish accent, standing beside the woman.

"It's a demon, I say!" shouted a man standing at Pierce's feet. "We ought to throw it overboard!"

"It's a bad omen, it is," said the Irish sailor.

"Aye!" said several others.

The woman continued to stare intensely at Pierce with Cedric-like curiosity.

Pierce tried to stare back, but saw only shapes of people and possibly two of each. There was no depth of perception or clarity of detail. The sensation of the bullet in his brain was peculiar. It was the only thing he could feel—hot and cold at the center of his brain. Paralysis prevented him from feeling anything else below his neck. Thinking was difficult, all his memories seemingly erased.

"If it is a demon, we should behead it," said Diego with a light Spanish accent.

"No," said Nora. "He handily disabled our ship, injured and killed many of my men, caused that merchant ship to get away, received deadly bullet wounds and sword wounds, yet here he is, alive by the looks of it. I want to know why. What is he, who is he, and why would he sacrifice his life for those on that merchant ship? Secure him in chains and box him in my quarters."

"But, Captain, he...he cannot be trusted," muttered Diego.

She ignored Diego, moving away toward the stern.

Three men wrapped Pierce in chains and lifted him into Captain Nora's quarters. At the foot of her bed sat a gleaming chest of bronze—two feet wide, six feet long. Etched onto the curved lid were the initials: N. S. W. B.

Pierce saw the initials on the lid just before he was dropped into the box.

"Leave the lid open and go," ordered Nora, "and let no one disturb me. I'll come out when I'm good and ready." When the door closed, Nora poured herself a glass of rum and dragged a chair to the box. Turning the back of the chair toward Pierce, she sat down like a man, her legs apart, and gazed down at Pierce's face. The bullet hole in his forehead appeared to be healing. She held the glass over him. "Do you fancy rum?"

Pierce said nothing.

"From my experience, you suffered...five, six...possibly seven mortal wounds. You should be dead. Perhaps you will die. Perhaps you are paralyzed. Perhaps the bullet in your head left you dumb, blind, deaf, and mute. But, I wonder...can you hear me?" She knelt down and touched his forehead, dragging her finger in a circle around the entry wound, watching intently for any signs of movement. When she touched the wound, Pierce's eyes blinked. She pulled away and sat back down in the chair. "Blink if you can hear me."

Pierce blinked.

"Are you a demon or sea god?"

Pierce would not blink.

"Are you an ordinary man with extraordinary luck?" When Pierce would not blink, she held the glass of rum over his head. "I will ask you once more, and if you do not respond with so much as a blink or grunt, I shall pour rum into your head wound and set it aflame. Now, do you fancy a drink or no?"

"No," Pierce managed to say.

"Remarkable, you can speak. What is your name?"

Pierce closed his eyes and swallowed. The bullet was no longer in his head. Did it vanish or fall out at some point?

"What is your name?" repeated Nora.

"What is yours?" said Pierce in a raspy voice.

Her face lifted with a smile and she wagged her finger like a metronome. "Unless you are Socrates, answering a question with a question is hardly appropriate."

Pierce closed his eyes and felt his wounds. A bullet in his arm, two more that punctured his lungs, stab wounds through his midsection, he was healing quickly and glad for taking a nourishing gulp of pirate's blood earlier. "My name is Pierce van Fleming."

She placed the glass on the floor and placed her chin down on the chair's backrest. "Fascinated to make your acquaintance, Mister Fleming. Where in England is home?"

"Manchester, by way of Flanders."

"I am Nora Burns of London Town, by way of plunder and murder. I am captain of this ship, and you are my prisoner." She observed him from head to boot. "Now, Mister Fleming, I cannot help but notice your wounds healing before my eyes. I am neither religious nor superstitious, but *you* are obviously a miracle of sorts. So, tell me, what *are* you exactly: demon, sea god, freak of nature?"

The question confounded Pierce as a deluge of memories flooded back. He searched his mind for the satchel and saw it, floating in a space of nothingness. He was terribly weak and becoming weaker by the minute as his body healed its wounds. His magical powers were ineffective even when he was in excellent health, and he feared he would not gain enough strength to break free of the chains.

"All right, Mister Fleming. Perhaps it is better if you start the dialogue. Please, ask anything you like. I shall be forthright with my answers."

After a minute of silence, Pierce opened his mouth and said, "Why am I in this box?"

Nora sniffed. "It is actually a coffin. A Spanish gunship left it in a tender for me to retrieve. It contained a message from one of the captains responsible for murdering my father. Two initials engraved on the lid are mine, the other two stands for 'Sea Witch.' That is what they call me. I find it amusing, don't you?" She lifted her glass and sipped the rum. "Made to frighten me, but I think the box is rather beautiful."

"It is too short."

Nora leaned back and smiled. "You are too tall, and I cannot let a demon loose on my ship. That is what my crew believes you to be, a demon. You do understand." She finished her rum and placed her hand on the lid. "Please hold your breath and rest, Mister Fleming, while I tend to my crew's paranoia." She closed the lid and walked toward the door. "I shall return shortly to resume our discussion."

Nora met Diego and Ernesto at the wheelhouse to discuss their prisoner and the next course of action.

Aware of crewmen staring, she covered her mouth when she spoke. "His wounds heal rapidly, but I still don't know how or why."

"What have you learned about him?" asked Diego.

"He is English."

Ernesto inhaled a trembling breath of fear. "He is ungodly. We should throw him overboard before it is too late, before he destroys us!"

"Now, now, Mister Ernesto, let's not jump to curses and revelations," said Nora. "That man saved that merchant ship, and I want to know why. He will remain in chains and in that box until I say otherwise." Noticing Ernesto's undiminished concern, Nora placed her hand on his shoulder. "If he proves to be a demon, we will do as you suggest. But please allow me time to discover the truth. Agreed, Mister Ernesto?"

Ernesto nodded warily. "Aye, Captain."

"Good. Kindly set a course for Culebra. We need supplies, healthy crewmen, and repairs." She turned to Diego. "Lieutenant, mend the mainsail. We shan't flounder about like a clipped goose."

"Aye, Captain."

Back in her quarters, Nora removed her boots and uniform and washed her face over a pail of water. After she dried off, she approached the box. "Mister Fleming, are you awake in there? Would you like to resume our discussion? Mister Fleming?" She heard nothing. She knocked on the lid and called out his name again. Cautiously, she unlocked the box and opened the lid.

Pierce's eyes were closed. He appeared dead to her. She held the oil lamp to his face and saw that his wounds had vanished, not a scab or scar to be seen. She placed her hand on his forehead. He was cold. She lifted an eyelid. His eye was blue and clear, not glazed and lifeless. She unbuttoned his shirt, but the chains were wrapped so tightly she could not assess his wounds. She leaned into the box and placed her ear on his chest. Instead of a heartbeat she heard his voice.

"What are you doing?" said Pierce.

Startled, Nora lifted her head into the lid and fell back on the floor. She vigorously rubbed a growing welt on her head and sat up slowly.

"Are you all right?" asked Pierce with a tone of amusement that surprised Nora.

"I thought you were dead, and I prefer not to sleep with a dead man at the foot of my bed." She moved onto the chair, this time with her back against the backrest, and continued to rub the soreness from her head.

Pierce moved his eyes to meet hers. "How long do you intend to keep me in chains? Better question, what do you want from me?"

"Powers of rapid healing and invincibility," said Nora, no longer rubbing the welt on her head. "I also want to know why you allowed the merchant ship to escape. Was she transporting something of value? Were others like you aboard her?"

Pierce smiled. "Only innocent people were aboard that ship. They deserved to finish their journey unhindered and unharmed."

"Nobody journeys through life unhindered or unharmed, Mister Fleming. Now, tell me, why sacrifice your life for that ship? What or who was it transporting?"

"It was transporting nothing special, no one special, just ordinary cargo from Holland and Flanders, including an American whiskey distiller and a Dutch family. I saw nothing remarkable aboard that ship."

Nora smirked. "That is a lie. For one, you are remarkable. I watched you impossibly heal from impossible injuries in minutes. I want to know more about that, and about your uncanny speed and strength. My men saw you jump fifty feet and move faster than a wild animal on the rigging. How? Do you have magical powers?"

"Suppose I do."

Nora furrowed her brow and stared intensely at Pierce. "I want them."

"If I gave them to you, how would you use them?"

Nora thought for a moment. "I would use them to defeat my enemies."

"Then you are not deserving of such powers."

"Then you will remain in chains and in that box. If you are alive by morning, I will have my men suspend you over a fire, cook you, and eat you, because thanks to you, we are running low on food rations."

Nora got up and poured a glass of rum.

"What happened to you, Nora? You were clearly privileged. What made you resort to piracy?"

With bottle in one hand and her glass in the other, Nora swirled the rum and stared at the flame atop the oil lamp. "If I had met you in a former life, at a party or ball, I might have allowed you to dance with me." She turned to observe Pierce once again, imagining his face shaven and clean. He was handsome, terribly so. She leaned forward for a closer look. His wounds had completely healed. He looked healthy and virile. "I might have laughed at your jokes, let you kiss my hand, and hoped you might return a scarf I would have strategically dropped as we parted ways."

"And now?" asked Pierce.

Nora laughed quietly with a slight shake of her head. "Now my crew wants you dead, especially Diego."

"Your Lieutenant, the man standing beside you when I was good as dead on the deck?"

"Yes."

"You love him."

"Is that a question?"

"An observation. I understand you."

"Nobody has ever understood me, not even Diego." She placed the bottle on the floor and drank more rum.

"In my first life, I was murdered at age twelve and resurrected the following year by my mother who was a necromancer. She erased my childhood memories and sent me to England to live in secrecy. My family and friends there were massacred by a vampire. She destroyed my second life, replacing it with my current life to walk with one foot among the living and the other among the dead. All vampires like me are deplorable creatures."

"Vampire?" Nora laughed and finished her glass of rum. "They are as real as unicorns—"

"Says the woman who thinks I am a sea god," quipped Pierce.

Nora refilled her glass, kneeled before the box, and pulled back her braids. "So, Mister Fleming, are you hungry? If I feed you, will I become a vampire like you? Will I inherit great powers?"

"No."

"Why?"

"I will not change you. Once cursed, there is no going back."

Nora scowled at him, the effects of the rum clearly effecting her emotions. "Yes, there is no going back! There is only this life, plundering and killing and running and pursuing. It's more exhausting than you can imagine."

"You can choose to stop."

She finished the rum and dropped the empty glass. "I will not stop until I have avenged my father. His killer is still out there."

Pierce followed the edge of the copper lid with his eyes. "What we do is not always who we are or who we aspire to be. Circumstances can force us to do regrettable things, but regret need not destroy us. Buried in your heart is the girl from London. Find her. Revive her. Surely, you would rather live in peace."

"Impossible," muttered Nora, lifting the bottle to her mouth.

"If it were possible, what would you do, Nora?"

Tears drifted down her cheeks as she lowered the bottle to her side. She let out a long sigh. "I would be a loving mother to my son."

"Where is he?"

She scoffed at his question. "Do you take me for a fool, Mister Fleming? I will never reveal his whereabouts."

"How can he be safe without his mother to protect him?"

"He lives with an elderly couple, pretending to be his grandparents. I trust them."

"Where is the father?" Her silence spoke words. Nora drank from the bottle again and lowered herself to the floor, leaning her back against the box. "Diego does not know..."

"How can he not know?"

"I was three months pregnant when I traded my frigate for this schooner, which was still under construction. During that time, the entire crew was ashore. Diego is by nature a jealous man, and I needed space to think. When he agreed to oversee the construction of this ship, I left for five months to have the baby. My seamstress was my midwife. She and her husband took custody of my child. I bought them a house overlooking the sea. I send money when I can."

"All the money in the world cannot replace a mother's love."

"Have you children of your own, Mister Fleming?"

"No."

"Then do not lecture me." Nora got to her feet and paced the room with bottle in hand. "I would trade all of this to have a normal life with my son." She stopped beside the box. "My fate is sealed. I am the Sea Witch, a pirate, with a Spanish bounty on my head. It is not the fear of being hanged that keeps me from my child. It is the fear of ruining his life, with knowledge of who his mother truly is..."

"I am sorry, Nora."

"I have no regrets, Mister Fleming. I intend to avenge my father and then end my wretched life." Her tired eyes drifted down to see Pierce. "Now, show me what you can do. Show me some magic."

"I am not exactly free to—"

"I am sorry for the chains and metal coffin, truly I am. But..." Nora tilted her head and drank more rum. "Show me."

Pierce closed his eyes and soon a leather satchel materialized over his chest.

Nora blinked, uncertain to what she was seeing.

"Captain, please take it. You will not be harmed. I assure you."

Nora clumsily reached for the satchel, but it moved to Pierce's boots. When she reached for it there, it vanished.

"You see, Captain, the bag of tricks you wish for will not allow anyone to touch it."

"Is there a way for you to give it to someone else?"

"I know not."

Losing her desire to stay sober much less awake, she yawned and stretched and then smiled so sweetly that Pierce could almost see the previous version of Nora before she embarked on her tragic course. "I shall retire for the night, Mister Fleming. I can let you sleep with the lid opened if you'd like."

"Please close it and lock it, just in case one of your crew tries to get at me."

Nora did as he asked and then got into bed and fell asleep.

# EPILOGUE IV - FINALE

While *Vengeance* made headway southward, the weather turned dark and lightning storms riled the sea. Nearing the isle of Culebra, hurricane force winds made it impossible to navigate safely. *Vengeance's* main mast fractured, the top half falling onto the aft mast. The jib was torn away. Finally, she struck a reef. As the storm dragged the sinking ship into deeper water, Nora ordered all hands to ready the tender.

"The boy first!" shouted Nora.

The boy deckhand got into the boat, followed by the rest of the crew until it was over capacity.

As the ship's boat was being lowered into the angry sea, Nora suddenly remembered that Pierce was still locked inside the bronze box. She tore away from Diego and waded through seawater gushing over the deck. She entered her quarters and found the large box sliding across the floor, half submerged in rising water.

Diego came and turned her away from the box. He held her tightly in his arms, kissing her passionately and whispering in her ear as the water rose above their waist.

"Te amo. Te amo, mi amor."

Pierce had realized they were in trouble when the storm pushed the ship into a reef, then back out to sea. *Vengeance* pitched violently and began to list without righting herself. The box slid across the floor and seawater started to seep in. He felt the water pressure build as the entire ship plunged into the depths.

Then, silence.

The box settled at the bottom of the sea with a gentle thud.

Tightly chained, famished and weak, Pierce struggled to break free. He tried to pry a chain link open with his finger, but it was no use. He was too feeble to bend the iron. Panic overwhelmed him. He screamed, allowing water to fill his lungs. He struggled again to no avail. He begged for the angel of death to relieve him of his confinement, but she had only visited him in his dreams after becoming a vampire.

A revenant was bad enough, but a vampire? He was thrice born and wishing he had never been born in the first place. What a horrible life to be dealt, he thought.

He felt something on his chest and realized it was the satchel. But he could not move his arms enough to even touch it. He tried to remember some of its contents, a spell that might free him, but he had not taken the time to study any of it. He felt stupid and powerless, incapable even of bringing his hands together and blasting the box or himself to pieces. He sighed. Is this how it ends? Countess Marie de Vos once told him that if he dared returned to Flanders he would be bound in chains, locked in an iron box, and buried alive. Was this her farewell curse?

He squirmed and struggled to free his hands again. He imagined Nora and Diego floating within eyeshot of the box, embracing, food for the fishes.

Pierce tasted the salt water, tears of the gods, and over time he managed to fall asleep, a deep and prolonged sleep, months at a time, years at a time. Each time he woke in utter darkness, entombed in a box at the bottom of the sea, closer to death and never to die, a circular succession of emotional torment, of panic, anger, fear, penitence, helplessness, and hopelessness repeated over and over until he lost the ability to move even so much as a finger or eyelid or eye. A torture eternal, without hope of ever being rescued, as Cedric Martens had rescued him of his demons once upon a time.

Dear reader,

It means the world to me that you bought The Meridiem and took time out of your busy life to read it. I endeavor to write stories that are entertaining, intelligent, and thought provoking. My goal is to develop characters that are interesting, original, and memorable. I would love to know what you thought of this story. Please leave a star rating on Goodreads and the online bookstore you purchased this from, and if you can follow up with an honest review, please do! Your feedback is very helpful to me as a developing author of fiction.

Thanks again for your support!

C. A. Lear